THE OFFICIAL MOVIE NOVELIZATION

HALLOWEEN ENDS

THE OFFICIAL MOVIE NOVELIZATION
HALLOWEEN ENDS

BY
PAUL BRAD LOGAN

TITAN BOOKS

Halloween Ends – The Official Movie Novelization
Print edition ISBN: 9781803361703
E-book edition ISBN: 9781803361710

Published by Titan Books
A division of Titan Publishing Group Ltd
144 Southwark Street, London SE1 0UP

First edition: October 2022
1 3 5 7 9 10 8 6 4 2

A CIP catalogue record for this title is available from
the British Library.

Printed and bound in the United States.

For David Gordon Green, without whose generosity, support, and inspiration this would not have been possible.

And to Sarahy, for putting up with all of it.

AFTER THE MASSACRE

November 1st, 2018: Early Morning. Before the Light.
As the paramedics wheeled her to the ambulance, Allyson looked up and saw her mother staring through the upstairs window of Judith Myers's bedroom. As Halloween night ended, Allyson felt relief knowing *he* had been killed. And even though the pain and horror of losing her father and her friends would not completely set in until much later, Allyson took solace in the fact that it was over. Finally.

Allyson's eyes moved across the yard as more people gathered. Then she heard a voice announce from the distance that "Michael killed them. Killed them all. They're all dead." When Allyson's eyes moved back to the upstairs window, her mother had vanished from her view, forever.

Allyson had a feeling that something had gone horribly wrong, but did not know for sure until an officer ran out of the Myers' home and yelled for backup because he'd "just found another body upstairs!"

At that moment, the medics closed the ambulance

doors, sealing Allyson inside. All sound faded into a vacuum-like hum. The sirens disappeared. The squawking bursts of 'walkie' talk disappeared. And the screams that reverberated around Haddonfield, as more of Michael's violence was discovered, disappeared. All that existed was the hum. And Allyson existed inside it.

*

Hugo and Ozzy were on their morning garbage route as another pack of flashing lights and screaming sirens raced by hunting for Michael Myers. The sun had barely come up, and the dim light cast an ominous glow across Haddonfield.

Ozzy's wife Olivia had woken him with the news about Michael.

"They can't make you go to work with that monster on the loose."

"Olivia, they have not called to tell me I am not going in, so that means I *am* going in."

"You checked your emails?"

"My emails are full of junk. They did not email me. They did not call me. I have to go to work."

"Baby, I don't want you goin' in today. They showed a picture of that maniac on TV with that awful mask over his face… I can't get him out of my head. I'm scared. He's still out there. Stay home with me, please. Just call in sick."

"I do not have any more sick days. And if you want to ever get back to Portugal so you can feed those ponies again, then that means I have got to go into work. Even when there is a maniac in a monster mask on the loose in Haddonfield."

Ozzy kissed Olivia sweetly. "And you do not have to worry about anything when it comes to me and him because Michael Myers has never met a guy like Ozzy." Ozzy flexed his biceps to show off his muscles. Olivia was far from convinced.

"And in addition to that, Hugo has been on a strict high-performance diet, he's pumping iron, and he is lean and mean, trust me."

"You're trying to be funny, but this isn't funny to me."

"Listen, if we cross paths with that psycho, which I guarantee we will not, but hypothetically speaking, if we do meet Michael Myers, we will win."

"Win? I just want you to survive!"

"Olivia, you don't need to worry because me and Hugo are ready for anything. I promise you. There is *nothing* to worry about. Make your coffee, watch your morning shows, stay away from the news, and I will see you this afternoon."

Hugo, who had broken his diet two days into it and hadn't lifted a weight in decades, gobbled down four partially cooked Toaster Strudels and chased them with an ice-cold glass of Strawberry Quick while watching the local news cover the Michael Myers massacre.

"Jesus Christ," Hugo murmured in disbelief when they announced the body count from the massacre. "How the hell's someone kill that many people in one night? How can that happen?"

A shadow moved across his kitchen window, and Hugo almost had a heart attack.

It's him! Hugo's mind instantly went into fight mode, and he dove into a crouched position and crab-walked to the utility drawer, where he removed the first two things he grabbed: a screwdriver and a packing tape dispenser.

Hugo paused for a moment, considered his two makeshift weapons, and then he carefully rose.

Hugo peeked nervously over the window ledge, but the darkness prohibited him from seeing anything. He quickly killed the kitchen light and looked back through the glass. His eyes slowly adjusted. He looked across his small yard, mostly filled with dead grass, a dying oak tree, and a tiny toolshed that he hadn't used since the early nineties. He saw nothing else.

Hugo stepped outside and looked to the shed. Enough light made it into the doorless storage room to let Hugo see some rusty garden tools but not much else. He gripped his weapons and timidly approached.

"Someone hiding in there?" Hugo called out. His voice shook with fear. "I'm armed," he announced, hoping to frighten any intruders.

Hugo focused on the doorway and waited for a reply. He prayed he would not see that masked face he had seen on the news emerge from within.

A breeze rustled the leaves of his dying tree as time slowed to a crawl. Hugo's eyes remained fixed on the doorway. Waiting. Expecting any second to meet that psycho. He gripped his weapons tighter—

The opening notes to 'Far Behind' from Candlebox, Hugo's ringtone, broke the silence abruptly.

Hugo frantically grabbed his phone to silence it and dropped his weapons. Hugo's eyes shot back to the door.

What the hell are you doing out here? What if he is in there? Hugo's mind screamed. *You're gonna kill the boogeyman with a screwdriver and a tape dispenser?!* Hugo's mind questioned his hasty decision. *Go inside, you idiot! Go inside, now!*

Suddenly there was movement in the toolshed. A thin shadow. Then some tools rattled.

Hugo froze. Unable to run away.

Please God, Please God, Please God.

Each second that passed made his heart beat louder. His eyes grew wider... And then—

Reeee-aaaahhhh!

Hugo screamed as a mangy cat leapt out of the darkness and raced by him.

Hugo spun around and lost his balance. His face kissed the brick wall, and he fell and banged his head against the tape dispenser.

"Shit!" he screamed.

*

"Jesus Christ, man, you are lucky that it was some drunk guy and not Michael Myers," Ozzy told Hugo as they hung a left into an alley. Embarrassed by the truth, Hugo had told Ozzy a drunk guy had knocked him over. A story that, based on Hugo's bruised face and scraped arms, Ozzy found spurious.

Hugo held a frozen burrito against his injured eye to stop the swelling.

"All this boogeyman shit's got me on edge," Hugo confessed.

"Olivia was giving me attitude about even going out today."

"You ask me, Olivia's right. Nobody should be out right now. Least of all us."

Another pair of sirens raced by.

"They will find him," Ozzy confidently told Hugo. "You can't get away with anything in this town. Olivia's cousin, John Michael, had a warrant for unpaid parking tickets, and they found him in his girlfriend's RV parked at a KOA. Can you believe that? If they can find John Michael hidden inside an RV parked at a KOA, they can most certainly find Michael Myers."

Hugo looked at the glint coming off the trashcans from the morning light. *At least Halloween's over*, he thought.

Ozzy stopped at the first set of cans, and Hugo hopped out.

As soon as Hugo reached the trash, he stopped dead in his tracks.

A figure sat slumped against the chain-link fence, bleeding from multiple wounds. The dawn light gave his mask a sicker, paler appearance. Hugo recognized it instantly. The same masked face he'd seen on the news. The same mask he could not get out of his mind.

"Mother—!"

Hugo bolted back to the truck.

"What?" Ozzy asked, concerned.

"He's there, man!" Hugo stuttered as he jumped inside. "Michael Myers is out there!"

"What are you talking about?" Ozzy said as he craned his neck around Hugo.

"I'm tellin' you, he's lying against the fence. Let's get the hell out of here!"

Ozzy smirked and climbed out.

"Ozzy, what the hell are you doing?!"

"I am going to see for myself whether or not you are having some fun with me."

"I am not having fun! This isn't fun! Let's get out of here!"

Ozzy opened the door and stepped out. "Don't worry." Ozzy removed a canister from his belt. "I am prepared with pepper spray."

"What is your problem, you fool?!" Hugo screamed.

Ozzy came around the truck and approached the fence.

Hugo banged against the window. "Don't be an idiot!"

Ozzy reached the fence but didn't see anything except a dark, thick liquid collected on the ground. It could have been oil or blood or any number of things.

Hugo pressed his face against the window. Watching with horrific anticipation.

"Dumb son of a bitch…" Hugo whispered under his breath when he saw Ozzy squat down and

13

disappear from his view. Hugo quickly climbed into the driver's seat.

"I'm gonna leave your butt if you don't get the hell in here right now!" Hugo shouted.

"There is nobody here!" Ozzy shouted as he stood back up.

"What?" Hugo quietly asked in disbelief.

"I am telling you that I am standing here right now, and there is nobody here. The joke is on you, funny man."

Ozzy looked down the length of the fence in one direction and then in the other. He didn't see anything out of the ordinary.

Hugo's worry grew. "I swear I saw him." His eyes nervously moved across the horizon, looking for the slightest hint of what he'd seen. But he didn't see a thing.

"He was there," Hugo said again. "And if he's not there now, then I'm telling you he's hiding. Please, Ozzy, let's just get out of here."

"Maybe you got a concussion after all," Ozzy suggested as he grabbed the cans and headed back to the truck. "Should I drop you off at the clinic to get your head examined?"

"Quit joking around!" Hugo yelled as he lost his temper.

"The boogeyman's gonna get you," Ozzy teased as he disappeared behind the truck.

Hugo rechecked his injuries in the mirror. He winced as he softly touched his swollen eye and bruised face. Could he have seen something that wasn't actually there? Had he gotten so worked up by all the news coverage that he'd somehow imagined Michael Myers in the flesh? In all his forty-eight years, nothing like that had ever happened before.

"Maybe I did get a concussion," Hugo mumbled as he slurped the rest of his Strawberry Quick from his Thermos and considered the possibility. First, he'd mistaken a freaking cat for the monster, and now this.

Hugo smirked and looked back to the mirror. Ozzy hadn't yet returned.

"Ozzy, what's the holdup?" Hugo yelled through the window.

He received no reply.

"Hey, Ozzy?!" he shouted again.

A moment passed. And still nothing.

"Ozzy? Are you playing a joke on me?"

Nothing.

"All right then, you want to be funny," Hugo said as he grabbed the long metal trash-picker pin and stepped out of the truck. "Let's see how funny this is."

Hugo approached slowly. His eyes darted everywhere, certain that Ozzy would soon jump out from a hiding place and yell, "Boo!"

"You better not be joking around back here. You might get stabbed. I got the picker in my hand."

Hugo's footsteps crunched loudly over some loose gravel from the unkempt road. It was the only sound he could hear. Paranoia crept in and made it hard to walk smoothly. Hugo tripped over his feet. "Goddammit, Ozzy, stop messing around."

Hugo reached the back of the truck but didn't see his partner. The alley looked empty.

Hugo heard a *drip-drip* from behind and turned. There he found Ozzy's body, crammed into the rear loader with his stomach sliced open and his guts spilling everywhere. Ozzy's can of pepper spray had been brutally jammed inside his throat, crushing his trachea and dislocating his jaw. Ozzy's eyes were blood-red, suggesting the pepper spray had been at least modestly effective.

"Oh God," Hugo cried out and took off.

When Hugo came around the truck, he met Michael Myers.

Michael made no immediate movement. He simply stood there. Watching.

"*No!*" Hugo screamed and jabbed the picker into Michael's neck. Michael crashed against the chain-link fence. Hugo jumped over him and raced for the door.

Hugo hurried into the cab, but before he could put the truck in gear, the trash picker smashed through the window and pierced Hugo's temple.

Hugo's head slumped toward Michael as the blood streamed out. His eyes flickered as his hemorrhaging brain shut down.

The shape before him watched blankly through black eyes.

Michael removed Hugo from the truck and arranged him alongside his friend in the loader. He then pulled the lever and engaged the hydraulics, which lifted the bodies into the compactor. Ozzy and Hugo's carcasses were crushed in the belly of the machine.

Michael climbed inside the truck and drove past the unsuspecting police cars. He vanished into the early Haddonfield morning.

LOVE LIVES TODAY

On November 1st, 2018, the manhunt for Michael Myers began.

The Michael Myers massacre became a national news story. Outlets covered the story relentlessly, and television networks scrambled to create dramatized versions of the story for their movies of the week and endless news specials.

The FBI and police forces from surrounding cities aided in the search. Hero-hungry vigilantes arrived in droves armed to the teeth, confident that they could find and kill the monster faster than the law.

But after months of searching, nothing.

Michael had seemingly vanished without a trace.

An abandoned garbage truck near the river on the edge of town was discovered shortly after the search began. But no sign of Michael Myers.

Farther away, buried deep in the surrounding woods, police came upon another grisly scene inside a dilapidated hunter's cabin.

The authorities combed the woods and dragged the river.

And still, nothing…

Laurie Strode led a crazed charge to slay Michael, aligning herself with fringe groups. She had prepared alone in the years leading up to Michael's escape, but now, she had a bloodthirsty army to join in her efforts. And after the death of her daughter, Laurie's own bloodlust became far more savage.

"The police in Haddonfield don't know what the fuck they are doing. It's up to us to bring him down," became Laurie's mantra as she rolled through the streets, hunting for the man who had taken everything from her.

Sheriff Barker resigned, and a new sheriff, Nate Scott, arrived with the promise that he could bring down Myers. He implemented county-wide curfews, choked traffic with routine roadblocks, and worked with the state to deploy the National Guard. But in the end, he proved no more capable of capturing Michael Myers than Barker. And all his efforts did nothing to provide a clue to where Michael could have possibly gone.

Had Michael Myers died? Had his injuries proved too fatal for any man to survive, even the boogeyman? Some residents assumed so. Others believed he had changed shape and was hiding in plain sight. And many more feared his imminent return.

The local loudmouth, shock-jock WURG DJ, Willy the Kid, helped circulate wilder theories about what had could have happened to Michael Audrey Myers, but there were plenty more rational explanations to keep people terrified.

Paranoia swept through Haddonfield and led to a mass exodus from the city after Michael's massacre. Those who remained directed their fears onto their neighbors. The town turned ugly.

The city bulldozed the Myers' home, and in its place they erected a community garden and memorial dedicated to the victims of Michael's rampage. A sign that read 'Love Lives Today' greeted visitors to the garden. Photographs of the victims of the massacre were shellacked onto the fountain wall that rested in the center of the memorial, but it did little to erase the legend, which only grew in strength as Michael remained missing.

Teenagers with a taste for the macabre became the only visitors to the garden as it soon fell into disrepair. Mostly goths, punks, and misfits who were fascinated by the stories of a loner who had become an icon. Some of them tattooed his name onto their bodies. Others wrote songs about him. Graffitied images of Michael's mask sprung up throughout Haddonfield, painted onto walls and billboards. Even though you could not see the boogeyman, you could not avoid his presence.

All the while, Allyson remained confined within the hum…

COREY CUNNINGHAM

Halloween Night, 2019

Corey Cunningham saw only a few trick-or-treaters as he rode his bike to the Allen house. Most parents opted to keep their children at home rather than risk the possibility of another nightmare taking place.

Joan, Corey's mother, begged him to stay home too, but Corey looked for any excuse to get out of his house. So, when he got the request from Mrs. Allen to come and babysit their boy Jeremy, he accepted immediately.

Corey needed one more year, *just one more year*, to hopefully have enough money to get the hell out of his momma's house and into an engineering program at a university. Corey had been working overtime mowing lawns and doing odd jobs to make that happen, and he reminded himself of this goal as Joan screamed at him to "Stay home with your mother, Corey!" *Caw-ree* is what it sounded like through Joan's severe Northeastern accent.

Corey could hear her voice echoing inside his head as he pedaled through the neighborhood. He could not escape her overbearing control. His whole life, there she was, on top of him, unwilling to let him go. Even away from home, he could hear her. Always.

Corey did not know much about his father. Wally had left the picture when Corey was just a child. Joan told Corey that Wally had driven his motorcycle off the road and died, but that wasn't true. Truth was that as soon as Joan gave birth to Corey, Joan lost interest in Wally. And late one night, she told him to hit the road. Wally, a Vietnam vet twenty years older than Joan, was far more interested in watching *M*A*S*H* reruns and drinking beers with his buddies in the motorcycle club than being a dad, so he did not put up a fight. Wally left as soon as she said the word 'leave', and he never looked back. All Corey knew about his dad was that he had been the produce manager at the grocery store where Joan ran the register, he had a tattoo of a duck, and he loved Merle Haggard, which Corey discovered when he found some of the things Wally had left behind.

With Wally out of the picture, Corey became Joan's sole obsession, and obsess she did. Joan rarely let Corey out of her sight. She strictly forbade him from participating in any after-school activities, and sports were entirely out of the question. Corey went to school, he came home; that was his life. And when Joan worried that school was becoming too intrusive in their relationship, she would lie and tell Corey he had an illness and demand he stay home so she could care for him. Sometimes Joan even tampered with the thermometer to read hotter than his actual temperature to further convince Corey that she was right.

"But, Momma, I feel fine," he'd plead, desperate to get out of the house.

"Listen to your mother. She is the only one who will take care of you. The *only* one. You are a sick boy. A very sick boy. And you will stay home with your mother."

At home, Joan had complete control. That's where she thrived. Joan dressed Corey every morning until he turned thirteen, and he had little say in the matter. Even when he turned thirteen, he had to beg his momma to let him pick out his own clothes.

Joan fed Corey each night at six sharp. Always a dinner served with milk. Then she tucked Corey into bed at 8:30PM on the dot, never a minute later.

"Nobody will ever love you the way I love you," Joan would tell Corey as she sat in the chair close to his bed, watching him until he fell asleep.

Joan had grown up in a large family. She was the oldest of six siblings, and Joan loathed the lack of attention she received from her parents. *Loathed it*. And with each new addition to the family, Joan saw her desired attention diminish further.

Nothing her parents did could ever make Joan feel special enough, and when the last of the children arrived in the form of a snotty little monster the family called Mickey, Joan began acting out in more devious ways. Sometimes she would steal her sisters' favorite toys and bury them in the lot behind their home. Then she would hide and watch them cry when they couldn't find them. God, it made her feel good when they cried. When they were miserable. All those little shits did not deserve to be in her family, and seeing their pain delighted Joan no end. Joan would then lie and tell her parents that she had seen her brothers steal the toys, and point them in the direction where she had buried them. Watching her brothers get into trouble gave her an incredible thrill. And sometimes they would cry too. That was even better.

"I'm the only one who doesn't do bad things," Joan would tell her parents.

But Mickey's entrance into the family was the final straw. Because no matter how hard Joan fought for attention, there would always be somebody new. So, Joan put the full force of her ire onto the newest addition.

Joan would pinch the baby and watch him scream when nobody was looking. At night she would sneak to his crib and shake it violently until he woke up crying. Joan never missed an opportunity to torment the child. And eventually, she took that torment too far.

"Keep an eye on your brother," Joan's mother instructed as she hurried off to grab her things one morning before school. Any time Joan heard the words *keep an eye on your brother*, her temper flared. On that particular morning, Joan's temper burst into flames.

Joan sat next to the little monster, trying to enjoy her Cream of Wheat cereal, while he chirped and drooled and thrashed about in his highchair like a foul little weasel.

Mickey had a habit of pressing his little feet against the table and tilting his highchair back. Everybody in the family had gotten used to making sure he was never too close to the table that he might actually push himself over.

Joan looked down and saw Mickey's legs darting out, reaching for the table but unable to touch it. It inspired a sinister idea.

When Joan got up to put her bowl in the sink, she gave Mickey's highchair a little push closer. Just to where his feet could touch the table. And then she walked away.

"Momma, I'm going to the bathroom!" Joan shouted as she hurried to the bathroom.

"Make it quick! We need to leave soon!" Joan's mother yelled back.

Joan stood in the bathroom, looking at her reflection in the mirror. Wishing that her family would love her the way she wanted to be loved. Wishing that it was only her.

Joan did not expect anything to actually happen by scooting Mickey's chair closer to the table, but then she heard the crash. And when she heard her mother's screams followed by her brothers' and sisters' cries, she knew something had happened. Something awful.

Joan came into the kitchen and saw the blood on the floor. Mickey had toppled over and cracked his head open. Joan's mother held the child in her arms, pleading for him to wake up. Joan's brothers and sisters were bawling their eyes out.

Mickey never woke. And Joan never got her attention.

Joan left home after high school and severed all ties with her family. She moved from the Northeast to the Midwest, and Corey never learned anything about his extended family.

Corey had just turned fifteen when Joan married Ronald Prevo, another Northeastern transplant. Joan let Ronald know as soon as he came into her life that he would remain firmly on the sidelines when it came to Corey's upbringing. Ronald gladly obliged.

With Ronald in her life, Joan eased up on Corey ever so slightly, but she did not release her grip entirely.

Any friends that Corey wanted to see outside of school had to go through Joan first. And when Corey got a crush on Lauren in ninth grade and brought her over to work on their history project together, Joan stayed in the room with them, monitoring Corey's interest. When Lauren left, Joan told Corey that he should be embarrassed to keep company with such a nasty girl. After that, Corey kept his love interests and friendships to a minimum and secretive.

That is how Corey Cunningham turned out to be a socially awkward twenty-one-year-old with no car, who lived at home, dreamed of getting away, and ended up agreeing to babysit a nine-year-old kid on Halloween night.

Corey passed by more darkened homes. More

FOR SALE signs. It seemed like everybody but Corey was getting out of Haddonfield.

Corey didn't share the same paranoia about Michael Myers as the rest of the town. On a subconscious level, Corey just didn't feel special enough to end up as part of Michael's story.

During the first few weeks after the Myers massacre, Corey avoided the news stories. But the stories about Michael's violence were inescapable, and Corey soon learned the names of the victims and the survivors, and he imagined their grief and nightmares. When he heard the reports of Michael Myers, he could not help but wonder, *how could such evil exist in the world?*

Corey had spent *that* Halloween night at home in his room, writing a paper about *The Scarlet Letter* for his American Literature class at the community college. He was asleep in bed by the time the boogeyman unleashed his wrath.

Corey pedaled quicker, wanting to be early so that Mr. and Mrs. Allen could get into their evening.

The Allens lived on the good side of the town, where the homes were bright and well-kept. Everything looked clean. Corey had been mowing their lawn since the previous spring, and the Allens were by far his favorite clients. They took an interest in him that made him feel less embarrassed about where he'd come from and how he'd been raised.

Corey thought of the Allens as the perfect family. Even when he occasionally overheard one of their arguments about a bill or a forgotten appointment, they didn't do it with the same venom as Joan did when she got upset.

Even though Corey had only known the Allens for half a year, he felt close to them. Corey viewed Roger Allen as a man capable of handling anything. Mr. Allen never looked worried. And he was funny, too. Corey didn't have to fake a laugh like he did with some of his other clients. Mr. Allen's jokes were good.

Theresa Allen couldn't have been friendlier. And she always had plenty of heartfelt advice to impart. Mrs. Allen possessed a nurturing quality that Joan painfully lacked.

Corey could feel real love in that house, and it made him feel like that kind of love was possible in his own life.

So, when Mrs. Allen called Corey and asked if he could fill in for their regular babysitter, who had bailed because of a stomach bug, Corey couldn't say 'yes' quick enough.

Corey didn't know their son Jeremy well, but he seemed like a nice enough kid. Jeremy had spent a large part of the summer at different camps. He was busy with soccer practice, piano lessons, fencing class, and his private tutor during the school year, so Corey had never really gotten any one-on-one time with him, but he looked forward to getting to know the little guy.

"I can't thank you enough, Corey!" Mrs. Allen told Corey for the second time as she dashed around the home hurriedly putting together the final touches on her flapper costume for Mr. Allen's company costume party. Being able to come through at the last minute made Corey feel needed.

"Roger! Corey's here!" Mrs. Allen yelled as Corey stood in the entryway.

Corey poked his head into the living room and found Mr. Allen, dressed as a train conductor, playing the piano effortlessly. Mrs. Allen might have been frantic, but Mr. Allen was in no hurry whatsoever.

Mr. Allen sipped his beer. "New gig, huh? Hope he's better at childcare than he is at yard work!" Mr. Allen jokingly told Mrs. Allen. "Oops," Mr. Allen feigned embarrassment, "did I say that out loud?"

Corey laughed and shoved his hands in his pockets as he dodged Mrs. Allen, who ran back to grab her pearls.

"You know, you should consider some perennials next spring," Corey suggested to Mr. Allen. "Hydrangeas could balance that dogwood in the side yard."

Mr. Allen couldn't give a shit about perennials or dogwood, but he appreciated Corey's enthusiasm.

"You decided on a school yet?" Mrs. Allen asked as she fastened her necklace.

"Not yet. I'm applying to a few engineering programs. We'll see. I'm just saving money this year, so I can go next fall. Hopefully, I'll have enough and—"

"Jeremy! The sitter's here!" Mrs. Allen cut Corey off as she checked her makeup in the mirror by the entryway.

Jeremy didn't respond, and Mrs. Allen looked to the upstairs balcony. "Jeremy?" she asked with some confusion.

Corey stepped closer and looked upstairs too.

The stairs curled and climbed all the way up to a third-floor attic. The height made Corey a little dizzy.

"*Boo!*" Jeremy jumped out from the nook behind the stairs wearing pajamas and a wolfman mask.

Mrs. Allen shrieked. Corey jumped too but tried to play it off.

Jeremy giggled maniacally and sprinted by his mother.

"Jeremy, come back here!" Mrs. Allen screamed as she followed him into the living room.

Jeremy popped out of another door and launched a paper plane which fizzled mid-flight and crash-landed into the side table.

The kid lifted his mask and looked at Corey with big, hopeful eyes.

"Corey? Can you show me how to make a Thunder Bomber? The number one of all time? My dad can make the best ones!"

Mr. Allen whispered through the living room door, "They're really not that good."

Corey smiled. "I'll sure give it a shot, little dude." He tousled Jeremy's hair.

Jeremy turned and raced upstairs to retrieve a stack of paper.

"Corey, can I talk to you for a sec?" Mrs. Allen asked with a more serious tone as she stepped back into the entryway. Mr. Allen strolled in to join her.

Mr. Allen snatched a mini-sized Twix from a bucket of candy and ate it as Mrs. Allen wrote a number down on a notepad.

"We'll leave the candy on the porch so the trick-or-treat kids can help themselves," Mr. Allen told Corey as he dug through the treats, looking for some Rolos. "We don't expect many this year—hey, Theresa, didn't you buy Rolos? I don't see any."

"Help yourself to anything in the fridge." Mrs. Allen ignored Roger's question.

"She made zucchini bread. It's actually good," Mr. Allen added sarcastically.

"Okay, here's my number. If there's an emergency, call me, we'll just be right down the street. We'll probably be home around ten-ish."

"It's a company party. It'll be sooner than that," Mr. Allen joked.

"But I do need to tell you one thing…" Mrs. Allen continued. She glanced upstairs to make sure Jeremy was out of earshot.

Corey grew curious.

"Since last Halloween," Mrs. Allen lowered her voice, "and all the events with you know… *Michael Myers*," she whispered, "Jeremy has been afraid of the dark. He's started wetting the bed at night, and, well, bedtime has just been really difficult."

"I can read him a story or something. Does he have a favorite book?"

"I think he enjoys the handbook on how to wear out one's patience," Mr. Allen said with another wink.

Corey smiled. Jokes.

"Roger, come on, knock it off," Mrs. Allen scolded.

Roger playfully zipped his lips.

"Once he goes to bed, it's usually fine," Mrs. Allen added, "but he saw the picture of that man with that awful mask on TV and, well—*he's just really sensitive*." Mrs. Allen sounded exhausted.

"I think many of us are right now," Corey replied calmly. "It's probably just normal kid imagination stuff. You know, his mind is trying to deal with all this scary stuff."

"We're just extra careful with everything right now, so no TV, and no candy, or fruit juices—he's already had two. And the normal stuff, you know, no running up and down the stairs, no jumping on the bed or anything else that could land him in the emergency room…" Mrs. Allen searched for her phone. She realized it was in her hand and continued, "You guys can play until eight-thirty, eight-forty-five at the latest, then he should be in bed or else he'll be a monster in the morning."

"Easy money." Mr. Allen unzipped his lips to eat the Rolos he'd finally found at the bottom of the bucket.

"Hey! Are you gonna come play with me or what?!" Jeremy announced as he came downstairs with a bunch of paper and a no-nonsense expression.

"Sounds like a threat," Mr. Allen joked and took the candy outside. "Good luck, pal!"

Corey turned to Mrs. Allen and assured her, "It's Halloween. We're gonna have a good time."

Famous last words.

As soon as the Allens walked out the door, Jeremy went full gremlin.

Almost like he had a checklist in his head, Jeremy began methodically crossing out everything Mrs. Allen had forbidden him from doing. He immediately dove into the trick-or-treat candy and ate half of it, then he chugged two more fruit juices. Corey tried to be the good guy and politely suggested other activities, but Jeremy ignored him and continued his ruckus. He bolted up and down the stairs, did front flips on his bed, and then... he insisted on watching a movie. Corey felt powerless to stop any of his behavior.

Away from Jeremy's doting and loving parents, it turned out that Jeremy Allen was a rotten little brat.

When Corey pled with Jeremy to follow his mom's rules, Jeremy lashed out with a flurry of insults.

"You are stupid, you have no friends, and you are poor!" Jeremy yelled when Corey took the rest of the fruit juices and put them where Jeremy couldn't reach them. "And you're being mean cause you're not as rich as me!"

"Come on, dude, I'm not being mean. Why are you being that way?"

"*Come on, dude!*" Jeremy mocked. "What twenty-year-old doesn't have a car? Oh, I know! A broke-ass, poor nerd who doesn't have any friends on Halloween. And that's why you gotta ride a stupid, little girly bike all the way over here. If you had a friend, you wouldn't be here trying to tell a nine-year-old what to do."

"You're not being nice," Corey informed him, thinking it might do something. It didn't.

"Good, I don't want to be nice. Because it's fun to be mean to a stupid, poor babysitter like *you*!"

Corey regrouped and tried again.

"Hey, why don't we make some planes. Come on, it'll be fun. What about that Thunder Bomber? Let's try to make the number one of all time. What do you say?"

"I say: fuck no."

"Don't use that language."

"I want to watch a movie."

"I can't let you do that. Your mom said 'no'."

"White trash."

"Jeremy!"

"I'm not gonna obey another thing you say until you let me watch a movie. It's your decision."

"Fine. But not anything scary. Just a cartoon or something short—"

"—No. I want to watch an adult movie. A rated-R movie. And I want it to be scary. If you don't let me, I'll tell my mom how bad of a babysitter you were. I'll tell her… you were the worst babysitter I've ever had in my entire life."

It was a standoff. And Corey worried that if he called Jeremy's bluff and Jeremy did lie and tell his mom all the things he threatened to tell her, well, then Corey's relationship with the Allens would be kaput.

"Okay," Corey gave in, "but you can't say a word about it. Promise? And you have to be in bed before they get home. Got it?"

Jeremy gave Corey a sinister grin.

"Got it?" Corey repeated again.

"Yeah, yeah, got it," the little shit replied.

Corey scrolled through the guide on the TV, hoping he could find something innocent. Something not too scary…

"Stop. That one," Jeremy ordered when he saw the first movie that grabbed his attention, *The Thing*. "That's the movie I want to watch tonight. Play it right now."

Corey saw that the movie had been made in the eighties and figured an older movie couldn't be too scary. Corey was wrong. Dead wrong. And half an hour into the movie, it had been scary enough to freak Corey out more than Jeremy. Jeremy might have been startled by the special effects, but the unrelenting sense of dread got under Corey's skin and profoundly unnerved him. Corey worried that Jeremy would be just as affected.

"All right, this is actually completely inappropriate for kids. I'm turning it off," Corey told Jeremy.

"You touch it, I scream."

"Come on, Jeremy."

"You touch it, I will kill you," Jeremy threatened.

"This movie is way too scary for you."

"I'm not scared. You're the one who's scared."

"Yeah, right. I'm twenty-one years old. I don't get scared," Corey lied.

"I bet you're scared of… Michael Myers."

Corey smirked and shook his head. He played along to show Jeremy how unafraid he was and teased back, "The boogeyman is gonna get you."

"What, are you stupid? He's not gonna get me," Jeremy said with a sneer. "Michael Myers kills babysitters, not kids. And guess what? Michael Myers is out there right now. It's Halloween night. That's when Michael Myers kills. And also guess what? I bet he's watching you right now. Because you know why? Because I've seen him. He's waiting. And when you're not looking, he's gonna be there with his big knife to get you."

Corey grew more uncomfortable with the conversation. "I am shutting this off, and we can play hide-and-seek or something for a few minutes before you go to bed. Your parents are gonna be home in—"

"*No!*" Jeremy shouted with such force that it caused Corey to sit up. "I'm not playing around, and I don't feel like doing dumb kid's stuff like playing stupid games with a wimpy-ass white trash boy babysitter."

"You're being a real jerk," Corey said as he got up. *Little shit* is what he really wanted to say.

"I can be a jerk if I want to. It's my house. You wish you had a house like mine!"

"Five minutes. That's it," Corey told Jeremy as he glanced at his phone. 9:00. He'd broken another one of Mrs. Allen's rules without even noticing.

"You suck at babysitting," Jeremy lashed out.

"I'm not a babysitter! I mow the lawn!" Corey yelled as he went to the kitchen to get a reprieve from the unrelenting little heathen.

"You suck at that too!" Jeremy shouted back.

Corey looked at the beer in the fridge. He took a deep breath to calm his strained nerves.

Instead of the beer, Corey grabbed the last bottle of chocolate milk. He gulped half of it down, praying it would provide some comfort. It didn't. So, Corey turned to the zucchini bread on the cutting board. Mr. Allen was right. It looked delicious. Corey picked up the knife to slice himself a piece when Jeremy let out a murderous scream.

"HELP!"

Corey jumped. The scream startled him so badly he nearly cut his hand.

"What is his problem?" Corey whispered under his breath. "What are you doing in there, Jeremy? No horsing around!" Corey yelled. "Five more minutes! I'm serious!"

A crash sounded from the living room, followed by a *clang* from the piano.

Corey dropped the knife and raced out of the kitchen.

Corey saw light strangely flickering inside the living room as he approached.

"Jeremy?" he asked uneasily.

Corey entered the room and found the lamp on the ground. Jeremy's wolfman mask sat on the couch, and everything on the coffee table had been knocked to the floor. Jeremy was nowhere to be found.

"Jeremy? This isn't funny! Stop messing around." Corey looked around the room but didn't see him hiding anywhere.

A tapping noise came from the entryway. Corey stepped cautiously in that direction and discovered the front door open just slightly, swaying in the breeze. Tapping against the frame.

"Jeremy?"

Corey peeked out. He didn't see anything. The yard was empty. The driveway was empty. The streets were empty. It made Corey feel like everyone on Earth had disappeared.

Corey closed the door and looked back into the house. *Was the little shit playing a joke, or had something bad happened?* Corey's worry grew.

Corey ascended the stairs.

"Jeremy!" he called out again. Nothing. And each time he received no reply, it pulled his nerves tighter.

Corey looked into Jeremy's room. He checked beneath the bed and the closet. He did not see a thing besides hundreds of toy dinosaurs.

"Come on, man! If you're hiding, this isn't funny. Cut it out, Jeremy!"

Corey grabbed the bathroom door, and it gave resistance.

"Are you in there?" Corey called out. "Jeremy?"

Corey pulled a little harder, but still the door didn't open. Corey clenched the handle, hoping to hear Jeremy's giggle inside. But nope. Just silence and more dread.

Corey removed his hand and stepped away from the door, not wanting to acknowledge his more worrying thoughts. The thoughts that told him maybe someone had broken into the house to kidnap the kid. And maybe, just maybe, they were now hidden behind the bathroom door.

"Hello?" Corey quietly asked through the door.

Corey knew that if anything happened to Jeremy on his watch, the Allens would never forgive him. So, he sucked up some courage, put his hand back on the handle, steadied his nerves, and gave the door a good yank. This time it popped open. Corey reached frantically for the lights. He found the switch and flipped it. Corey's eyes nervously ran across the room, but he found nothing except for the bathtub with a closed shower curtain.

Corey stepped closer to the bathtub. He cautiously put his hand on the curtain. Corey had seen way too many movies where a character entered a similar predicament, and he knew it rarely fared well.

Corey pulled the shower curtain back before thinking about it any longer. But he did not find anybody hidden behind it. Nobody could have hidden behind it because the tub was filled with more toys than were in Jeremy's closet.

"Spoiled brat," Corey said under his breath as he continued his search. "I'm calling your parents. Seriously. It's gonna ruin their night. They're going to be really upset, and you're gonna get in trouble."

Corey checked every room, bathroom, and closet upstairs but found no trace of Jeremy.

When Corey approached the third-floor landing, another *clang* from the piano rang out from the room below. Corey hurried back downstairs.

Corey came off the stairs and stopped at the entryway. The front door had been opened again. By that point, the name *Michael Myers* began running through Corey's head on a loop. And while Corey might not have felt special enough to be a part of Michael's lore, he knew without a doubt that Jeremy Allen certainly fucking was. And maybe Corey had been cast as a peripheral character in Jeremy's story.

Suddenly, everywhere Corey turned, he felt sure someone was watching him. And he became painfully aware of the size of the home. If Michael Myers had indeed broken in, there were a million places for him to hide.

Corey returned to the kitchen and discovered that the knife he'd used on the zucchini bread was missing. *No.*

"Come on, man," Corey said as his fear ramped up. "Jeremy, please be okay," he whispered to himself.

As Corey ran by the entryway, he noticed Mrs. Allen's phone number on the side table. He reluctantly pulled out his phone and dialed the number.

Corey could hear the worry in Mrs. Allen's voice the second she answered. He tried to sound like he had things under control, but Corey couldn't hide his panic.

"I'm so sorry. I know it's against the rules, but I let Jeremy watch a movie and… Well, I think he got scared. And now, I can't find him anywhere."

"I hope everything is okay. We're on our way now."

Corey hung up and continued his search, more feverishly now, running from room to room, turning on every light in the house, desperately looking, desperately hoping he could find Jeremy before the Allens returned home.

When Corey reached the second floor, he heard footsteps above. Corey leaned over the railing and looked up. He could see light coming from the attic.

"Jeremy?!" Corey shouted as he sprinted up the stairs toward the room.

For a moment, Corey thought the game was over. He expected to reach the attic and find Jeremy Allen hiding inside. But Corey's relief disappeared when he made it to the third-floor landing, and instead of finding the boy he'd been tasked with looking after, he found the missing knife from the kitchen lying on the floor inside the attic.

"Jeremy, what are you doing in there?" Corey asked nervously as he approached. "I called your parents. They're on the way home now. They're gonna be real mad about this," Corey told him, thinking that if all of it was a stupid prank, then Jeremy might reveal himself knowing the trouble coming his way.

But he did not. And Corey stepped into the attic.

Corey picked up the knife. The handle felt warm and clammy. It had been freshly gripped.

Corey examined the small space. It might have been a mostly empty room, but there were more than enough shadows and corners to conceal oneself.

Corey apprehensively stepped deeper into the attic. He gripped the knife tighter.

"Jeremy?" His voice cracked. "Where are you?"

Wham! The attic door slammed shut. Corey bolted for the door and grabbed the knob. It did not turn. Locked.

Tidal waves of panic crashed over Corey as his head darted around the room.

"*Help!!*" Corey screamed as he kicked the door. Each time he glanced back over his shoulder, he felt sure he'd find Michael Myers coming for him.

Corey kicked the door harder. His panic turned to terror.

The floorboard creaked behind him, either a product of his own frantic movement or the boogeyman's emergence.

A surge of adrenaline spiked, and Corey struck the door with all his desperate strength. The door swung open.

Corey had just enough time to see Jeremy's surprised expression on the other side of the attic as the door smashed into the boy and sent him flying backward over the stair railing.

Corey heard the front door open. Then he heard the horrible sound of Jeremy's body hitting the floor. And then, everything turned to fog. Shock set in and made things dreamlike.

Jeremy's body laid nonsensically on the ground, looking more like a child-sized doll than a human being. Blood spilled out from beneath his little head. The chandelier above lit him elegantly.

Corey peered over the stairs to the floor below, still holding the knife. He found the Allens standing over their now-dead son. Looking up at Corey. Observing the monster that had killed their beautiful little Jeremy. The horror…

"WHAT HAVE YOU DONE?!"

Mrs. Allen's scream sliced Corey in two.

UNTITLED

Haddonfield was once a peaceful town. But then, one Halloween, many years ago, all of that was lost. And darkness began.

Michael Myers was pure evil. He took our dreams and turned them into nightmares.

I ran from my fears and hid from the world. As he was locked away in his prison, I disappeared into mine.

Forty years later, he escaped, and Haddonfield was once again forced to confront this man in a mask.

His senseless brutality ravaged my community. And it killed my daughter.

It's hard to say where Michael Myers ends, and the boogeyman begins. Every truth of our tragedy is challenged by lies and legends. The lines of good and evil have become blurred.

The people of this sweet little town fell into a plague of grief… of despair… of suspicion. Evil is contagious. It is handed down and passed around.

*

Laurie sat at the computer in her office, considering the opening page to the manuscript she had been writing. Officer Frank Hawkins had been the one to suggest Laurie start writing an account of her experiences to process all her grief and trauma. Frank had begun journaling a year after his recovery when his niece Monique sent him a Brené Brown podcast and he first heard of the idea. He decided to give it a try and found it a pretty effective tool to give his feelings a name and move past some of his darker impulses, like his need for vengeance, and get to a place of acceptance.

"Give it a whirl, who knows what things you'll learn," Frank told Laurie when he ran into her at Nichol's Hardware one year after Michael's massacre.

Frank tried to check in on Laurie during that year, but she had once again cut most of her connections as she hunted for Michael. Those connections included Frank, who couldn't participate in the search due to his intensive rehabilitation.

Frank worried about Laurie's sanity, and he couldn't help but wonder what might happen if they never found that monster. Then what would become of his friend? And where would her vengeance go?

Laurie blew off Frank's therapeutic suggestion as New Age bullshit.

"Writing about him is not going to kill him," she told Frank.

But then, on one particularly dark night of the soul, when Laurie ran out of choices to make and wondered if she would live to see another morning, she cut herself open and wrote.

When the sun rose and Laurie saw what she

had written, she wrote more. *His evil consumes me, and I have nothing left. And I will never see my little girl again.* Inspired or at the end of her rope, Laurie did not stop writing, and she soon discovered that it helped exorcise some of the demons festering inside her soul.

*

As soon as word got back to Laurie that Michael Myers had killed her daughter, Laurie stormed out of the hospital to hunt him down. Laurie gave up any hope that the Haddonfield Police Department could capture Michael, and she took it on herself to kill the monster. But after a year, she, too, had found no trace of him.

Laurie drove the streets of Haddonfield, searching. Observing the fear. The madness. The paranoia. Swept up in all of it herself. Haddonfield had become a town ruled by the boogeyman.

The pain of all that loss hollowed Laurie. And as much as she tried to drink it away, she could not escape the emptiness she felt inside. Everything in her life had grown out of her need to find and kill Michael. And when she couldn't, she discovered she had little else to live for.

Frank had seen that frightening void in Laurie's eyes the day he ran into her at the hardware store, and he worried how far she'd take it.

"There is another way, Laurie," Frank told her as he helped himself to a cup of coffee from the breakroom. "Hell, I'm living proof."

"You're a different breed," Laurie smirked.

"I used to think so too," Frank smiled, "but the older I get, the more I realize we're all the same. We just tell ourselves differently."

It angered Laurie that Frank had given up, and she left without saying goodbye. Why was it all on her again? Had no one learned their lesson?

Laurie sat in her truck watching Frank laugh with some employees who loaded paint cans into his car. Frank didn't appear to have a care in the world.

"Living proof," she whispered quietly.

Frank wasn't the first person to suggest Laurie take another route. Lindsey Wallace, who had been just as determined to bring Michael down after what she had experienced, pushed Laurie into therapy.

Panic and depression took control of Lindsey's life when she couldn't escape the nightmares that haunted her. Therapy had helped pull her out of that pit, and on the other side, Lindsey found many more fulfilling things to take its place. An interest in Tarot reading and other mystical rituals gave her profound insights into a spiritual journey. And the more she pursued those interests, the less she concerned herself with Michael's story.

For Laurie, things came to a head one pitch-black night at the bottom of a bottle of Scotch. Laurie stood in her tiny, one-bedroom apartment. There were no signs of life anywhere in her home—not that you could really call it a home. It was just the fourth place Laurie had moved into after getting kicked out of the previous three. She had no furniture outside of the mattress on the ground. No photos, no books, no hints to a past except for the holes in the walls—Laurie's go-to anger management tool. A duffel bag stuffed with guns and survival accessories sat next to her mattress and told you everything you needed to know about where her mind was.

Laurie punched a new hole through the wall and then stumbled into the kitchen to find another bottle. But there were none left. Laurie opened the fridge and found only empty shelves and leftover hot sauce packets.

"Allyson," Laurie mumbled into her phone.

"Grandma, it's three in the morning." Allyson groaned on the other end. "What is it?"

"Allyson, I need to know you're safe."

She sighed.at Laurie "You're drunk… again."

After the massacre, Allyson had tried for months to take care of Laurie, but it always ended the same way. Drunk and yelling.

"Allyson—" Laurie fumbled the phone and dropped it. The coordination it would take to bend down and pick it up was too complicated for someone in Laurie's inebriated condition, so she slumped to the floor and rested her head by the phone to continue the conversation on the ground.

"Who're you talking to?" Laurie heard a man ask on the other end.

"Is that Doug?! *Doug?!*" Laurie called out. "Let me talk to him. Doug! Are you looking after her? Are you keeping her safe?!"

"Grandma, go to bed. You're gonna wake up your

neighbors again, and then you're gonna get kicked out. I'm not gonna go bail you out this time. I told you."

"But Allyson. He's... the boogeyman is out there..." Laurie slurred her words.

"Grandma, I can't do this anymore. I've got school in the morning. I'm not gonna answer these calls anymore."

"He's out there. Baby. He's still out there."

There was a long, quiet pause.

"I know... and so are we," Allyson said and hung up.

Laurie screamed and pounded her fists into the kitchen floor until her knuckles bled. The downstairs neighbor returned the noise by yelling, "Shut the fuck up, you crazy bitch!"

Laurie dragged herself into the living room, ripping her clothes off in an explosion of emotion. Her bloody knuckles painted her skin red. Laurie pulled herself off the ground and studied her reflection in the cracked mirror, leaning against the wall by her mattress. And she wept naked.

When Laurie woke the next morning, she found a message drunkenly scrawled onto the mirror, written in blood:

He's still out there. And so are we.

Laurie washed her hangover off with an ice-cold shower. Then she got dressed, sat down on the floor, and wrote more. She didn't stop until night fell. Afterward, she called Lindsey and told her that she needed help.

Laurie entered the same exposure therapy program Lindsey had undergone, and she faced the demons that most frightened her. During that process, she learned how to unclench her fists and let her monster go.

Laurie got sober, she sold all her weapons except for the gun Frank Hawkins had given her in the hospital for protection, and then she moved into a home with Allyson.

*

As Michael's evil turned the town in on itself, I worked toward a different path. I chose not to let fear rule my life. It was time to start breathing. I found a home. A place to live. Not a trap. Not a place to hide. A place where new memories could be made.

The connection I have with my granddaughter gives me joy and hope. It's a second chance at motherhood. She means everything to me. Everything...

Laurie re-read those words. And then she typed: *Michael Myers was simply the personification of evil. It is up to us whether we lock the door and say goodbye or let him inside.*

Laurie paused as she measured those words. Then she made an adjustment.

... let it inside.

Laurie looked at the photographs and clippings she had put up around the office to help her recall the stories and memories. There were high school pictures of the friends she had lost. Family photos of those in her life and those no longer with her. And crime scene photos and obituaries explaining in gruesome detail what had happened.

*

"Fuck," Allyson said under her breath as she banged her elbow against the bedpost while hurrying to tie her shoes. She investigated the redness and shook off the pain. She glanced at the clock. *Shit*. There would be no way to make it to work on time.

Allyson stole a look in the mirror. Some of the nurses Allyson worked with, like Deb, wore the scrubs well, but on Allyson they felt like a costume that didn't fit. As much as she wanted to tear them off and find something new, Allyson straightened her top and linked her laces.

Allyson could never quite go all the way with her feelings. When she decided to chop all her hair off and dye it jet black, she cut half an inch and kept the natural color. When she wanted to burn every single thing in her room, she cleaned the house and watched a marathon of home renovation shows instead. And when she wanted to scream out "*Fuck everything*," she just smiled and whispered.

A motorcycle roared by their home, and Allyson drifted into a fantasy. A fantasy that put her on that bike, driving the hell out of Haddonfield. Wind in her hair, nothing confining her, free to go wherever she wanted—

BEEP! BEEP! BEEP!

The fire alarm shrieked with deafening ferocity. *Fuck!*

Allyson jumped up and tore out of her room. She nearly crashed into Laurie bursting out of her office.

"*Sorry–sorry–sorry!*" Laurie yelled as they ran to the kitchen.

Smoke filled the house.

"What'd you do?!" Allyson yelled back.

"It's okay, it's okay, it's okay! I forgot to set the timer. It's the pie!"

Allyson ran for the fire extinguisher in the walk-in pantry as Laurie grabbed the oven mitts. Laurie threw open the oven and pulled out the charred remains of a smoking pumpkin pie. Huge black clouds of smoke billowed.

Realizing there was no fire, Allyson set the fire extinguisher down and hurried to disarm the smoke detector.

Laurie dropped the pie in the sink as the smoke continued to rise.

"I don't think I can save this pumpkin pie," Laurie said, looking at the botched dessert.

"Why are you even baking a pie? You don't know how to bake," Allyson asked as she wafted the smoke out the door,

"It's a Halloween tradition. I'm trying to—"

Allyson rolled her eyes. "I think that's more of a Thanksgiving tradition, Grandma."

"I mean, I know we have it on Thanksgiving, but pumpkins are everywhere on Halloween. Why can't we eat them in a pie?"

"I gotta go. I'm late for work. Are you okay?" Allyson asked tersely.

"I'm great. Never been better. Don't be late and don't worry about me. I think I still have another pie crust. Do you have your costume?" Laurie yelled as Allyson grabbed her bag.

"I told you, I don't want to go alone," Allyson said over her shoulder as she ran out the door.

"So, take someone!"

"Please don't bake any more pies!"

*

Allyson's car rattled loudly as she drove to work. When the overly chipper morning DJ unleashed a flurry of cheesy sound effects to announce the beginning of his program, she turned off the radio. Allyson preferred the rattle to the noise on the airwaves. The radio felt too exhausting. Everything felt too exhausting. Work. Home. The same thing, day in, day out. So depressingly mundane that it made Allyson feel dead inside. Weeks turned into months that turned into years, and Allyson, without even realizing it, suddenly found herself four years away from the night when she had lost so much. Since then, life had become something to endure rather than experience.

Few things brought Allyson any joy. And even fewer things made her care. She lived in a town full of horrible memories with a grandmother who tried so hard to show the world she'd gotten past her trauma that it sometimes seemed more like performance art than a cathartic new perspective. A grandmother who had been so stricken with grief over the loss of her daughter that she became an overbearing presence in her granddaughter's life.

Allyson hadn't always thought of things that way. No, when Laurie started going to therapy and quit drinking, Allyson bought the new Laurie whole cloth. And she felt relieved that Laurie had finally taken her finger off the trigger and had done something to take care of her well-being.

But living under the same roof and dealing with Laurie constantly imparting wisdom and advice had taken a toll on Allyson. And Allyson saw no way out. She worried that if she left her grandmother, Laurie would fall back to drink and depression and God knows what else. But if she stayed there, Allyson would probably suffocate to death.

Allyson stared at Haddonfield as it raced by her window. *What a miserable place*, she thought, as she did each time she drove to work. Neighborhoods were abandoned. Potholes appeared like landmines down every street. Vagabonds and panhandlers roamed the sidewalks. The stench of decay lay like a heavy blanket over the destroyed town.

And everywhere Allyson turned was another reminder of that horrific night. Allyson navigated the city strategically to avoid the most upsetting memories. She drove the long way to work to avoid passing by the park where she had discovered so many dead bodies. She took Cuthbert to Prospect Avenue to slip past Haddonfield Memorial Hospital without having to look at it. And even though the city had bulldozed the Myers' home, Allyson never even considered driving down Lampkin Lane where it once lived.

A police car *blipped* its siren behind Allyson. Allyson looked in the rearview and saw its flashing lights. She pulled off the road onto the shoulder, just before the old bridge overpass.

"Great," Allyson muttered and shifted angrily in her seat. She glanced at the time. Dr. Mathis was going to unload on her for being late again. And she had been doing everything she could to stay on his good side ever since he brought up the idea of promoting her to charge nurse. Allyson thought that maybe a minimal raise and new title might do something to soften her malaise. At least that's what she told herself when she had to put up with Dr. Mathis's bullshit.

"Come on, let's get this over with. What's taking you so long?" Allyson said irritably as she watched her rearview.

Allyson's gaze drifted past the mirror to the old bridge road and then to the wilder landscape on the other side. Her eyes situated on the expanse of untamed Haddonfield that existed around the county line, where there were no roads or sidewalks or homes. Just tall trees and grass that grew freely. Allyson imagined getting out of her car and walking into it. She wondered what would it feel like to emerge on the other side in a new place where all those memories didn't live?

Allyson fell deeper into those thoughts, and then she saw something move in the landscape. Her eyes focused on a shape, partially hidden by some shrubs.

Is that a person? Allyson questioned her judgment and stared harder. The shape was too far away to make out any details, but Allyson tried all the same. It had been four years, and even though Michael Myers was not at the forefront of Allyson's mind daily, she consistently found herself asking, *would he return?*

Allyson intensified her focus. She leaned across the passenger seat to get a better view. Allyson grabbed the two wedding rings attached to her necklace and squeezed. They were her parents' rings, and Allyson kept them close to her heart. Anytime she felt an overwhelming sensation coming over her, she squeezed, hoping they would help her fight the feeling.

Allyson studied the shape. And then it moved again. She squeezed harder—

Tap–tap–tap.

Allyson jumped, startled by the officer knocking on her window. When Allyson turned back to the shape, it had disappeared.

"You're under arrest!" the officer yelled as she rolled down the window. Allyson found Officer Doug Mulaney on the other side. Her ex-boyfriend.

"For being the prettiest girl I know," Doug winked.

Allyson smirked at his dorky charm.

Doug was another memory Allyson wished to avoid.

Allyson had stumbled into a relationship with Doug after he helped her through that Halloween night four years before. Allyson needed someone, and there was Doug. As Laurie recovered, she pushed Allyson and Doug together, hoping that Doug could ensure her granddaughter's safety.

Allyson, numbed by the tragic loss, mistook Doug's kindness for a devoted connection. Soon after Allyson graduated, she found herself living in Doug's apartment, trying to make a home amongst his hunting gear, tae kwon do equipment, and the many framed photos of his parents Conrad and Darlene, who Doug religiously called every single evening to give them a rundown of his day.

For a short while, living in Doug's world was what Allyson needed. It turned out to be the perfect place to disappear. While Doug patrolled the streets of Haddonfield and joined the manhunt for Michael Myers, Allyson hid on his couch behind a blur of television game shows. Allyson had no responsibilities other than suggesting what they'd eat for dinner when Doug got home. And usually, he'd already made the decision.

Doug's apartment also proved to be a valuable refuge from Laurie's spiraling madness. The Laurie Strode that Allyson had grown up with had always been a polarizing presence in her family's life, and there was rarely a moment when you couldn't feel the tension radiating off her. But that Laurie was nothing compared to the Laurie after 2018 when all you could smell was the booze on her breath, and all you could see was the blood in her eyes. Laurie had become a woman completely unhinged by pain and anger. Allyson never understood why her mother had kept Laurie so far away until then.

Allyson spent the remaining months in high school doing everything she could to help her grandmother, but it always led to a fight. And Laurie could fight. Their conflict became routine, and Allyson grew to resent Laurie. So, while Laurie hunted the streets like a madwoman trying to galvanize the police force and sketchy militia types like Derek and Lee (who both looked like they could rival Michael's savagery), Allyson stayed put on Doug's couch, debating whether to get kung pao chicken from Yummy House or burgers from Mr. Reuben's Restaurant.

Any time Allyson left the apartment, she tried to disguise herself so she would not draw unwanted glares. After Michael's massacre, Haddonfield devolved into a circus of paranoid finger-pointing and wild conspiracy theories fueled by rage and fear. And no matter what she did, Allyson couldn't disguise herself well enough to avoid the looks or mute the gossip that swelled around her. When nobody could find Michael, some Haddonfield residents turned their anger toward Laurie, and the narrative shifted from a woman who had undergone an unspeakable tragedy to a woman who had provoked a deranged lunatic into releasing such unimaginable annihilation.

"Had you all just called the police instead of treating things like some sort of game, my boy would still be here!" Cameron's mom screamed at Allyson when they saw each other at the cemetery.

Others in Haddonfield looked at Allyson with so much pity it made Allyson sick to her stomach. Allyson hated those looks almost as much as she hated the derisive stares.

But Doug never looked at Allyson like those other people. Doug never judged. He just counted his blessings that he got to be with the prettiest girl in Haddonfield. And when Allyson would wake up screaming, certain that Michael Myers had broken into the apartment, Doug could always calm her down.

"I won't ever let anything happen to you," Doug would softly tell her as he held her in his arms.

Even though Allyson never reciprocated those feelings, she couldn't deny the need to feel so protected.

But as Allyson crawled out from beneath her mountain of grief, it became harder for her to pretend she had deeper feelings for Doug. And all Doug's quirks that had brought her such comfort in the beginning quickly turned into nails on a chalkboard for Allyson. Suddenly, she couldn't stand to look at his hobbies cluttering the apartment. Or listen to those endless, annoying phone conversations with his parents who lived just ten minutes away. Who they saw all the time! And she hated the way he dressed. Every time they went out, Doug wore dress shoes and jeans, and he tucked his shirt into his pants with no belt; a look Allyson grew to despise so much that she ended up buying him at least a dozen belts throughout their relationship—and he still wouldn't wear them!

But more than any of those irritating habits that got under her skin, Allyson wanted distance from the person who'd seen her at her lowest. Doug became yet another reminder of that terrible night.

Eventually, Allyson broke things off passively by telling Doug she needed a break to work on herself.

"You don't have to like me as much as I like you," Doug told her, sensing her exit. "I'm fine with that. I can make that work. And then, who knows, maybe you'll start to get more into me over time. I'd at least like the chance to see if that might happen."

"Doug, it has nothing to do with you," Allyson lied. "I just need some time."

But once Allyson got out of the relationship, she never went back. And because she'd never firmly ended the relationship, Doug believed the door was still open.

"You doin' all right?" Allyson felt obligated to ask as Doug stood at her car.

"Oh, yeah, I can't complain. It's been pretty chill around here, which is the way we like it."

Allyson feigned interest and looked at the clock.

"How's your grandma?"

"She burned the pumpkin pie."

"Well, you tell her I said hi."

"I will," Allyson said as she looked back at the clock and calculated how late to work she'd be.

"I called you the other day. You get my voicemail? Or my texts?"

Allyson sighed. "I know. I owe you a call, and I've been meaning to…"

"I just want to know you're okay."

"I'm okay," Allyson said, becoming more annoyed with the conversation. "Is this why you pulled me over? To—"

"No." Doug looked into her eyes. "I pulled you over 'cause I miss you. Do you miss me?"

Doug switched gears before Allyson could answer. "I'm just kidding. Pulled you over 'cause it looks like your muffler's about to fall off your car. Wanted to give you a heads-up. If you don't get that fixed, you're gonna have a problem on your hands."

Allyson smiled and nodded politely. "Thanks for looking out for me."

"I like looking out for you."

Doug remained at Allyson's window long enough to make it awkward.

"Well, I gotta get to work. I'm late," Allyson finally told him.

"All right, you get out of here. Don't let Mathis give you any guff. He does, you call me, all right? And if he doesn't, you still call me. 'Cause you owe me a call. And maybe a margarita too."

Allyson maintained her bogus smile, and as Doug walked away, her eyes returned to the place where she'd seen the shape. She saw no sign of him, but she wondered again: *would he ever return?*

CHOCOLATE MILK

Corey Cunningham ignored the stares he received as he rode his bike through the streets of Haddonfield on his way to work. In the years since the accident, Corey had become a local pariah. He abandoned his plans for college, became more reclusive than he had been before, and took a job at Prevo Auto Body Shop working with his stepdad.

"Hey! Corey Cunningham! Who you gonna kill this Halloween?!" a driver heckled and veered toward him. Corey swerved, just barely missing the car.

Behind the windows throughout the neighborhood, Corey could feel eyes watching him. Judging him. Corey didn't look.

Rumors swelled all around Haddonfield about Corey after Jeremy Allen's death. Stories were made up about Corey's evil nature and how he used his job as a babysitter to terrorize children. With one boogeyman missing, the town found a new one in Corey Cunningham.

Even though Corey had been proven innocent during the trial, it didn't stop the rumors. Some people simply didn't believe it. Others speculated that his family had paid off the judge to get the ruling. And then some of the more insane theorists believed that Corey belonged to a secret Cult of Samhain along with other important figures in Haddonfield, including judges, sheriffs, and people in local government. This theory, a favorite amongst wackos, helped answer the question: *Why does so much violence happen on Halloween in Haddonfield? Why is it then that these monsters strike?*

It became easier for some people to conclude that a wicked cabal must control and release their boogeymen on Halloween for sacrificial purposes rather than accept the senselessness of such evil. These theorists believed the boogeyman killed to appease an evil god that the cult worshipped. The more intense wackos took that story even farther by suggesting that Michael Myers wasn't actually a human being, but rather a supernaturally malevolent force conjured by the cult to infect whoever they desired. And if you were to find one of the hell caves beneath Haddonfield where they believed the cult conducted their ceremonies, you would find their next vessel waiting. This is why, according to the believers, nobody had found the body of Michael Myers.

The biggest and loudest instigator of this Cult of Samhain business was the WURG DJ and all-around troll Willy the Kid, aka Sean Shrider, who used his nightly broadcast to entertain and fuel the most outrageous ideas. Back when he started out in Tampa as a morning DJ, Willy developed a reputation for pissing people off, and the station got so much kickback that they let him go after less than a year. So, Willy the Kid took his schtick to a smaller market. And then an even smaller market. And then he reached the end of the road in Haddonfield.

*

Ronald's mouth lit up as the spicy dan dan noodles from Yummy House lived up to their name.

"Holy Jesus!" he yelled as he burst out of his office and hurried to the vending machine in the garage.

"Oy, Ronald, are you all right?" Atilla, a mechanic at the shop, called out from behind a Chevy.

Ronald shoved some coins into the machine and grabbed a Mountain Dew Code Red. He drank half of it in one fell swoop to put out the spicy fire in his mouth.

Buuurrrrp! Ronald belched loudly.

"Want some dan dan noodles from Yummy House?" Ronald asked Atilla. "They're too hot for me. Gonna give me reflux."

"No, thank you. I just had a lovely snack. Do you have eyes on Corey? My friends with this Chevrolet Cruze need the muffler removed, and they'd like that done sooner than later."

Ronald glanced at the clock. Corey was late again. Third time that month.

Another mechanic at the shop, Simmons, pulled his hair into a ponytail and grabbed a mug of green tea next to the coffee pot. "Yeah, and I need him to empty the oil pans when he's done with that."

Ronald grimaced. He grabbed his takeout and walked out of the garage.

As Ronald approached the dumpster, he noticed a shadow moving behind it.

"That you, Corey?" Ronald asked.

He received no answer.

"Who's there?"

A moment went by and nothing.

Ronald began to circle the dumpster when the old vagabond stepped out.

Ronald jumped back.

The man stood before Ronald with wild eyes and a weathered expression.

"You can't be back here. This is a private business," Ronald told him.

The man's eyes remained on Ronald's. He made no gesture to suggest he understood.

"Hungersome?" Ronald asked as he offered the vagabond his leftovers.

The man looked at the food and then hsi eyes went back to Ronald.

Ronald's phone buzzed and caused him to jump again.

Ronald shoved the container into the man's hands and watched him slip through the broken fence behind the shop as he answered his phone.

"What is it, Shannon?" Ronald asked as he headed back to his office.

Corey came through the gate, pushing his outdated ten-speed. The chain needed fixing again.

"Hold a sec, Shannon." Ronald dropped the

phone to his side. "Corey, you're late. You're late. Again!"

Corey nodded and pushed his bike into the garage.

As he zipped up his jumpsuit, Corey could hear Willy the Kid's voice greeting Haddonfield through an old boom box's busted speaker sitting on a waylaid Dodge Dart that Simmons worked on.

Corey had gotten used to ignoring Willy's voice, especially after the DJ dedicated an entire week to discussing the Corey Cunningham case during the previous Halloween season. Callers phoned in and offered up their ideas about Corey's involvement in the cult, and Willy embellished them all.

"We all know what happened that night was no accident," Willy smirked. "That's the conspiracy right there, that an *accident* happened, and we sure ain't buyin' it. Nah, not that nonsense, 'cause we know that Corey Cunningham locked that little child in the attic and terrorized him while his evil cult hid in their hell cave and offered the boy up to their dark lord. That's what we know!"

Corey lowered the welder's helmet over his face, turned on the gas tank, ignited the torch, and went to work on the Chevrolet.

Corey stared at the roaring flame cutting through the steel. Sometimes he daydreamed about taking that torch to other parts of his life. Though he didn't put any specifics on that thought, he enjoyed it all the same.

The muffler broke free and slammed to the ground with a thunderous crash.

"Hey'ya. *Hey Corey!*" Ronald yelled as he killed the radio.

Corey lifted his mask and saw Ronald waving him outside.

Ronald yanked off a canvas tarp to reveal a 1975 black and orange Kawasaki 350.

"It's a fixer-upper, but what do ya think?" Ronald asked.

"You want me to work on it?" Corey asked, confused by the question.

"I used to drive this thing when I was a hundred pounds lighter," Ronald belly-laughed. "Used to get laid on it, if you can believe that."

Ronald smiled at those memories.

"It needs some work, but get it registered, new plates." Ronald studied Corey's expressions. "You like it? I got no use for it no more. Maybe with a good engine pushin' ya, you can make it to work on time. Know what I mean?"

Ronald put his foot on the ratcheting lever and kick-started the motorcycle.

Corey beamed at the gesture.

"Wow, Ronald, thanks."

The engine sputtered and died.

"Like I said, needs some work. Have fun, kid."

Corey couldn't take his eyes off that motorcycle as he swept up the garage toward the end of his shift. All he could think about was blasting away.

*

After work, Corey stopped at the Quickie-Go gas station for some treats. He stared at the shelves debating what to get for a solid five minutes before he finally decided on a Slim Jim, some Nerds, and his all-time favorite, chocolate milk.

"You're Corey Cunningham, aren't you?" asked the woman behind the counter, a new hire that Corey hadn't seen before. She looked at him suspiciously as she rang him up.

Corey smiled politely and slid his money under the plastic shield. He'd been coming to the Quickie-Go almost every day after work since he'd started the job specifically because, at the Quickie-Go, nobody ever said anything to him. But now this? Corey grabbed his loot and left, knowing he'd have to find a new place to get his treats.

*

Stacy revved the engine on Terry's dad's convertible LeBaron as she drove the Haddonfield High drumline out of the school parking lot. Terry had spiked his fruit punch with too much Everclear during lunch and worried he might fuck up his dad's car if he drove, which, if that did happen, would likely result in Terry's dad murdering Terry. So, Stacy volunteered to drive, and Terry watched her with more scrutiny than their driving instructor had.

"You're pulling the blinker down too hard. You're gonna break the lever," Terry said when she signaled her turn.

"You needs to chill," Stacy told him. Then she looked in the rearview at Billy and Margo in the back. "Can y'all please tell Terry to cool his fucking cheddar?"

"Just be careful, all right, my dad will kill me if he sees so much as a nick on this car. It's his baby."

"Yeah, we know. I'm bein' careful," Stacy reiterated.

"Hey, Terry," Margo called out from the back, "can I copy your biology homework?"

"Fuck no." Terry laughed. The rest of the gang laughed too.

"Well, fuck you then," Margo responded.

"Shit, you wish," Terry teased. They always teased Margo. Always. If each group had to have a punching bag, Margo played that part splendidly within this group.

"Stacy, stop by the gas station so we can get some beer," Terry told her. "I want to keep this buzz going."

"Facts. I'm not marching unless my buzz is legitimate." Billy seconded the motion.

*

Corey leaned against the Quickie-Go storefront with the Slim Jim in his back pocket, about to chug his milk before going home to avoid getting an earful from Momma about spoiling his supper. His plans changed when the convertible LeBaron sped into the lot, and the four members of the Haddonfield High drumline jumped out.

"What do you mean you don't have your ID? How are we supposed to get beer?" Terry snapped after Billy told him he'd lost his fake ID.

"I figured we'd just steal some," Billy told him, not really giving a shit about Terry's concern.

Stacy slammed the door shut. "Stacy, seriously? That's how you close a door? Are you trying to break it—"

Terry noticed Corey against the wall as they approached, and got an idea.

Sensing unwanted attention coming his way, Corey put his head down and hurried to unlock his bike.

"Hey, man. What's up, dude? What's goin' on? You got a sec?" Terry asked.

Billy twirled his drumsticks and whistled a catcall to get Corey's attention.

Corey ignored them and continued unlocking his bike.

"Hey, man, I'm talking to you. Hard of hearing?" Terry said as he reached Corey. Corey reluctantly looked up.

"Hey," Corey said quietly.

"He can talk!" Terry said triumphantly. Terry fished a crumpled twenty from his pocket and flashed it.

"So, here's the deal," Terry continued. "We are seniors. Got so much to celebrate. We've been practicing like crazy for our show—*go Haddonfield High!*—and we're loading up on our way to the game tonight. We are very excited, as I'm sure you can imagine, and we were hoping you'd be a cool new friend and buy us some refreshing beers. To help us celebrate this wonderful occasion." Terry gave him a used car salesman's grin. "So, my new friend, what do ya say?"

Corey politely smiled and shook his head. "No, thank you."

"No, thank you?" Terry smirked and looked at his gang. "You are kidding, right?"

Corey had only ever been in one fight back in eighth grade when Jesse stole Corey's clothes from his locker during PE and threw them in the toilet. That encounter had gone so wrong that Corey promised himself he would avoid any future conflicts if possible. So, making good on that promise, Corey grabbed his bike to move away from the gang. But it didn't work. The gang sidestepped alongside him.

"Why are you being like that? Why are you being so unfriendly?" Terry asked. "We're all friends here. Are you not our friend?"

"No," Corey politely replied, not paying attention to the actual question.

"No? We're not friends?" Terry cracked, acting fatally offended.

"No, we are, I just… I can't. I'll get in trouble."

"You won't get in trouble. We do this all the time. It'll take two minutes. Two minutes, pal."

"I'm sorry," Corey anxiously replied.

"You're serious?" Terry couldn't believe that his typically intimidating presence hadn't done enough to persuade this nerd to do what he needed.

Stacy homed in on Corey's look, and it dawned on her who they were dealing with. "Oh shit! I know you!"

The second Stacy recognized him, they all recognized him.

Margo spit laughed, "You're Corey Cunningham!"

"I know you did something messy," Billy taunted.

"Oh, oh yeah," Terry said as he got closer. "You're that psycho babysitter."

"You killed a kid, and you won't buy us some fuckin' beers?" Billy shook his head in mock dissatisfaction. "So whack."

Corey's stomach sank. He tried so hard to be anonymous, and now this.

Terry stepped closer, deciding to go full tilt. After all, who would give them shit for messing with someone as evil as Corey fucking Cunningham?

Corey pressed himself against the wall. He had nowhere else to go. He squeezed his glass bottle of chocolate milk with one hand and made a fist with his other. A furious anger swelled inside. As the drumline inched closer, Corey squeezed tighter. His anger deepened. He could feel it in every ounce of his being.

Terry whispered into Corey's ear, "You didn't just kill him, did you? You did other stuff. Disgusting stuff. We heard the stories. You a pedo, huh? You a pedo creep?"

Corey's anger exploded through his grip and the bottle shattered in his hand, slicing his palm wide open. Chocolate milk and blood sprayed over Terry's letter jacket.

"Are you fucking kidding me with that?" Terry said in disbelief. The rest of the drumline howled in laughter.

Before Corey could process his wound, Terry pushed Corey into the wall. Corey lost his footing and slammed to the ground. The debris in the parking lot opened his gash wider and filled it with shards of broken glass and bits of dirt and asphalt.

"Hey, assholes! Fuck off!" a voice yelled from behind.

The gang turned to find Laurie Strode gassing up her pickup truck. Her authority momentarily quieted them.

"We're not doing anything." Terry raised his hands and smiled.

Billy—who'd never been able to endure a tense, quiet moment—busted up, and the rest of the gang started laughing all over again.

"What the hell is your problem?" Laurie asked them.

They quietly repeated the name 'Michael Myers' as they scrambled to the door, snickering.

Terry gave Corey a parting wink. "Hey, Psycho— meet Freakshow, a match made in heaven."

"Ta-ta for now," Stacy told Corey with a faux proper English accent.

"Hey Margo, you wanna go to the school play on Saturday night?" Terry jokingly asked as he entered the store.

"Why, yes, I do," Margo excitedly answered, happy to be included and not bullied for a change.

"Well, have a good time!" Terry screamed and high-fived Billy.

"Fuck you, Terry," Margo said as she entered the store. "You guys are such pricks, you know that?"

Once they were inside, Corey could hear them chanting, "We're from Haddonfield, couldn't be prouder. Can't hear us now, we'll yell a little louder!"

Laurie approached Corey. "So, which one are you, the psycho or the freakshow?" she jokingly asked as she helped him up.

Corey gave her a nervous, shy glance and returned to his injured hand.

"Never mind, I know," she said with a sly smile.

Corey tried to pull some of the bigger pieces of broken glass out of his wound, but the pain burned too bright to touch.

"You don't fight back? Gotta watch out for assholes like that. They're contagious," Laurie said as she took his hand to examine the wound. She couldn't disguise her horror at the size of the gash.

"It's not that bad," Corey told her, hoping she'd leave him alone.

"I know a clinic close by. Why don't I give you a ride?" Laurie told him.

"It's fine. I don't need—"

Laurie turned her attention to the commotion coming from inside the store as Terry argued with the clerk about price gouging.

Margo backed her rear-end up to the door and dropped her sweatpants to moon Laurie.

"Kiss my ass, Laurie Strode!" Margo squealed with laughter.

Laurie smirked and then discreetly removed a pocketknife and unfolded the blade. She glanced toward the store to make sure no eyes were on her, and then she looked at the LeBaron.

"Hey," she asked Corey as she held up the knife, "you want to do it, or you want me to?"

Corey smiled and took the knife.

Laurie grabbed Corey's bike and loaded it into her pickup as Corey carefully approached the car.

Corey raised his arm, thought two seconds about it, and then jammed the knife into the tire. The escaping air hissed viciously.

*

Laurie ground the gears of her stick shift as she whizzed through the streets of Haddonfield. She reached past Corey, opened the overstuffed glovebox, and managed to retrieve a cassette tape. She inserted it into the archaic stereo system and cranked the volume.

Corey hung his hand out the window to avoid getting any blood on the upholstery. Laurie had wrapped it sloppily with the napkins from Sonic she found in the crease of her seat.

"You like Dan Fogelberg?" Laurie shouted over the loud volume of Dan Fogelberg's 'Better Change'.

"Who?" Corey yelled back over the music.

Laurie grinned. She waved to the crossing guard

as they passed by a school. "Hey, Tyrone, keepin' 'em safe?!"

"Yes, ma'am!" Tyrone shouted and waved back.

Corey stared at Laurie, mystified by her effortlessness. So many people thought of Haddonfield as the home of Michael Myers, but sitting shotgun in Laurie Strode's truck, Corey saw another candidate for that title.

"Corey, right?" Laurie asked.

"Yeah. And you're Laurie. Laurie Strode," Corey shouted.

"The one and only." Laurie laughed and took a quick left. Corey slid into her.

*

Inside the Grantham Primary Medical Clinic, Allyson pulled the lamp closer to see inside Julian's ear.

"Mom says I got all that wax in there 'cause I wear my headphones all the time. As soon as I get out of my bath, when my ears are still wet, I put 'em in, and I even wear them when I go to bed. But I can't live without my music, so I just gotta deal with the wax."

Allyson smiled. Julian had more swagger than any fifteen-year-old she knew. And when he lay on the exam table, she couldn't help but think about her friend Vicky who'd been killed by Michael the night she had babysat Julian. But Julian, despite that traumatizing encounter, had grown up and appeared to be more adjusted than most of the people she knew who'd lived through the nightmare.

Julian pulled on his gold chain as Allyson searched for the source of the obstruction. "One day, I'm gonna be a big deal record producer. And I'm gonna take my money and invest it wisely, not like those other people who go spend it on disposable things. I'm gonna be prudent with my money. Like I bet you can't even tell this chain is fake, can you?"

Allyson squinted as she looked deeper into his ear. "You fooled me," she said, not really paying attention to his boasts. Allyson had already done the ear-syringing, and nothing came out. But she could definitely see something stuck inside his ear.

"Here, let's tilt your head, Julian," Allyson told him as she helped direct the angle. Then she gently shook it.

"Wax supposed to just fall out?" Julian asked.

Julian adjusted his posture, but nothing happened, and Allyson moved his head back to its upright position. Julian pulled out his phone and sent a few text messages as Allyson continued her investigation.

"But people think my chain is real. So, I buy this for fifty bucks instead of five thousand, and then I put the rest of my money into a Vanguard account. Prudence. That's how you create an empire big enough to climb out of dumb Haddonfield."

The tilting worked enough to let Allyson see the impediment more clearly.

"Don't move, Julian," she said as she grabbed some long tweezers and inserted them into the shallow part of his ear. "I think I see it."

Allyson clamped the tweezers and grabbed hold

of the object. "Got it," she said as she removed a tiny spider from his ear.

Julian fell back and put his hand over his mouth. "Oh shit! I had a spider in my ear?"

"Looks like it," she said as she dropped the spider into a cup and examined it. "Maybe it just wanted to hear what you were listening to."

"Nurse Allyson, I think I'm gonna pass out."

Allyson wet a cloth and handed it to Julian. He melodramatically leaned back and draped it over his head.

"What if it laid eggs in there?" he questioned from under the rag.

"Are spiders so bad?" Allyson joked.

"Is there such a thing as a good one?"

"I actually think spiders are pretty cool."

"All right. If you think they're cool, then I think they're cool too. But I still don't like it living inside my ear."

"Fair enough."

*

Allyson passed by one of the other nurses, Deb Jennings, who was trying on a novelty black cat mask.

"What do you think?" Deb asked Allyson as she headed to the door. "Hot or not?"

"Sure." Allyson didn't have much patience for Deb.

"You should try it on!"

"That's all right."

Deb had been trying to convince Allyson all week long to go with her to the costume party at Velkovsky's. Laurie had been haranguing her to go as well.

Allyson knelt and carefully dumped the spider out of the cup. The spider looked confused at its new outdoor surroundings and stood motionless.

"Go on, see what's out there," Allyson quietly encouraged.

The spider took her advice and disappeared into a crack alongside the building.

When Allyson came back inside, Deb shoved the black cat mask into her hands.

"Try it on."

"Will you leave me alone if I do?"

"No, but I'll be *very* happy."

Allyson gave in and reluctantly slipped the mask over her head. "There, are we good?"

"Are you kidding?! It looks great on you!" Deb squealed.

Allyson rolled her eyes and looked at her reflection in the glass partition next to reception. The mask only accentuated Allyson's gloom. And it caused her heart to grow a little heavier.

Deb didn't seem to get Allyson's reluctance to celebrate Halloween and kept egging her on.

It's not even that Allyson didn't want to participate. Allyson wanted to participate more than anything in the world, because that would have meant she'd become a 'normal' person—not a zombie tattooed with emotional scars, and riddled with anxieties and images that she couldn't shake.

At that moment, Laurie came through the doors. "Hey, look who's getting in the spirit," she said when she saw Allyson in the mask.

Allyson quickly removed it, embarrassed to be caught in the Halloween get-up.

"I brought you something," Laurie said. On cue, Corey Cunningham stepped into view.

Deb, who'd returned to organizing the paperwork at reception, glanced over her shoulder to witness the reveal. She quickly turned back and whispered to Allyson, "Is that your grandmother with Corey fucking Cunningham?"

Corey sat down and munched on his Slim Jim.

Allyson had never thought one way or the other about the stories she heard surrounding Corey Cunningham. But the guy who sat anxiously in the waiting room, eating a stick of beef jerky, looked as scared and vulnerable as she often felt.

Allyson signed Corey in and took him into the exam room to wait for Dr. Mathis.

Corey fidgeted nervously as he sat on the examination table.

Allyson gently removed Laurie's crude bandaging. "Pretty bad, huh?"

Corey turned his head so he wouldn't have to see the blood.

Allyson found his squeamishness adorable.

"The doctor will be here soon, and we'll get you out of here and on your way before you know it." Allyson leaned a little closer. "Everything is gonna be okay. Trust me."

Corey smiled. Unlike most strangers, Allyson immediately put him at ease. So much so that he didn't look at all happy when Dr. Mathis entered the room, interrupting his moment with her.

Dr. Mathis barely acknowledged Corey as he plopped down in his seat and wheeled himself closer. Pompousness oozed from his every gesture.

Allyson couldn't stand him, but he was the first doctor to make her an offer after she finished the nursing program. Allyson had seen Dr. Mathis on different news programs after Michael's massacre, talking about the victims he knew and acting like a victim himself. Trying to make a name for himself out of their tragedy. Dr. Mathis even wrote a book about the experience. In *On the Hunt for Michael Myers: a Doctor's Story of Survival and Justice,* Dr. Mathis inserted himself into that 2018 night and spoke about his close call with death, which was nothing more than his Halloween-themed party being blocks away from the park where Dr. Mathis's nurse Marcus and Marcus's wife Vanessa were brutally murdered.

I am certain that after Michael Myers killed my employee and his wife, he walked past my house. Did he look inside? I have a feeling he probably did. And had he come through my door, there is no doubt in my mind that he would have met his match. Because I am not afraid of a man in a Halloween mask. I never will be. And if Michael Myers ever returns to Haddonfield, I will be waiting, Dr. Mathis wrote in chapter four.

In his very thin book, Mathis also psychoanalyzed Michael by asserting all the well-worn cliches.

*It is my expert medical opinion that Michael Myers
wanted nothing more than to sleep with his mother. And
when his request was denied, he took vengeance out on
the women in Haddonfield.* In Mathis's estimation, this
explained why many of Michael's victims had been
women.

Dr. Mathis enjoyed his local celebrity status,
but he wanted more. So, when Laurie Strode's
granddaughter came into his office looking for a job,
Dr. Mathis hired her on the spot, thinking she might
bolster his credentials in the Myers mythology.
When Mathis brought up the idea to Allyson of a
follow-up book where he would explore the Strode
saga in Michael's story, Allyson showed no interest.
Eventually, Mathis stopped bringing up Michael
Myers around her, and they quickly settled into a
cruddy boss–disgruntled employee relationship.

After Allyson got hired, she heard the stories about
Dr. Mathis's sexual inappropriateness, which he'd only
recently curbed for fear of damaging his reputation.
Allyson never had to deal with that side of him.

"He's a little older than the type I normally
fuck, but he's also kind of a babe, you know," Deb
confessed to Allyson over margaritas one day after
work. Allyson tried not to throw up. "And he's rich
as shit. That goes a loooong way. He's also smart, and
I'm the type of woman who finds intelligence really
sexy. Like I'd totally let him *#metoo*. And you know
what Lydia told me? She told me that Dr. Mathis
had invited that nurse who used to work with him—
you know, the guy who Michael Myers stabbed to

death—Lydia told me that Dr. Mathis had invited him and his wife to like a sex party or something he was having on that very night."

"His name was Marcus. Hers was Vanessa," Allyson said, recalling that night and growing angrier with the conversation.

"Yeah, and think about it, had that guy just gone and had a fucking blast with Dr. Mathis, him and his wife would still be alive today. Isn't that fucked up?"

Allyson considered looking for other jobs every day, but she barely had enough energy to get to the one she had, much less searching for something new. And when Mathis brought up the promotion, Allyson hoped it would make her job a little better.

"All right, let's take a look at that hand."

Dr. Mathis lacked any finesse as he grabbed Corey's hand forcefully and studied the injury. Dr. Mathis pulled it and poked it with no regard for Corey's level of sensitivity. Then, without warning, Dr. Mathis jammed a needle into the wound to numb it for the stitches. Corey, whose eyes were on Allyson, was surprised by the sudden, painful sensation and reflexively kicked his legs into a table of tools knocking it over.

They clanged loudly against the floor, both startling and annoying Dr. Mathis. He took his anger out on Allyson, who scrambled across the room to pick them up.

"Jesus Christ!"

"I'm sorry. So sorry." Allyson hurried to clean up the mess.

"I'm sorry. That was my fault," Corey told Dr. Mathis.

"No. It was me."

Allyson fumbled with the gauze, and it unspooled across the floor.

"Stop it! Goddammit. Idiot! What a mess," Dr. Mathis rudely scolded Allyson.

Allyson froze. Her face turned bright red. When her eyes caught Corey's, she quickly looked away.

Dr. Mathis tore off his gloves. "Clean it up. Give him a tetanus shot. I'll be back."

Dr. Mathis stormed out of the room, and an intense silence hung in the air for a few moments while Allyson grabbed a new pair of gloves and reorganized the tools that had fallen off the tray.

"You shouldn't let that guy talk to you like that," Corey quietly advised.

Allyson hid her face as she put things away, hoping Corey wouldn't see her shame.

Corey wanted to say something, anything, but the only words he could find were inspired by Laurie. "I'm just sayin', working for a guy like that... it makes you sad. Even if you don't think it does. You've gotta watch out for assholes like that. They can be contagious."

Allyson smiled, recognizing her grandmother's philosophy. She looked up at Corey. "I've put up with worse."

Allyson situated herself to clean his hand and admitted, "I'm just dealing with it for the time being until I get this promotion."

"Is it worth it?" Corey asked as their eyes met again for a charged moment.

Allyson returned to his hand. She removed the saline from her kit and cleaned the gash tenderly. Then she grabbed her tweezers and carefully pulled out the bits of trapped glass and debris from his wound.

"So what'd you do? To your hand?"

"I was at work, then I had an injury," Corey told her as he looked away.

"So your job sucks too. Where do you work?"

"What?" Corey said he looked back at Allyson.

"How'd you hurt it?"

"Mechanic shop," Corey replied to her earlier question.

"Oh, really? My car has been rattling."

"It's just your exhaust system clamp has probably come loose. It's an easy fix. It's super cinchy. You just need a lift and two screws."

"Cinchy?"

Corey found a small laugh. So did Allyson.

As Allyson cleaned his hand, Corey looked through the window and noticed Deb watching him with judgmental eyes. He turned away.

Allyson saw her too. "Don't mind her. She's harmless."

"I don't like the way she's looking at me," Corey said quietly with his head down.

"She's just jealous," Allyson told him.

"Why?" Corey asked, confused.

"'Cause I got to treat your hand, and she didn't."

Corey blushed a little. Allyson got a little embarrassed too, wondering if she'd accidentally gone too far.

Flirting? she thought. *You don't even know this guy. What is wrong with you?* Allyson reeled herself back and focused on finishing up the job.

*

"So, I'll see you tomorrow night?" Deb asked Allyson as she reapplied some lipstick.

"I doubt it," Allyson told her as she collected her things.

"You are no fun, whatsoever." Deb rolled her eyes. "Rather stay at home with old grandma than come have fun with a cool bitch like me. Lame!" Deb bounced across the hall to Dr. Mathis's office and knocked on his door.

"Yeah?" Mathis called out from inside, busy working on his fantasy football lineup while scarfing down a salad from McDonald's.

Deb entered the office. "Thought you could use a lunch date!"

"Mi casa, tu casa," Mathis replied with a laugh. "Pull those blinds and have a seat."

Allyson watched the blinds in Mathis's office close. Then she grabbed her things and left.

Allyson found Corey walking up and down the sidewalk outside the clinic, looking perplexed.

"Hey," she called out. "Lost?"

"I can't find my bike. I think your grandmother took it by accident."

Accident. Allyson smirked.

"You can't ride a bike with one hand, anyway, can you?" Allyson asked.

Corey looked at his bandaged hand.

"Come on, I'll give you a ride."

Allyson used her car as a closet, and she had to move a pile of clothes, junk mail, and a collection of leftover takeout bags to the back seat to make room for Corey.

Corey stared out the window, listening to her car's rattle as they drove through Haddonfield.

"Oh, yeah, I can definitely fix it so it stops rattling."

"Well, maybe I'll bring it in."

"Yes!" Corey said a little too excitedly. "I mean, you should," he added, a bit more tempered.

Allyson passed by the Haddonfield High drumline hobbling down the road in Terry's deflated LeBaron. Corey hid a laugh.

"Friends of yours?" Allyson asked.

Corey just shook his head and kept smiling.

It had been a while since Allyson enjoyed anyone's company, and she wasn't quite ready for it to end. She flipped on her blinker and pulled into the drive-thru of Bernie's Soft Serve close to the bridge road.

"I need a chocolate vanilla swirl. Want one?" Allyson asked.

"Yeah. I'd love one," Corey said, as he never got to enjoy his chocolate milk.

Once they got their soft serve, Allyson pulled over on the side of the road, and they stared at the nothingness surrounding them as they ate.

The afternoon sun came through the window and made it almost feel like spring. Sort of like things were coming to life, Allyson thought.

Allyson put on one of the playlists Lindsey had made her, and they listened to the Cocteau Twins, Siouxsie and the Banshees, Slowdive, and This Mortal Coil while they ate.

"So, what do you do, Corey? Outside of working at a mechanic shop?"

Corey poked awkwardly at his soft serve, not sure how to answer. "I don't know. Not really anything, I guess."

"Yeah? Same here."

Allyson saw a vagabond pushing a cart of junk toward the underpass beneath the bridge. Past him were some abandoned warehouses. On the speed limit sign in front of them, someone had crossed out the numbers and replaced them with the word *DIE*.

"This town…" Allyson said as she scraped the sides of her cup.

"I know…" Corey quietly agreed.

They finished their desserts, and sat quietly and comfortably for a few moments listening to the music. Both appreciated the sensation of not needing to mask their pain and malaise behind false expressions and idle banter. Together, they could just be.

*

"Thanks for the ride. You didn't have to do that," Corey told Allyson as she pulled to a stop in front of his house.

"Sure, I did. My grandma stole your bike. It's the least I could do."

Corey laughed.

"What's your number?" Allyson asked.

"Phone number?" The question surprised him.

"So I can give you a call about my car. The rattle. And bring your bike."

"Oh yeah, sure."

As Corey gave Allyson his number, he noticed the curtains in his home open just slightly. Momma was watching.

Corey abruptly ended the moment. "Thanks again, and thanks for the ice cream and my hand. I gotta go," he told her as he dashed indoors.

Joan moved away from the window the second he came inside.

Corey's quick exit left Allyson wondering if she'd actually experienced a connection or had just imagined one.

But then Allyson looked upstairs and found Corey approaching the window, smiling. He waved innocently. It made Allyson smile too. She waved back. And then downstairs, Allyson saw the living room curtain open again as Joan returned to her lookout.

*

Allyson arrived home to find Lindsey's car parked out front, which always made her happy. Lindsey and her had grown incredibly close over the years, and Allyson credited her with convincing Laurie to get help.

89

Allyson came inside to find Laurie elbow-deep in pumpkin guts as she carved another jack-o'lantern. Lindsey relaxed by the coffee table, sipping a glass of rosé and shuffling through a deck of Tarot cards.

"Well, that was quite a move, Laurie," Allyson jokingly said as she passed by her grandmother.

"What did I do?" Laurie asked with mock confusion.

"You weren't trying to set me up?"

"What? He was injured and needed help. Where else was I gonna take him?" Laurie said with a smile, revealing her true intentions.

Allyson sat down by Lindsey and took a sip of her wine.

"Don't believe a word she says. She's a strategist," Lindsey said as she pushed her deck toward Allyson.

"Okay. Whatever. I thought he seemed nice. And cute. What's the big deal? It worked, didn't it?" Laurie laughed. "I can see it on your face."

Allyson took a card from the deck and flinched.

"Oh no, I got the death card!" Allyson tossed the card onto the table.

"No, that's not bad. In Tarot, it means one major phase is ending, and a new one is going to start," Lyndsey informed her. "Puts the nail in the coffin of that police officer you were dating."

"Ugh. I ran into him on the way to work."

"Maybe next time, don't fall for someone at your own crime scene," Lyndsey recommended as she poured herself a refill.

"You know what you need, Allyson?" Laurie

advised, "You need to find someone that can let go. Someone that makes you want to take off your shirt, show grief your fucking tits, and say—" Laurie raised both her middle fingers and yelled, "Let's go!"

Laurie cracked up as the sinewy pulp of the pumpkin innards slithered down her fingers. Allyson couldn't help but laugh too. Partly because of her grandmother's wild idiosyncrasies, but mostly because she couldn't get Corey's smile out of her mind, and it felt good.

*

Corey sank in his seat at the dinner table, queasy from the sight of the bright red dollop of marinara clinging to the rim of Joan's glass of milk. Corey hated spaghetti suppers. They always made him sick. He moved the food around on his plate, not wanting to eat it. He looked at his own glass of milk, wanting that even less.

Joan made her spaghetti sauce recipe by frying up an entire box of bacon and then adding a package of hamburger meat, a couple jars of pre-made marinara, several very liberal shakes of garlic powder, and then almost a full cup of sugar. It made the meal sickly sweet, and incredibly greasy. The odor always lingered in the air for hours after they'd eaten.

"Why aren't you eating, Corey? It's your favorite. You love your mother's spaghetti."

Corey shoved a couple of forkfuls in his mouth. The noodles dangled from his lips, and he quickly slurped them up while trying not to get sick.

"Those noodles are too long. Here, give your plate to your mother," Joan said as she grabbed his dinner and cut his spaghetti into tiny bite-sized pieces.

Corey kicked his shoes off under the table and dug his socks into the carpet. The sensation helped calm his growing nausea.

Corey glanced at his reflection in the glass door of Joan's curiosa cabinet, which was filled with all varieties of eerie-looking rabbit figurines. There were antique dolls, ceramic sculptures, and glass ornaments. Rabbits in all shapes, sizes, and colors. And they always looked like they were watching Corey. When he was younger, he would turn them away so they wouldn't be staring at him. Joan would inevitably make the discovery and turn them back. Eventually, Corey grew tired of rearranging hundreds of figures every day and gave up on it. Now he had to stomach their looks the same way he had to stomach his mother's spaghetti suppers.

Ronald dumped half a can of parmesan cheese over his portion to kill the sweetness and then spooned several heaps of the spaghetti in between slices of white bread to make a pasta sandwich. He took a bite, and big globs spilled out and splattered onto his plate.

"Ronald." Joan snapped her fingers. "No messes."

Ronald scraped half the pasta out of his sandwich.

Joan turned back to Corey's hand. "Is it infected? Did your hand get infected? What did the doctor say?"

"I'm fine, Momma. It's gonna be terrific, he said. You don't need to worry, he said."

"Ronald, were you not watching him?"

Corey had lied and told Joan that he'd hurt his hand just before leaving work. He reckoned that would be better than telling her he had been pushed around by some high school kids.

"I can't keep my eyes on him every second."

"Well then, I might have to send him back to work for DeVon at the call center if you can't give him the proper supervision. Got it?"

"Got it." Ronald nodded as he slurped up a noodle.

"Thank God he still has his mother to take care of him. Jiminy Cricket. Corey, you practically amputated your hand on treacherous equipment. I don't care if it was an accident, don't be so cavalier about parts of your body."

Joan dug the ladle into the bowl of spaghetti and dropped a massive portion onto Corey's plate.

Splat!

"Momma, that's enough," Corey groaned.

"Can't you taste the bacon?"

Corey stabbed the spaghetti with his fork.

Ronald grabbed another piece of bread.

For a moment, the family ate silently.

And then Corey's phone buzzed in his pocket. He discreetly removed it and checked the incoming message under the table. Corey's face lit up.

Hey, it's Allyson from the clinic. Don't forget to change your bandage. Hope you're not in too much pain. I'll bring your bike to the shop if you're there tomorrow.

Corey could not text 'Yes!' quick enough. And then he wrote more:

It was nice to meet you.

A second later, he received a text back:

It was nice to meet you too ☺

"What is this with the telephone? Who is calling my boy under the dinner table? Who is this person you are texting?"

Corey stayed silent.

Joan angrily grabbed her dish and took it to the kitchen.

"Boys that keep secrets don't get custard for dessert."

Joan dropped the dish in the sink and filled it with water. Ronald leaned close to Corey and whispered, "Don't tell her about the motorcycle then."

Corey nodded.

Joan came back in for round two.

"Is it that girl who brought you home? Is that who's sending you messages? What the heck was that all about?!"

"Just someone who worked at the doctor's office," Corey sighed.

"Well, I have a very bad feeling about her. As soon as I saw her out there with you."

"She's nice, Momma."

"I'll make that determination." Joan shook her head and looked down at his hand. "Doctors." She blew a raspberry and continued, "You should have come home to your mother and let me take care of you. Not those doctors with all their ideas. They're no good. They don't care for you the way I care for you. How many times have I told you this, Corey? They make matters worse, not better.

94

I make it better. Your mother is not happy with this at all."

Joan's glare bounced between Ronald and Corey. When they gave her no reaction, she returned to the kitchen.

"Get your laundry together, Corey! I'm gonna put in a load. Whites and delicates!"

*

Corey stared at himself in the bathroom mirror, wondering if Allyson could see past his awkwardness. Why had she been so nice to him? Corey worried that if she saw him again, all those things she'd missed in their first meeting might be more apparent. And what if she could then see the psycho everyone else saw whenever they looked at Corey?

No sign of personality could be found anywhere in Corey's room. A few generic posters hung on Corey's wall. A limp baseball pennant. A painting of a duck. A photo of his dad on a motorcycle. Corey had no interest in expressing himself through décor. Didn't see a point.

Out of the antiquated clock radio on his dresser, Willy the Kid blathered on about the crazy surprise he'd been promising to reveal all week long. And then, finally, the time came...

A static burst sounded followed by a voice with an English accent, full of concern. "The evil has its hold on Michael. It will not release its grasp. This is no longer a task for a doctor. This is a task for God." Corey listened.

"That's right folks, your own Willy the Kid has procured the Dictaphone logs of the one and only Dr. Loomis! And I'm gonna let you in on all the juicy details."

The recordings continued, "They don't know what they have here. Behind these bars. What kind of dark power it possesses. They treat it like a boy. They treat it as a person. This is no boy. This is no person. It is evil. And it is waiting… And when it begins, it will not stop…" Another static burst popped.

For a moment, silence. And then Dr. Loomis continued, "Wednesday, October 31st, 1984. 11:30PM. Tonight it got out. For one hour, they could not find it. And then there it was. Standing at the end of a corridor which they had previously searched. Still. It had wrapped its face in white linen. It said nothing. They do not know how it got out. But I promise, it will get out again… And it must be stopped."

Corey stood at the window staring at the flashing red light on top of the WURG radio tower in the distance as he got drawn into Dr. Loomis's analysis.

"I have lost all hope in Michael's recovery. Each day it waits. I sit before it, and it looks through me. I fear its madness is becoming my own. At night I do not know who or what I am becoming. Who or what I am? I fear I cannot stop this madness. I can no longer sleep. Not knowing what I know. I have stared into its eyes. And now the abyss stares back at me... Whatever evil force lives inside Michael, it wants but one thing. Death. And I pray each night it will burn in hell!"

Corey grabbed the dumbbells Ronald had bought him the previous Christmas and curled them. Somewhere in the back of his mind, he hoped that people wouldn't see his flaws if he got a few more muscles. Maybe.

"Where are you, Michael?" Willy taunted. "It's almost Halloween. Will we see you this holiday? Or will you send someone else into the night to do your dirty work? Is the cult of Samhain receiving my radio waves? Can you tell Michael to come out and play?" Willy paused. "Michaeeeellll... Michaeeeellll..." Willy laughed again. "All right, Haddonfield, I'm opening up the hotline, and let's hear some more of your theories. Big Texas, you're on with Willy the Kid!"

Corey moved to the pull-up bar in his closet.

"Willy! Long-time listener, big fan. I just wanted to make sure people know that the man who escaped Smith's Grove in 1978 was not the same man who killed all those people. In fact, Michael Audrey Myers himself was murdered that night, and the heavy breather with the mask was a hitman. The same man who poisoned Pope John Paul the First just weeks before. It's all tied up with the powerful financial institutions of the Vatican. Just ask the Archbishop of Chicago, for cryin' out loud! I can't believe the CIA hasn't put two and two together."

Joan stepped into the doorway with a bowl of vanilla custard. She put it on his dresser, and turned off the radio. She had no patience for Willy the Kid.

Joan collected Corey's dirty clothes scattered around the floor and stuffed them into a laundry basket. She noticed that he'd put the photo of his father back up, and she tossed that in the basket as well.

Corey ignored the theft, as he'd expected it to happen when she discovered it.

Corey looked at the shiny film on top of his momma's custard. Joan somehow made the custard less sweet than her spaghetti. Still, he sat down in his bed and shoveled it into his mouth.

*

The red light from the radio tower came through Corey's window rhythmically as he lay in bed, working on what he'd say to Allyson when he saw her the next day.

Corey watched the flashing red light wash across his wall, wishing for something different. Anything different than what he had.

Corey couldn't sleep… again. He turned back and forth in his bed, but his thoughts kept him awake. His thoughts always got louder at night. Corey surrendered to his insomnia and climbed out of bed. He got dressed and snuck past Joan and Ronald's bedroom, where he could hear both snoring. Then he quietly left the house.

Corey walked through his neighborhood. The lights in the houses were out. Most were empty. He didn't look at any of them. He just kept his head down and walked as he always did, trying to remain unseen.

Corey came to the Allen house, which had been vacant since Jeremy's death.

The lawn had died and turned yellow. So had the flowers Corey had planted years before. He looked at the impressive house, up to the attic where it had all gone wrong. The home towered over him with threatening menace. The one home in Haddonfield that once made him feel okay had turned on him too.

Corey slipped through the opening in the gate and approached the entryway.

The windows had been boarded up long ago, but one plank had fallen and was propped against the wall. That's the entrance Corey used.

It felt colder inside the home than outside as Corey passed by the piano, caked in dust. You could see the outline of the television against the wall. Corey ran his finger over it as he moved into the entryway.

Paper planes of all different sizes littered the floor. Corey waded through them as he walked to the stairs.

Corey ascended the spiraling staircase up to the attic, never taking his eyes off the bloody stain on the ground. The stain they hadn't been able to wash away.

Corey reached the attic and pushed the door open.

The wooden grate against the wall in the attic

broke the moonlight into thin sheets that reached across the floor. Corey grabbed a dusty stack of paper that he kept on the shelf and then moved back to the third-floor landing.

Corey sat down, cross-legged like a kid, and meticulously folded a piece of paper into an airplane. Making sure every angle was precise. Studying the wings with focus.

On some nights, the wind slipped through the cracks in the home and parroted the screams the Allens had made as they discovered their dead child. On other, quieter nights, like this one, Corey could hear the silent devastation filling each room. It helped to soften the noise his thoughts created.

Corey launched the plane, and it wobbled through the air, crashed against the stairs, and then nosedived to the ground.

Corey grabbed another sheet and proceeded to do the same thing. And he continued with one sheet of paper after another until he'd created another small paper plane graveyard on the ground below.

When he'd finished, Corey leaned over the railing and stared at all the folded papers covering the floor but not quite masking the stain of blood.

Corey grabbed the railing and hoisted one leg over. And then he brought the other leg over. He held onto the wooden spindles and looked down. It looked so far away from him. This had been another ritual Corey had engaged in since the Allens deserted the house. But he had not yet worked up the nerve to let go.

Corey closed his eyes and leaned back, holding the railing tightly, telling his hands to release their grip. But they wouldn't listen. No matter how hard he tried, Corey could not let go.

NELSON CHRISTOPHER

On October 30th, 2018, Nelson Christopher regained consciousness a short while after the bus transporting the Smith's Grove inmates to Glass Hill crashed.

Nelson peeled himself off the floor of the bus. A few of the inmates remained on board. Many more wandered around the wreckage outside. But Michael Myers had escaped. Nelson knew that as soon as he came to.

Nelson's head was heavy from the collision, and he stumbled through the bus as blood trickled down his face and fell over his eyes.

Dr. Sartain had been shot and lay unconscious on the ground. Nelson stepped over his body and left the bus.

Outside, Nelson found more death. An officer had been killed. He lay dead in the grass, covered in blood. A little farther on, a boy had been murdered and discarded like a piece of litter on the side of the road. His head smashed so severely that it no longer made sense as a part of the human body.

"He done this. Michael done this…" Nelson mumbled incoherently. "He killed them all."

Nelson looked up to the stars twinkling softly in the night as if they weren't looking down on all that violence. And then he continued wandering down the road to find his God.

A few hours later, he heard the sirens approaching. Nelson tried to hide in the bushes, but the police arriving at the scene spotted him. They picked Nelson up along with the rest of the inmates and took them to Glass Hill.

*

On Halloween night, some thirty years earlier, Nelson Christopher walked into Oshman's Sporting Goods inside the Russellville Park Mall, wearing a dirty white plastic Halloween mask and carrying a small hatchet. He grabbed the gate at the entrance of the store and pulled it down. Then he jammed a screwdriver through the lock so no one could get in or out. Through the mask, his eyes were oil black.

Everybody in the store turned at the sound of the gate crashing closed.

"Heed my call!" Nelson yelled as he stepped onto the counter and waved his hatchet. "I be the one to bring you to the other side!" Nelson swung his hatchet into the light socket. Sparks exploded. A chorus of screams sounded. Music to Nelson's ears. Their fear tasted good. Nelson hoped his violence might reveal the dark kingdom he'd been seeking.

Everybody ran toward the back, and Nelson climbed off the counter and stalked in their direction.

"I am your death merchant. Your boat captain to the next world," Nelson said as he swung his ax and chopped the stationary bikes and tents during his march to the terrified hostages.

"The fires of hell await. There we'll find him. Together, we'll serve."

Security guards raced to the gate and worked to get it open.

Nelson stopped before he reached the panicked crowd. He placed his hand upon a shelf of racquetball gear and raised his hatchet into the air. "The fires of hell await!" Nelson bellowed and then brought the blade down on his hand, chopping off three of his fingers.

"These are mine!" Nelson screamed as he lifted his detached fingers. "And they soon will be yours."

Just then, the gate sprung open, and security rushed in and stopped Nelson before he could do anything more.

Not long after that incident, Nelson was determined to be criminally insane and locked up at Smith's Grove.

*

Nelson's father, Erik, was a minister at a small fundamental church in the backwoods of Illinois. Nelson's mother died young by her own hand. When she couldn't recover from a depressive spell, she went to the woodshed early one morning before the sun came up. She stood in the darkness and called out, "God, deliver me to your kingdom."

Her cries woke little Nelson and brought him to her.

"Momma," the boy whispered as he approached the open door.

His mother's pale skin cut through the blackness and showed itself to Nelson. The faint light made it look like she had donned a mask.

Her expression remained stern, and Nelson saw that she held the handle of a hatchet in both hands.

"Go back inside and tell your father what you've seen," she said firmly.

And then she swung the hatchet forcefully toward her face. The blade caved her head in and buried itself in her skull. Her body crumpled to the ground right before her child. Nelson watched her dark blood wash out of the woodshed and marry itself to the dew on the grass.

The trauma destroyed the family. Panic overtook Nelson, and he was given to night terrors. The loss sent Erik into a psychotic rage. Voices began speaking to him. Told him that his wife had been turned evil and that her offspring contained the same dark energy. Jill, their oldest daughter, escaped Erik's madness. But Nelson, just a young boy, could not get away.

"My son is contaminated with sin and controlled by evil," Erik told the elders at the church before performing a series of cruel cleansing rituals to rid his son of the demons he believed had infected Nelson's soul.

"No, Daddy, no!" Nelson screamed as Erik

plucked him out of his sleep and dragged him toward the bathroom, where Nelson could hear the elders of the congregation singing hymns. The candles burning inside made Nelson believe hell awaited. It likely did.

Erik dunked his son in scalding bathwater as the elders prayed. Nelson cried out in agony as the water scorched his skin. His eyes begged for help. The witnesses remained firm. Devoted utterly to their preacher.

"Get out, you devil!" Erik screamed madly as he whipped the boy across the back with his belt. "*Out!*" Erik took the boy's head and pushed it underwater. Nelson thrashed wildly.

Every night, Erik locked his son in the woodshed where Nelson had seen his mother take her life. There, upon the bloodstained floor, stricken with fear and grief, Nelson slowly lost his mind. He believed everything his father told him about his evil nature and vowed to exact revenge upon the righteous for the unholy treatment he'd received.

On Halloween night, when Nelson turned sixteen, and while locked inside his woodshed prison, he could hear the trick-or-treaters roaming the streets of his neighborhood. Little goblins, witches, and monsters shared stories about the boogeyman while they collected their candy. On the night when evil mischief filled the air, Nelson swore his soul to the darkness. "You get me out of here, I will find your king, and I serve him. I spread my evil where you send me. Let me know the boogeyman."

Jill came to her brother's rescue years later. She found Nelson still confined to the woodshed while their daddy sat sick in the house. The congregation had long since abandoned the family, and their daddy lived a hermit's existence. Only venturing out to feed his son slop and to pray for the evil to release its hold on Nelson. A ritual he'd never stopped performing.

Nelson's condition horrified Jill. Gaunt from malnourishment, Nelson stood hunched over. His skin nightmarishly pale. His long stringy hair fell over his bony shoulders and he could barely form a coherent sentence. When Jill brought him to her home in Russellville, Nelson regularly lashed out angrily without warning. Nelson needed much more than his sister's love to save him, but he refused her attempts to get him psychiatric help. Finally, she had to force him out of her house when she came home one night and found him wielding a knife, threatening to "kill them all."

Nelson moved onto the streets, and over the next several years he confirmed himself to the darkness to which he'd been cursed while scavenging out of dumpsters and taking whatever charity he could find. He grew angrier by the day. Voices in his head alerted him that the time had arrived to become the driver to the next world.

On Halloween, the anniversary of when he'd promised his soul to the darkness, those voices in his head screamed. And Nelson could ignore them no longer.

Nelson stole a hatchet and a plastic Halloween mask from Hill's Hardware Store. He filed the clown paint off the mask and made it dirty white.

"This face mine now," Nelson said as he looked at his reflection in the store's glass window. "I can't see me no more."

And then Nelson journeyed to his sister's house.

Jill screamed when she found her brother at her door, wearing the grotesque mask and holding his weapon. Demanding to know how to get back home so he could send to hell the people he had promised to kill.

"Daddy's dead, Nelson. He died five years ago," Jill informed him.

As soon as Nelson heard those words, he raised the hatchet to strike his sister. Jill slammed the door, and Nelson swung the hatchet into the wood, splintering it. Trying to break inside. If he couldn't take Daddy, he decided to take Sissy instead.

The neighbors ran out when they heard the commotion, announcing they'd called the police.

"I shall begin a wicked reckoning, and I find you then," Nelson mumbled to the darkness as he left the neighborhood.

Nelson passed by packs of trick-or-treaters, and marched to the Russellville Park Mall.

*

Dr. Sartain preferred experimental techniques over methods and medications that had undergone clinical analysis. And when he received Nelson and conducted his first interview with the new inmate, Sartain's mind raced with possibilities. Not about Nelson's recovery, which he had little interest in exploring, but rather in using Nelson as a tool to better understand Michael Myers.

"You have eyes like his," Dr. Sartain told Nelson as he led him to his cell.

Michael stood in the shadows against the wall, watching as the two approached.

"Michael, I would like you to meet Nelson Christopher." Sartain grinned. "He shall be residing on the other side of your wall."

Michael made no reaction to Sartain's provocation. He remained still. Faceless. But Sartain could sense his gaze.

Nelson took residence inside his barred room, muttering incoherently about good and evil. Soon, he found himself drawn closer to the wall bordering Michael's cell.

"You a man or a monster?" Nelson whispered through the wall. "Or you da' devil? Tell me, mister. Are you the darkness? If so, I be your driver."

Dr. Sartain watched their exchange from a monitor in his office, but he observed no response from Michael. Sartain's most prized psychological artifact remained in a near-comatose state. Upright but inactive. Watching but nothing more. It seemed that no matter what Sartain did, he could not wake Michael. And his obsession with Michael grew stronger as Michael refused to show him the cold brutality Dr. Loomis had warned about.

Determined to use Nelson as an instrument to arouse the evil inside Michael, Dr. Sartain engaged in more hideous tactics to encourage Nelson's role in the process. The same tactics he'd used on Michael when he took over his care. Sartain determined that if he could release the monster inside Nelson, perhaps Michael would unleash his.

Orderlies were directed to keep the inmate awake.

Once they'd put Nelson into a sleep-deprived state, Dr. Sartain and his associates fed the inmate nightmarish images and videos. The bloodier, the better. And as Nelson reached a state of complete psychosis, Dr. Sartain restrained Nelson in front of Michael's cell.

"I see you lookin' at me, mister. You know me don't you? I be your driver! Let me take them to hell! I bring 'em there for you," Nelson screamed at the motionless shape in the shadows. "I kill too!" Nelson screamed excitedly. "You da' monster, I see that," Nelson whispered. "I'm a monster too!"

Nelson's ravings had no effect on Michael. After a while, Dr. Sartain abandoned the experiment and returned Nelson to his cell. But the monster whet Nelson's appetite to spread more fear.

Crazed, Nelson beat his hands against the barrier separating the two. Trying to break into Michael's cell but unable to punch through the walls. Even though Michael told him nothing, Nelson grew more certain that he had found his answer.

"I do what you want. I be yours. I be your Michael

Myers!" Nelson screamed into Michael's cell as he broke his remaining fingers against the wall.

At night, Nelson stayed by the wall of his cell, declaring his devotion to Michael Myers.

*

In 2018, the state transferred Nelson from Glass Hill to the Gunshor Dalia Facility. Then, a year later, Governor Fialkait discharged many inmates who'd been previously held at Smith's Grove after a class action lawsuit arose.

Nelson was released to the streets of Haddonfield.

Nelson came to the underpass beneath the old bridge road either by pure chance or cosmic fate. He'd been digging for cans when a storm rolled in, and he took shelter beneath the overpass.

Once there, Nelson sensed something he hadn't felt since the night the bus crashed. The presence of the evil he'd devoted himself to.

Nelson peered into the opening to a tunnel beneath the underpass, and he knew he'd found his God when he heard Michael's breath inside.

Nelson crawled through the tunnel and observed the darkness. Farther inside, he found the shape in a foul and rotten form, slumped and decaying. Covered in mold. Infected by the wounds he'd sustained the year before.

"I'm here. I'm here too…" Nelson called out. "I be your Michael Myers. I take care of you."

Nelson made a new home beneath the bridge, and he took on the role of Michael's caretaker.

Nelson returned to the bridge with the leftover dan dan noodles Ronald had given him.

"Hungersome?" Nelson yelled into the tunnel, repeating what he'd heard Ronald say.

Nelson crawled through the opening and deposited the food at the foot of Michael's domain. A shaft of light broke through a grate above and allowed Nelson to see a sliver of Michael's pale gray mask.

Nelson climbed back out of the cave and sat down by the arts and crafts project he'd begun several days earlier. Nelson had broken into Nichols Hardware Store and stolen some tarp and rope so he could fashion his own mask.

Nelson trimmed the eyeholes he had cut into the tarp, and he widened the slit for his mouth. Then he wrapped the covering over his head and tied the neck together with the rope.

Nelson looked at his reflection in the shattered rearview mirror he kept on his shopping cart. He studied the mask through the cracks of broken glass.

"The fires of hell await..." Nelson quietly mumbled. "For that Michael Myers to wake."

Nelson stepped out from beneath the bridge and looked at the stars through his mask. And he sang the song he'd sung as a child when locked inside the woodshed back home:

> *"There's a hole in the boat*
> *And we can't keep afloat*
> *Ooo-lie-fee-ist in the sea*

Nail my hands to the door
And my knees to the floor
To stop that water till we reach the floor

There's a hole in the boat
And a lump in my throat
Ooo-lie-fee-ist fear thee

Nail my neck to the deck
And my cheek to the leak
To stop that water so the ship won't sink

There's a hole in the boat
And a lump in my throat
Ooo-lie-fee-ist fear thee

When all is lost
And the water won't stop
We'll sing this song till it coughs us up."

Nelson chuckled to himself and then disappeared back beneath the bridge.

DEATH IS IN THE AIR

Things were slow at the Prevo Auto Body Shop, and Ronald let Corey spend the day working on his motorcycle.

"Corey, tell me, what do you plan on doing with this old piece of useless junk?" Atilla asked as Corey tried and failed to start the motorcycle again.

"I plan on riding it."

"Hey, Atilla," Simmons interrupted, "I need you to come look at this wagon. I swear Ronald told me they wanted it cherry red, so that's what I did. But it's this uptight couple, and they're saying something different. They say they wanted beige."

"Right, let's hear what these geezers have to say, and we'll do what we need to do, won't we?"

"Copy," Simmons said as he hurried off.

As the day wound down, Ronald joined Atilla and Simmons for a six-pack at their barbecue pit campfire while they watched Corey try to get the bike going.

Corey started it, and again it sputtered and died.

"Hold on, hold on, hold on," Corey said as he jumped off the motorcycle. "I think I got it."

"He's a real easy rider over here," Simmons heckled.

"No bollocks, Corey, this time you get it started," Atilla added.

"Go easy on the kid," Ronald stood up for Corey.

"We're just having fun. Corey can take it. Can't you, Corey?" Simmons asked.

Corey finished checking the fuel valve.

"I think this is it," Corey said as he jumped back on. Before bringing his foot down, he heard a loud rattle pulling up to the shop. He glanced over his shoulder and saw Allyson stepping out of her car.

"Hey, there," she said, waving to Corey. "I brought your bicycle."

Corey pulled his bike out of Allyson's car and introduced her to Simmons and Atilla.

"That yours?" Allyson asked, pointing to the motorcycle.

"Yeah, it's a project I'm working on."

"Can I see?" Allyson asked.

"Yeah… yeah… um… you like motorcycles?"

"I think they're pretty cool."

Corey hesitated as he climbed back on. He put his foot on the lever and prepared for another attempt. Corey closed his eyes and whispered, "Come on, please start." He took a deep breath and then kick-started it once more. This time the motorcycle came to life.

Simmons and Atilla raised their beers and cheered him on.

Ronald pumped his fist triumphantly. "There you go, kid! Yeah!"

Corey's smile reached from ear to ear as he sped around the yard.

Allyson laughed and clapped with the guys, amused and excited by Corey's joy.

"Think you found yourself a good luck charm!" Simmons yelled to Corey.

"You ever ride?" Ronald asked as he leaned over to Allyson.

"No, always wanted to."

Corey pulled up to Allyson. "Get on."

Allyson hesitated and then said *screw it* to herself.

Corey scootched back and let Allyson get in front of him.

"Okay, now what?" Allyson asked as she looked at the bike.

"Be careful, Corey. Your mother will rip me a new one if anything happens," Ronald said as he walked back to the shop.

"I'll be super careful, Ronald," Corey told him. And then he explained how it worked to Allyson. "Right hand gas, left hand front brake…" Corey paused, "…no, fuck, shit, sorry right hand gas *and* front brake. Left hand clutch. Right foot brake. Left foot is the shifter thing. Simple."

"That's not simple at all. Show me again."

Corey placed her hand on the handlebars and put his over hers. "I'll show you this way. Ready?"

"I don't know."

"Hold on."

"What?" Allyson yelled over the engine.

Corey rotated her hand, and the motorcycle lurched forward.

Allyson screamed and then laughed, "Shit!" Her heart leaped into her throat as a shock of panic raced through her. *What are you doing?* Allyson's thoughts shouted.

Corey shifted gears and the bike accelerated.

"Slower!" Allyson yelled, but Corey didn't hear her. He pushed the bike faster, and Allyson gripped tighter.

"Slower!" she pled louder. But Corey still didn't hear.

"Slower!" Allyson finally screamed at the top of her lungs, absolutely terrified.

Corey slowed the bike to a roll and then stopped. "Are you okay?"

Allyson had trouble catching her breath. "That was just more intense than I thought it would be."

"I'm sorry, I didn't mean to— Are you sure you're all right?" Corey asked, noticing how the color had left her face.

"No, I'm good. I liked it. I think—"

Honk honk!

"Hey Corey, come give us a hand!" Ronald yelled.

Corey turned to find a tow truck rolling up to the garage pulling Terry's LeBaron, tire still deflated.

Terry and his dad followed behind.

"I used to have to give that asshole insulin," Allyson told Corey when she saw Terry's dad.

"My goddamn son drove three fuckin' miles on a flat because he doesn't know how to change a tire on a goddamn automobile," Terry's father yelled as he slapped Terry against the back of his head.

"That's very dangerous. You could lose control and cause an accident," Ronald calmly explained.

Terry turned and discovered Corey watching him. Corey quickly looked to Allyson.

"I'm gonna go help Ronald real quick, then I'll fix your rattle—your car—I'll fix the rattle on your car," Corey stuttered.

"Don't worry about my car. I came to see you."

Corey's smile grew so big it hurt. For a moment, he forgot about Terry. It was only Allyson. The only person in the world.

*

As soon as Corey got into Allyson's car, he regretted his decision to go with her to a Halloween party. He rolled the window down and up, and then he fidgeted with the A/C, trying to find a comfortable temperature.

"How many people you think will be there? Think there will be many people there or not that many people there?"

"You're stressing," Allyson told him calmly.

"I'm not stressing," Corey lied.

Corey looked out the window and then turned back to Allyson. "Can I just say... I don't go out much."

"We're just gonna say hey to a few friends, grab a

drink, and then lurk in the shadows. You know, like normal people do." Allyson smiled and whispered, "It's gonna be fun. We need this."

Corey nodded. "Yeah. Yeah. Okay... but it's just that people look at me... And..."

"Nobody's gonna see you, I promise. Because— hang on—"

Allyson reached behind her and retrieved a bag. She pulled out the black cat mask Deb had given her and handed a silly scarecrow mask to Corey.

"And if they do, you can use this mask to scare them away," Allyson joked.

Corey stared at the smiling scarecrow, not convinced it would keep him safe.

Allyson pulled up to Velkovsky's. Before they got out, she turned to him. "I know who you are, and you know who I am, so let's get over it and have a good time tonight, okay?"

Corey put on the mask. He looked at her through the disguise.

"Okay, then." Corey shrugged. "Let's have a good time."

*

The blaring music assaulted Allyson and Corey when they walked through the doors. People were everywhere. So many more people than Allyson expected.

Allyson's anxiety climbed, and in any other instance she would have bailed as soon as she entered, but when she turned to check on Corey, she could see

119

his unease even behind his smiling scarecrow mask. And it made hers less severe.

"This is how we turn normal," Allyson whispered to Corey.

Deb, dressed appropriately as a devil, ran up to greet Allyson.

"There you are! I thought I missed you! Who's under the mask?!" Deb directed her question to Allyson's date.

"I'm a… I'm a scarecrow," Corey answered sheepishly.

"Lemme see! Lemme see you! Take it off!" Deb teased him. Then she noticed the silly scarecrow's injured hand and his dorky clothes and awkward posture. She knew Allyson had brought Corey Cunningham. And she could not believe it.

"You supposed to be scary?" Deb goaded.

Deb turned to Allyson. "Is that him in there?!" She stared through the eyeholes of Corey's mask and asked, "Is it you?"

Corey's unease made her smile. Deb had fun watching him squirm. Like so many others in town, Deb had zero interest in Corey Cunningham.

Corey looked away. Another bully. Someone else to hate him. He wanted to tell her how he'd done nothing wrong. How Jeremy falling had been an accident. How he was a good person. The same things he wanted to shout each time he saw a look like the one in Deb's eyes.

"Lindsey's on fire with her palm readings!" Deb turned to Allyson. "She predicted that I'm gonna have a long and happy future! Let's see what your palm says, silly scarecrow!" Deb grabbed Corey's injured hand, but he yanked it back.

"I'm gonna get us some drinks!" Allyson yelled. She pulled Deb to the bar with her.

"Hey!" Allyson shouted at Lindsey, who had put together a fortune-telling station at the end of the bar.

"Oh!" Lindsey leaned over the bar and gave Allyson a hug. "So happy you came! What are you drinking?"

"Two vodka sodas!"

"Two?!"

Allyson turned to look toward Corey, who stood awkwardly in the middle of the bar, trying to stay out of the way.

"Guess who Allyson's silly scarecrow is!" Deb screamed.

"Tell me!" Lindsey looked to Allyson.

Deb continued to troll and asked Allyson, "Is it the guy who pissed in the water fountain at the mall?"

"Yeah, exactly," Allyson replied, annoyed. She had no patience for Deb's games.

"Or, or, or…" Deb teased it out. "Is it the guy that fucked the old lady at the nursing home?"

"Deb, drop it. Seriously."

"*No!* It's Corey fucking Cunningham, the guy that killed that kid!" Deb looked at Lindsey. "Can you believe it? Allyson brought a psycho killer to *your* Halloween party!"

"Shut up!" Allyson snapped. Then she calmed and told Lindsey, "It was an accident."

"If you believe that," Deb smirked.

Lindsey gave Allyson a look of concern.

"New beginnings, remember?" Allyson said as she pointed to the deck of Tarot cards. She felt so self-conscious it hurt.

"Is this a new beginning?" Lindsey asked. "'Cause it seems like something else to me."

Allyson gave Lindsey a look that read, *come on, you too?*

"Talk to Laurie. She's the one who encouraged this," Allyson replied back.

"Yeah, but Laurie's not you. I'll reserve judgment until I see him without a mask, but you could be with anyone."

"Yeah, well, right now I'm with him."

Allyson returned to Corey with the drinks. He gulped his down, desperately trying to quiet his nerves.

"Three–two–one–drink bitch!" Deb screamed as she took a shot of Jägermeister at the bar with a few random strangers. Allyson and Corey watched them all having a great time.

Allyson turned to Corey. He looked through the mask into her eyes. It was just the two of them, and fuck everything else. Regardless of all the opinions and gossip in the room about them, Allyson was determined to have a good time.

Allyson slammed her drink and pulled Corey into a photo booth.

A little buzzed and a little defiant, Allyson took on a more authoritative attitude as she pushed Corey to pose with her and instructed him to loosen up. "I'm serious. Smile!"

The Dead Kennedys' 'Halloween' exploded through Velkovsky's, and as soon as Corey smiled and the photo snapped, Allyson grabbed his hand. "Now I want to dance, come on."

"No–no–no–no–no! I don't do that!" Corey frantically protested.

"You do tonight! With me!"

Allyson dragged him out of the photo booth and onto the dance floor. As she started dancing, Allyson turned in Deb and Lindsey's direction to let them see how *okay* she really was.

Corey, on the other hand, terrified to call any attention to himself, stood cemented in place, pumping his fists up and down uneasily.

"No, no, no! Watch me!" Allyson yelled.

Allyson stepped behind Corey, grabbed his arms, and moved Corey like a marionette. She pushed her knees against the backs of his legs to get his feet off the ground. And it worked! Corey didn't look any cooler, but at least she got him moving.

Allyson spun back around to face him, and the two were off. As they got more into the dance, their inhibitions melted away. The blistering punk song inspired them to completely let loose. Soon it really was just the two of them, and fuck everything else. Their muscles pumped as they locked into one another. Moving in discordant rhythm. Perfectly together and perfectly out of sync with the rest of the crowd. Both dancing to escape all the bullshit they'd put up with, all the rumors they'd tried to ignore, and all the tragedy they'd experienced.

Masks came off.

Sweat poured down Corey's face as he strutted spasmodically around Allyson. His arms darted out at strange angles. In a state of frenzied ecstasy, his body gyrated wildly.

Allyson felt more alive than she had in years, and she pulled him closer.

Hearts pounding. Feet stomping. Their dancing screamed as loud as the music.

Corey gave himself completely to the moment and flailed his arms, flying. Pulsating. He threw himself to the ground and continued the dance on his back.

The other people dancing at Velkovsky's, those who didn't exist in Corey and Allyson's world, stumbled out of the way to make room for their violent choreography.

Allyson moved above Corey, grabbing the air around his face. Pulling it toward her. Absorbing the feeling.

Lindsey stood at the bar, watching with apprehension. Deb rolled her eyes at how out of control they looked. Secretly envious that Allyson had a date and she did not.

On the ground, Corey and Allyson's eyes met intimately. For a sustained moment. As not only the other people in the club disappeared, but so did the music, the walls, everything but the two of them.

When Allyson pulled her arms back, she hypnotically brought Corey up to a seated position.

Reality crashed back in. And Corey sobered abruptly.

Out of breath and dehydrated, Corey hurried to the bar to get a couple of beers. Allyson kept dancing. Still in that wonderfully isolated world where she didn't care whose eyes were on her or what they might be saying.

"*You!*" Corey heard someone close by say.

Mistaking the voice for Allyson's, Corey playfully replied back, "You!" But then he turned. And his blood turned to ice. It was not Allyson.

Jeremy's mother, Mrs. Allen, stood across from him. Staring at Corey as if staring at a monster. Wearing that same flapper costume she had worn the night Jeremy died. The years since that night had turned her face hard. Ravaged by grief. The strobing lights made her expressions inhuman.

Corey shook. Terrified. His eyes looked for Allyson. He couldn't find her.

"You're just in here dancing. Having a good time?" Mrs. Allen's voice came from her gut. And Corey flinched as each word hit him.

"I'm sorry," he said quietly.

"Sorry?" Mrs. Allen sneered. "You're sorry for killing my son?!"

Corey caved in on himself. Through the crowd, Corey spotted Allyson. Still dancing. Still free while Mrs. Allen trapped him against the wall.

"I wake up every day, and I can't get past the pain. It kills me. *Kills me!*" Mrs. Allen's voice went from guttural to demonic.

Corey slid across the wall and reached a door close by. The music, laughter, and horror grew louder as Corey grabbed the handle and twisted. *Locked*.

"Do you understand? You think you can come here— *No!* You do not understand if you think you can come here and have a good time with your friends?"

Mrs. Allen grabbed her drink and refueled. "I come here and drink."

Corey kicked the door, trying to open it. Trapped like he had been that night in the attic.

"And a judge might have said you were innocent, but I know you were not. I know it was no accident. It was *not* an accident. You pushed my little boy because you got mad and lost your fucking mind!"

Lindsey grabbed Mrs. Allen and pulled her back toward the bar.

Corey lost Allyson in the crowd. His head turned to the other side of the bar, where he saw Deb mocking him. She was clearly very happy now.

While Lindsey held Mrs. Allen, Corey fled.

"Innocent people don't do that!" Mrs. Allen screamed.

Corey crashed into the dancers blocking his path. *"Evil people do!"*

Allyson turned toward the commotion.

"Corey?!"

"Evil people!"

Allyson saw Mrs. Allen with Lindsey and ran to find Corey.

"Evil!!!"

Corey ran out of the bar. Mrs. Allen's voice followed him.

Allyson raced after him.

"Corey?!"

Corey heard Allyson's voice merge into Mrs. Allen's. Everything in his mind swirled to chaos.

Honk!

"*Corey, look out!*" Allyson screamed as a truck blasted by, just barely missing Corey.

"Stop! Slow down! Talk to me!" Allyson begged as she chased him.

Corey turned to Allyson. Anger poured off his face. "Is that why you took me there?! To embarrass me in front of your friends?"

"What?" Allyson asked, hurt by the accusation.

"You threw me in the middle of it and then you just… where were you? What do you want from me?" Corey screamed, desperate for an answer. Desperate for any way not to feel the pain stabbing him.

"I don't want anything from you. I just know what it's like to wake up every day and have everyone looking at you. Thinking they know you. Thinking they know what you've been through, when they don't."

Corey took a breath and listened.

Allyson continued, "But when I look at you… When I saw you the other day… I see a person who's trying to figure it the fuck out." Allyson struggled to articulate the connection she'd felt with him at the clinic.

Corey smirked. How could she not get it?

"The difference between you and me, Allyson, is that people treat me like, *who is this guy? Who is this monster?* And you? They treat you like a survivor."

"What are you talking about?!"

"And I get it. You survived Michael Myers. You're a victim. You're a hero with your struggles. And ask anyone... I'm just the psycho babysitter, the kid killer."

Allyson shook her head. Unable to say anything to make things better.

"I saw you, Corey. And your hand was hurt, and I felt it and I know you did too—"

"You think you can fix me, but you can't. So... I'll spare you the heartache."

Allyson stood there broken. Watching Corey slip away into the night. She grabbed his mask and held it.

*

Corey reached the bridge road. He couldn't shake the horror he had seen on Mrs. Allen's face. Everywhere he turned, Corey saw that horror. Everywhere. And no matter what he did, he couldn't hide from it. And he couldn't stand it one second longer.

As he stood looking over the railing of the overpass, staring into the darkness below, looking at it like the bloodstain on the floor in Jeremy Allen's house, Corey imagined all the different ways he could make it go away. There were the guns at Ronald's auto shop. Rifles and pistols. But Corey had never fired a gun. He had the expired bottle of anti-anxiety medication the doctors had given him after the accident. Back when Joan was open to the idea of medication and could afford it. But would it still be good? Good enough to make him disappear?

Corey shoved his hands in his pockets and felt the handle of the knife Laurie had given him. He pressed his finger against the handle and thought, *Just cut your wrists open and watch the blood leave your body. Lie down and watch your life drain from your veins.*

Corey felt a momentary sense of relief. Imagining not having to endure any more of the mess. The misery. The judgments. Then he scoffed, doubtful he could actually do it correctly. Wondering about the different ways he could fuck that up too.

A chilly wind cut across the bridge and stung Corey's face. Fall had arrived. The most frightening time of the year. Corey tensed to keep warm, but he really didn't care too much about being cold.

Corey could see the flashing radio tower in the distance. After the accident, Corey had spent so much time staring at it. Praying it would transport him someplace better. A lighthouse that he hoped might signal a way to anywhere but there. But now, he looked at it and didn't mean a thing. His tall beacon that once represented a shimmer of hope had turned into a meaningless structure with a red light flashing pointlessly into the night.

Corey moved from the tower to the stars. And he found they meant even less.

All was silent. Until it wasn't.

First came the accelerating engine. Then came the headlights crashing into him.

Corey turned. The LeBaron, tires fully inflated. Filled with the Haddonfield High drumline. Terry at the wheel. Barreling directly toward him.

Within seconds it reached him.

Corey jumped out of the way, and Terry swerved to miss him. Their laughter sounded like screams in the night.

Corey put his head down and hurried forward, but the LeBaron cut him off and screeched to a stop.

"Hey, kid killer," Stacy said as the drumline jumped out of the car and surrounded him.

"Hey, cool kid, what's up? Where ya goin'?" Billy asked.

"Come on, guys. Let's leave him alone," Margo fretted before they'd even gotten started.

Corey's eyes darted around. He no longer saw the radio tower. Or the stars. Or anything besides the darkness surrounding the bridge.

"I just want to apologize for… pushing your buttons. Corey, right?" Terry asked with a phony grin. "I wanna put the beef to rest. I mean, come on, Corey. Handshakes and friendship."

Terry extended his hand, but Corey refused to take it.

"Don't leave him hangin', dude!" Billy egged on.

Corey looked at the other members. Each with that look of hate in their eyes. Hate they couldn't mask behind their clowning.

Terry killed his smile and surprised Corey with a shove. Corey stumbled back and tripped over his feet. He hit the ground, and his glasses bounced off his face and slid across the street. Before he could grab them, Stacy crushed them under her foot.

Despite the escalation, all Corey could think about right then was how he would explain the broken glasses to Joan. She would have so many questions.

Billy kicked the broken glasses over the edge of the bridge, ending any hope Corey might have had about getting them fixed before Joan found out.

Corey had nothing left to lose.

"Spend all your beer money on that new tire?" Corey laughed nervously. Unable to stay quiet any longer as he got back up.

"What'd you say?" Terry asked, surprised by Corey's boldness.

"Wait-wait-wait-wait—you think you're funny? Huh? With your jokes and pranks?" Terry said, eye to eye with Corey. "Well, guess what? Your little stunt made us late for the game against Buffalo Grove. And I don't like to be late. If you knew me well, you'd know that. I like to be punctual."

"Facts," Billy agreed.

Terry continued, "A marching band is a formation where everyone is accountable for their actions." Terry quoted their band director, Mr. Dooley.

"Karma's not a bitch. It's a mirror," Billy added.

The gang stepped closer. Corey backed up against the railing. He felt it press against his back. He had run out of room. Worried what they might do next, Corey dug his hand in his pocket and pulled out Laurie's knife. He quickly unfolded the blade and thrashed it through the air clumsily, hoping it would scare them away.

"Get back! Get away from me!" Corey screamed.

His threat looked so awkward it even made Margo laugh.

"You gonna murder us? Huh? Same way you killed that kid?" Billy joked.

Corey waved the knife at Terry to keep him back. When he spun back around, Billy knocked the knife out of Corey's hand with his drumstick and sent it sailing over the edge of the bridge.

Corey spun around and saw the blade disappear into the grass below.

"Little psycho bitch," Stacy spat at Corey as the fury in the air intensified.

"I know why you act like you do," Corey said calmly as he turned back to Terry. "You act like an asshole 'cause your father treats you like one. It's contagious, right?"

The drumline gasped at the insult, knowing that Corey had just escalated the conflict to something much, much bigger.

"What did you say?" Terry saw blood.

"That's right. I saw it," Corey continued. "And I know what it looks like when people hate you. That's why you act like this. Because your goddamn dad hates you too."

The gang watched Terry. Not sure how he would react to the provocation.

Terry smiled and acted unaffected. For a second. Then he exploded forward. Terry tackled Corey at the waist. Corey went over the railing and plummeted to the ground below.

Fear set in, and the drumline raced to the railing and looked over. There they saw Corey on the ground. Still. Lit elegantly by the moon.

"Oh shit!" Billy screamed and laughed at the same time, not sure which response was appropriate.

"Terry, *what did you do?!*" Stacy yelled, horrified. Knowing how much trouble Terry had just created for them.

Terry's mind raced. He'd wanted more than anything to hurt the punk who'd fucked up his car, but now he saw the world closing in on him. He started brainstorming a way out of the mess, feeling a slight bit of confidence that if anyone were to find out what had happened, they'd probably take Terry's story over a child killer's.

"Little dick busted it," Billy kept laughing. The only one in the drumline seemingly having a good time.

"You just pushed him?" Margo asked in utter disbelief. The shock turned her mouth to cotton. "He okay?" she asked quietly.

Stacy turned on Terry. "Go down and look!"

Terry wheeled around and got in her face. "You go down and look!" He looked at the others and gave them the story they were to repeat if anyone found out what happened. "I didn't push nobody. He fell."

The gang silently agreed. Everybody but Billy, who kept giggling.

They hurried back to the car. Terry jumped into the driver's seat and tore across the bridge.

Billy's laugh rolled out of the car and disappeared into the night.

*

Corey lay on the ground, unconscious. Blood trickling from his head.

Nelson Christopher sat beneath the bridge, staring at the motionless body. He approached cautiously and peeked out from under the overpass. His eyes searched for witnesses. He found none. The laughter he heard had long since vanished.

Nelson laid his head on Corey's chest and listened for a heartbeat. *Good.*

He grabbed Corey's arms and dragged him toward the tunnel's entrance.

"Hungersome?" Nelson announced as he reached the opening.

He heard his God's rancid breathing from within.

DARKNESS

"The remains of a man now identified as twenty-year-old Ryan Couper of Haddonfield, Illinois, were discovered earlier this week inside the building that used to house the Cutway Meatpacking Plant. The man had been missing since Halloween night, 2019. Kimberley Hart, who Ryan was reportedly seen with the night he disappeared, is still missing at this time. Authorities have not yet named a suspect, but they have not ruled out foul play."

Photos of the missing persons in Haddonfield took over the screen.

Laurie watched the images with growing anxiety and then turned off the television. "Why are you doing this to yourself?" she said as she refilled her tea.

Laurie pulled back the curtain and looked out to her quiet yard, colored by the night-blue sky. The TV news did enough to give Laurie some worry about Allyson's night out. As much as she wanted to move on from the past, Laurie could not help but wonder, is he still there? Waiting. Ready to take someone else away from her.

Laurie returned to her office. She sipped her tea and tried to find distance from her thoughts through her writing.

As soon as I walked through the door of the Wallace house, I could smell the blood. That strange smell of rust and nickel that I would never forget.

Inside the house, I felt a presence. Observing me. Lurking in the shadows. A shape I could not see.

As I got closer to the room, I can remember something telling me to stop. Telling me to run. But I didn't listen. I had to know. I had to see for myself.

I found their bodies upstairs. Horrifically arranged for a maniac's amusement. Butchered to death by evil.

The fear strangled me. Instantly. I couldn't breathe, I couldn't blink, I couldn't do anything but be afraid.

The shape materialized from the darkness with nothing but a blank look and a murderous intention.

I tried to outrun it, but I couldn't. It just kept coming. And no matter where I went, there it was.

I died that night. And a new version was born. Something that would never see the world in the same way again.

Dr. Loomis had saved my life, but Michael Myers had taken control of it.

Each year after that night, his fear had a cumulative effect on me. Somehow growing in power.

The nightmares got worse. So bad that Mother could hardly stand me anymore. On more than one occasion, she kicked me out of the house and sent me to live with my aunt and uncle. My dad would protest, but the events

I'd gone through were too much for him as well, and he retreated into the background of our lives.

As much as I wanted to escape the memories and Michael's control, I could not leave Haddonfield. I felt confined to this place. And somehow, I knew that if I did manage to move somewhere else, the boogeyman would follow me there too. A change in location would never stop his pursuit.

Mother never understood the fear I lived with. She was grateful I had survived that night and would remind me how blessed I was every day. But the truth is, Annie, Lynda, and Paul had escaped. They no longer had Michael in their lives. But I did.

A year later, Daddy died. He had a heart attack while showing a property. A heart no doubt weakened by the pain he saw in my eyes.

I had no strength left to process his loss. And at the funeral, when I stood over his casket and saw that his eyes had turned the color of flesh, the same lightless look I'd seen in my friends, Michael Myers came back to me. I fell to the ground. Screaming. Causing a scene. Aunt Tamara and Uncle Jake had to carry me out. Mother averted her eyes.

The only person who brought me any comfort during that time was Dr. Loomis, whom I would call and visit when things went darker. Which they often did.

Dr. Loomis admitted that Michael had killed a part of him as well. Before he'd come to know evil, Dr. Loomis had been a successful psychiatrist and had helped countless people that the medical community had deemed irreparably damaged. But then he met Michael, and all that changed.

Loomis told me he'd never looked in the eyes of a human being and seen such a lack of humanity as he did with Michael. "There's nothing there but evil, Laurie," he would always say. "Pure evil."

Early one morning, he called me. He had disturbing news. This was the summer of '81... could've been '82. Those years remain foggy in my mind.

I met him in the parking lot of a K-Mart in between Smith's Grove and Haddonfield. Loomis kept his coat on despite the heat, making him look more uncomfortable.

Though I'm not sure if I ever saw Dr. Loomis comfortable.

The people in the parking lot avoided him. It was different than the way they avoided me. Moms would clasp onto their children's arms and pull them away. Maybe they could sense the evil residue clinging to his psyche. Or maybe it was the intense way he studied them.

Dr. Loomis greeted me the way he always did by getting right to business. It was never a 'Hi Laurie, how are you?' It was always a 'Michael is watching them, and they don't know what he's capable of.' On this day, he greeted me with the news of what had taken place at the sanitarium the day before. Michael's cell neighbour, whom Loomis had been working with, had killed two men and then taken his own life. Dr. Loomis presented me with this news as we sat in my car with the A/C blasting.

A boy in his late teens, Carl Serrot, had been institutionalized after an LSD trip led to a violent episode.

Carl, who'd taken several tabs of blotter, became hysterical during a screening of the movie Roadgames. *Believing the serial killer from the film had entered the* theater, Carl threatened and then assaulted the audience. Dr. Loomis began working with Carl once he arrived at Smith's Grove and quickly assessed that Carl's 'bad trip' had signaled the beginning of a schizophrenic disorder, which had been dormant in Carl until that night. And in Carl's violent threats, Loomis worried his condition could become deadly if not treated correctly.

"Carl's mind is now open to evil," Loomis deducted in his first sessions. "It is up to us to close that door and lock it for good."

After several months, Loomis told me he felt hopeful about the progress the two were making, and he pleaded with the state to move Carl to a much less restrictive facility to continue his work. A facility where true therapy could be administered. Loomis argued that Carl was not a killer, but his pleas fell upon deaf ears, as they always did.

Loomis's worry grew when the psychiatric administrator moved Carl next to Michael's cell. Loomis had long argued for wider separation between the inmates and Michael. "I believe he could be infectious if close to a susceptible mind." But again, nobody heeded his warning. In their subsequent sessions together, Carl confided that he'd begun feeling drawn toward his darker thoughts ever since the move. Dr. Loomis told me that Carl confessed to daydreaming about 'watching them all die'.

"Dr. Loomis, I want to see their faces just before they die. I want to see how scared they are," Loomis quoted the patient. "I want to taste their fear."

The progress Loomis had made quickly came undone by Carl's vicinity to Michael. Michael's presence had pushed open the door that Loomis had tried to close. Shortly after,

Loomis began noticing something else about Carl's shape. A vacancy appeared behind his eyes. The same sort of vacancy he believed lived inside Michael's eyes. A vacancy that hadn't been there when Carl first arrived. "I fear the look," Loomis said. And when he discovered gashes in Carl's hands, he became more insistent that something must be done, before "the evil overtakes him." During each of their following sessions, the vacancy in Carl's eyes grew more disturbing. And then, days later, Carl gave in to the evil. Loomis spared no detail in recounting the gruesome facts.

Two orderlies, Chris Miles and Gebert Bell, were bringing supplies into what they believed to be an empty examination room when Carl, who had snuck into the room during lunch, attacked. Carl's plan had most likely been to kill Dr. Loomis, but the two orderlies unfortunately arrived there first.

Carl wore a mask of bloody white gauze over his face. He had, as Loomis described, tried to remove his face using a scalpel he'd stolen.

Carl struck Gebert with a reflex hammer. He then trapped Chris when he tried to escape.

Security, who were searching for the missing inmate, heard the screams and came running, but they could not get into the room in time.

Carl pierced Chris's throat with a pair of dressing scissors. And then he moved to Gebert.

Dr. Loomis reached the door and ordered Carl to "turn away from the evil."

But Carl did not respond. Instead, he severed the carotid arteries in Gebert's neck and then drove the shears through his own eyes. Taking his life.

Inside Carl's cell, they found two bloody handprints on the wall. "He had made them by slicing open his hand," Loomis explained. "These two bloody handprints, pressed against the wall, trying to break through. Trying to get into Michael's cell," Loomis told me as he stared through my window into the blinding sunlight. And though Loomis had no proof that Michael had anything to do with it, he wasn't willing to deny the possibility.

Laurie stared at those pages. Thinking about Loomis. Thinking about her own paranoias. She looked up at the crime scene photos on her wall. The photos of Michael's arrest. The victims. And finally, to the photo of Karen, when she was just a child. Laurie could barely recall that time. Only glimpses remained in her mind. Glimpses that existed in between Laurie's drunken spells and her benders. Laurie could still hear the fright in Karen's young voice as she tried to comfort her mother after Laurie had suffered through another nightmare.

"Mommy?" she said again as I lay next to her bed sobbing. Trying to figure out how another nightmare could feel so real. How I could not protect my baby even in my dreams. And I did what I had the previous weekend, after I'd seen Michael in my nightmares. I took Karen to the car, and we spent the rest of the night inside it. If Michael showed up again, maybe I could get away. Every time Karen fell asleep, I wanted to wake her. I wanted her to be ready, always, for when he came back. As soon as the sun came up, I drove Karen back to Mother's house so she

could watch her. Mother wasn't happy to see me. She had plans with a guy she'd met in her ceramics class, and once again, I had 'screwed it all up'.

"I'm sorry, Mother, I can't do it. Not right now," I told her. She said the same thing she always said. "A mother needs to be better. Get ahold of yourself and be there for Karen." And I told her the same thing I always told her: that as long as he's alive, there is no help for me. Because I will never escape him. It was three months before I saw Karen again. She would send me letters written in the cursive handwriting she'd just learned, telling me how much she missed me and how much she wanted to stay with me. It hurt too much to respond, so I let the letters collect on my coffee table, and when they started spilling over the edge, I burned them in the fireplace. I drank myself to sleep every night, sometimes adding a painkiller to really turn things off. Nothing worked. Michael found a home inside my mind. And any time I thought he might have left, he'd appear once again. I just want to know, why won't he die?

"Why won't he die?" Laurie whispered. And then she continued to write: *What happens when I'm no longer afraid…*

Laurie's phone buzzed. "Hey, Lindsey." Laurie could hardly hear Lindsey through the loud music and noise at the bar.

"You didn't tell me you set up Allyson with Corey Cunningham!"

"And?" Laurie did not see a problem.

"And do you think that's a good idea?"

"I think everybody deserves a second chance."

"Well, we just had a scene up here. And you should know about it. Don't know how Allyson is handling it."

Laurie sat up, worried. "What happened?"

"Mrs. Allen was in here, and she saw him! She lost her shit, Corey ran out, Allyson chased her, it was a whole thing."

Laurie closed her eyes and sighed deeply. "Are they okay?" she asked quietly.

"They never came back. Thought I'd give you a heads-up."

"Thanks, Lindsey."

"I wish you would have told me, Laurie. I know your heart is in the right place, but I don't think this is a good idea for Allyson."

"He was proven innocent."

"That might be the case, but you know how it is here. People see him as the boogeyman, and I don't think Allyson needs that in her life."

Laurie heard some commotion coming from the kitchen and ended her call with Lindsey. "Allyson?" Laurie called out. No answer. The racket continued. Laurie headed downstairs and peeked into the kitchen. There she found Allyson angrily beating the shit out of their microwave. "Easy, easy. What are you doing?" Laurie asked.

"I can't get the fucking thing to work," Allyson said as she punched the microwave once more.

"And your plan is to beat it into submission?"

Allyson clenched her fists and slammed them

against the counter. "Everything in this fucking house is always broken."

"Hey, take a breath. Calm down," Laurie instructed.

"Just let me be mad. Why can't I be mad?! Why is that a problem for you?!" Allyson yelled.

"Fine, be mad. Smash whatever you want. I'm just gonna warn you right now that it can be an addictive habit."

"Thanks, fine, great. I'll just shut off all my emotions." Allyson leaned against the counter, stewing, as Laurie unplugged and re-plugged the microwave into the socket. Just like that, it came back to life. The food inside started spinning.

"There. Just needed a restart."

Allyson smirked and found a tiny smile.

"You did it. As always," Allyson said with some acid in her voice.

Laurie filled a kettle with water. "You want some tea?"

Allyson held herself and nodded.

"It didn't work out?" Laurie asked as she heated up the water.

Allyson shook her head. "I actually liked him."

"I know. I liked him too."

Allyson looked at Laurie. "Are we cursed?"

Laurie smiled. "No. We still got each other."

Allyson leaned into her grandma and found some comfort in her embrace.

Allyson lay against Laurie's shoulder as they watched *Family Feud*, ate popcorn, and talked deep into the night. It was moments like these that kept Allyson so close to her grandmother. When Laurie could open up and talk about anything in the most comforting way. The same way Allyson imagined Laurie must have been back when she was a teenage babysitter.

This is why they loved her, Allyson reminded herself.

But even as she felt comforted in that moment, Allyson could not rid herself of the disappointment about Corey. And as Laurie fell asleep under the Afghan blanket, Allyson replayed the night in her mind. For the first time in so long, Allyson had felt something that made her feel alive. And then it had been stripped away from her.

Allyson pulled out her phone to text Corey again, but just before she sent the message, she deleted it.

Allyson removed Laurie's glasses, careful not to wake her. And as she watched her grandmother sleep, she had but one thought. *We are fucking cursed.*

THE SHAPE EMERGES

On November 1st, 2018, when police unearthed the garbage truck Michael had used for his getaway, half-buried in the river on the edge of town, they focused their attention on the surrounding area. But after combing the space and dragging the river, they found no clues as to his whereabouts until several days later, when they came upon a hunter's cabin hidden in the woods.

*

Weakened by loss of blood, Michael crashed the garbage truck into the river and fell against the truck's horn. The siren yelled into the distance.

A little girl with bruised eyes, discolored skin, and busted lips heard the call. She stood in the hunter's cabin deep in the wood, watching her father sleep. Looking at the near-empty bottle of cheap whiskey on the floor beneath him. The source of her father's mean.

The cabin did little to keep the cold out. The girl, wearing only a light pair of pajamas, had grown accustomed to the discomfort. You could see the cold in her blue skin.

She pressed herself against the wall, listening to the horn, wondering if someone might be coming. As quickly as it began, the noise stopped and was replaced by the crickets and toads who'd been singing before it had begun.

The girl looked at her purple wrists and touched her tender head. Her dad had been extra cruel the night before.

The girl's father had taken her from her mother two weeks earlier. He'd been denied visitation rights on account of claims of abuse, and he sought to make his ex-wife pay for said claims. So, one night after the little girl and her mother had gone to sleep, he broke in and stole his daughter away. He used a kitchen knife to convince his little girl of his seriousness. The blade kept her quiet. She didn't say a word as he pulled her out of bed and drove off into the night, and she had not said a word since that night.

The man abandoned the car on the other side of an old meatpacking plant and fled into the woods. When he came across an empty hunter's cabin, he determined it to be an adequate place to lay low.

So far, that cabin had served them well. It had been almost a week, and nobody had discovered them yet.

Not long after the horn stopped, the girl noticed a significant change in the air. The crickets quit chirping. The toads got quiet, too.

A dark shadow moved past the cabin.

The girl stepped to the window. The farthest distance her rope restraints would allow her to move.

Her eyes moved past the trickling river and

arrived at the unfamiliar shape beneath the hickory tree. Lying in the willows. Covered in shadows. The man in the pale gray mask. Half-burnt, half-discolored. She didn't see a boogeyman. She saw a wounded animal.

She spoke to him in a whisper. "Have you come to take me away?"

The girl remained at the window until her father woke late that afternoon. Then she ducked behind the bed as he went outside to vomit the soured liquor in his belly, his waking ritual.

After he purged, the man went off to steal another bottle. He left the girl tied to the bed in the cabin.

When she returned to the window, she could no longer see the man in the mask. He had vanished. The only trace he'd left behind was the crushed willows on top of which he'd lain.

The girl turned to the door. The evening wind cut through the cracks and whistled awfully. The noise it created inspired her to sing, which she did quietly.

> *"Trick or treat,*
> *When we meet*
> *In the willows outside*
>
> *Trick or treat*
> *It's so sweet*
> *Where did you hide?*
>
> *Trick or treat*
> *I get beat*
> *Any time I cry*

Trick or treat
Smell my feet
Am I going to die…?"

Sometime later, her father returned with a fresh bottle and two cans of potted meat. He made a fire and cut the cans open with the knife he'd stolen.

At dusk, they ate. The little girl looked for the shape in the willows but still could not find him. She turned her attention to her father, who choked down his food. The alcohol made it hard for him to eat. Mealtime was always unkind.

Her father tossed an empty can into the distance and swigged from his bottle. The girl watched the embers from the fire dance close to his head. Wishing silently for them to cover him completely.

The alcohol kicked in at nightfall, and her father swayed wildly as he sat by the dying fire.

The little girl stood directly behind him. Watching. This night he would not beat her.

The girl sang her song. Her father ignored the words.

Behind the little girl, the shape appeared. Out from the darkness.

The fading campfire flickered across his mask.

A team of dogs cried out from a far distance. Their barks drifted through the woods and made it to the river where they'd set up camp. The manhunt moved in their direction.

"Them dogs come to find me?" her father slurred

as he turned to the noise. There he found his little girl standing over him with the blackest eyes.

"I don't like that look in your eyes," he mumbled.

The man's eyes drifted up to the horrifying shape behind the little girl.

"Who the fuck are you?" the man asked.

Michael Myers stepped closer.

The man grabbed the girl by the throat and held her there.

"You do this?" he screamed at the girl.

Michael stepped closer. Standing over the two.

"You get back. She's mine," the girl's father snapped at the man in the mask. "Did you bring him here?" he growled at the girl.

Just then, the man's pupils changed shape. He looked down and saw the kitchen knife buried in his gut. His little girl's hands pushed the blade deeper.

The attack surprised him, and his face turned ugly as he processed the pain. When his little girl removed the knife, he grabbed his belly and tried to stop the blood.

The girl looked at the blood trickling off her hands and the edge of the blade. Then she raised the knife and put the blade through her father's throat.

The knife slipped easily through his loose skin and caused him to choke as he tried to find the breath she had severed. His dirty yellow shirt turned red. His eyes stayed fixed on his little girl in terrified confusion. And then they lost their light, and he slumped forward into the fire.

The flames took to his scalp. His hair caught

fire and spread over his head to make an orange burning mask. The skin melted from his skull, and the girl could no longer see the face of the man who'd brought her such misery.

The little girl, barely out of breath, covered in her father's blood, turned to the man in the mask standing behind her. Her eyes black with hate. Just like his. She extended her hands and placed the large knife in his.

Michael Myers gripped the handle. He watched the blood roll down the blade and fall into the grass.

The dogs in the distance grew louder. Helicopters appeared in the sky as the manhunt intensified.

Michael looked at the little girl. He clenched the handle tighter.

*

Michael left the cabin and limped along the river. His wounds black and infected. Still clutching the knife, coated in more blood. Never looking back at his pursuers. Always moving forward. Deliberate, even in his injured state.

Michael eventually reached the abandoned meatpacking plant and hid beneath the floor in the chute used to catch the blood from animals. There he survived—barely—on the creatures that fell through his hole.

As police scoured the area, Michael sat waiting. Waiting for the night when he could surface to kill again. On the holiday that had first inspired his murderous rampage. On a night when a man in a mask would draw no attention.

A maniac with one desire: kill and feast on the fear of his victims.

*

Halloween Night, 2019

A light sprinkle drizzled and wet the ground as Kimberly Hart and Ryan Couper drove to the location where they had fallen in love to celebrate their first anniversary. That location being the abandoned meatpacking plant at the edge of town.

That previous Halloween had been a roller coaster for Kim, beginning with disaster and ending with love.

Cameron Elam had ended things with Kim the previous spring, but she hadn't lost her affection for him. And when the new school year began, Kim did everything she could to win him back, but nothing worked. He didn't answer her calls, and he didn't respond to the notes she slipped into his locker.

To make matters worse, Kim couldn't stand Cameron's new girlfriend, Allyson. She hated how everything in Allyson's world looked so fucking perfect. How Allyson looked so fucking perfect. It seemed to Kim that everything Allyson did, she won. School, soccer, boys. Allyson won all of it. And the cherry on the top: everyone loved Allyson. Allyson had friends in every clique.

On the other hand, Kim struggled with school, struggled to stay on the cheerleading squad, and struggled to maintain the relationships within her small group of friends. She was always in a fight with someone.

When Kim saw Cameron and Allyson arrive at the Halloween dance in their Bonnie and Clyde gender-swapping Halloween costumes, she made it her mission to win the game that night.

"Can I talk to you?" Kim asked Cameron as soon as Allyson stepped away.

Cameron tried to look past Kim and keep his eyes on where Allyson had gone, not wanting any trouble. "What, Kim?"

Kim pushed up against him and gently massaged his arm the way she used to do when they were dating. Cameron smiled but tried to resist.

"She doesn't have to know. This can be our secret," Kim whispered. "I just want to be with you."

Cameron's eyes met hers. Even though he had stronger feelings for Allyson, Cameron could not deny his attraction to Kim, and he momentarily let lust get the better of him. As Kim moved in for a kiss, Cameron did not refuse the advance.

I won, Kim thought as their lips met. But Kim had little time to celebrate her victory, because just as soon as they kissed, Allyson showed up to get in the way. And then Cameron left Kim to chase Allyson down.

Kim tried to stop him. "Please, Cameron, I want to be with you."

But she failed to convince him.

And that was the last time Kim ever saw Cameron alive.

The rejection crushed Kim, and she left the school dance alone.

*

As Kim walked home, she could hear sirens all around her, but she didn't think much about them. The massacre had begun, but the news had not yet spread.

Kim made it halfway home when Ryan pulled up alongside her. The hardcore band Cross Control blasted out of the speakers in his car. He reduced the volume and lowered his window.

"Kim, right?" It was hard to recognize her in her extravagant tiger costume.

Ryan wasn't hard to recognize at all. Kim remembered him from her first year in high school, when he was a senior and played guitar in a grimy punk band called The Grasshoppers. Back then, his type frightened Kim. But looking at him through the window of his car made her reconsider her stance on bad boys. Ryan looked kind of hot in his black denim jacket with his long sideburns and floppy hair.

"What are you doing? Walkin' home?" Ryan asked through the window of his vintage Plymouth Fury.

"Yeah."

"Get in. I'll give you a ride. Something's going on tonight. I don't think it's safe to be out. Cops are everywhere."

Suddenly, Kim's night didn't seem quite so bad.

"What are you doing back in Haddonfield? Are

you done with college?" Kim asked Ryan as he rolled through Haddonfield.

"College wasn't for me. I just needed to come home and figure some things out. It's like I gotta choice, you know. Try to make it with my band, or find a plan B, like my dad always tells me. But, honestly, I'm kind of like, fuck a plan B, know what I mean?"

"Yeah, I totally hear that," Kim said, trying to match his coolness.

"I like your costume," Ryan told her as he stopped at a light. "Are you a tiger or a cheetah?"

"Tigers have stripes. So, I'm a tiger."

"What a coincidence. Tigers are my favorite cat."

Kim blushed excitedly. "Mine too."

"Keep going straight?" Ryan asked regarding the direction.

"Yeah, but…" Kim trailed off shyly.

"But what?" Ryan asked.

"I don't know. My parents are gonna be awake, and they're gonna want to talk, and I don't feel like talking… to them."

"Feel like talking to me?" Ryan looked into her eyes.

Kim bit her lip and nodded.

Ryan looked out the window and considered his options. "Only thing is, I'm crashing at my folks' house tonight."

"Oh," Kim said, disappointed.

"But I know a place."

*

That's how Ryan and Kim ended up parked outside the meatpacking plant the previous year. The same place where Ryan and his band used to go late at night for nihilistic inspiration.

Kim and Ryan stayed there for hours, talking. Getting to know one another.

While the rest of Haddonfield was falling apart, Ryan and Kim were falling in love.

Over the next year, they were inseparable. Ryan wrote Kim love songs and made her lengthy punk playlists. Kim became his biggest cheerleader, and even picked up a guitar and taught herself how to play the beginnings of some of the songs he liked.

So, on Halloween night in 2019, Kim and Ryan returned to the scene of their first night together and made out in the back seat of Ryan's Plymouth Fury.

Like the rest of Haddonfield, Kim remained on edge about the possible return of Michael Myers. She'd been in a text chain with her friends, discussing what precautions they planned to take. Tara and Tess were driving into Chicago to spend the night in a hotel. Justin and Emily had installed cameras around their new home, and Travis planned to stay with his ex-military brother Alan. Kim didn't mention her and Ryan's plans to celebrate their one-year anniversary out in the wild for fear of being judged as irresponsible. But had she had it her way, Kim would have stayed home too. Because she was pretty freaked out just like everybody else.

So, when a shadow moved by the hazy window of Ryan's Plymouth, Kim saw it instantly. She jumped up and elbowed Ryan in the mouth.

"Jesus," Ryan said as he used his tongue to check for blood.

"What was that? Did you see that?" Kim wiped away the haze to look outside.

"Yeah, that was my lip."

"No, I saw a shadow."

Kim's eyes carefully moved across the area but didn't see anyone or anything.

Ryan, who had no fears of the boogeyman, remained calm to the point of being annoying and barely paid attention to it. "It's just Mother Nature, baby. All of God's creatures are out to celebrate our love tonight." He laughed. But when he saw that she still looked uneasy, he assured her. "We can't live our lives in fear. Because then we'll miss out on living," Ryan told her in an attempt to sound a little extra philosophical.

"Oh, babe, I want you so bad," Kim said as she climbed on top of Ryan.

"Isn't it crazy how life puts us where we need to be?" Ryan said as he kissed her back. "Had I not been driving at that exact moment a year ago tonight, we wouldn't be here right now."

"It's like fate, babe."

"Yeah, fate," Ryan said as he helped remove her shirt. Kim's bosom fell over Ryan's chest.

"Man, that is really hot," Ryan said as he buried himself in Kim's cleavage.

Kim again saw movement outside the window and pushed Ryan back.

"Fuck, someone *is* out there," Kim said as she pressed her face against the window and grabbed her shirt. "I saw someone walk by, I swear to God."

"The mainstream media put Michael Myers in your head, and now you can't get him out—"

"Babe, I will fucking knock you out if you say that again. I know what I saw. Somebody just walked by the window. Don't condescend to me."

"All right." Ryan sobered up. "I'll go take a look," Ryan said as he pushed his erection into a more comfortable position.

"No, no, no, let's just go back to your apartment. No looks."

Ryan could see the fear consuming her, and he caressed her arm.

"Okay," Ryan told her. "Let's go."

Ryan stepped out of the car to move to the driver's side. He heard the rhythmic squeal as a large *NO PARKING* sign above the industrial building swung back and forth in the breeze.

Kim got tangled up in her shirt, trying to put it back on.

"Holy shit!" Ryan yelled as he reached the door.

"Babe?!"

Kim cautiously climbed out and saw Ryan at the hood of the car, staring at something on the ground. Judging from Ryan's posture, she could tell it was something bad.

"What is it?" Kim asked nervously as she stepped closer.

"I don't know."

Kim screamed when she saw the figure on the ground. The figure in a thrashed garbageman's uniform. The figure's face obscured by long stringy hair. The name 'Ozzy' embroidered above the pocket of the figure's jumpsuit.

"This wasn't here when we pulled in," Ryan told her as he scanned the area. "I think we should call someone." Ryan looked around.

"No, we should get the fuck out of here and call someone on our way out," Kim decided.

"Maybe we just found Michael Myers."

Ryan gently touched the body's shoulder with the toe of his combat boot. The slight disturbance caused the head on the body to come loose, revealing a decayed skull hidden beneath the long hair.

Ryan stumbled back in terror. "Oh my God."

Kim turned back to the car and stopped.

"No. No."

Ryan heard Kim whimper. He spun around. Michael Myers stood before them. Next to the driver's-side door. In his hand, a rusty kitchen knife. His stance modestly askew.

Ryan and Kim backed away carefully.

"We don't want any trouble, man," Ryan blurted out.

Michael remained still. Watching.

"Babe?" Kim quietly cried out.

"It's gonna be okay," Ryan whispered. "It might

not even be him. Could be someone messing with us.

"Who the fuck are you?" Ryan yelled, trying to intimidate him.

The watching shape did not stir.

"Babe, stop, please," Kim begged, growing more frightened.

Kim grabbed her phone and hit the emergency button... but nothing. She had no bars.

And then, he stepped forward.

Trapped between Michael Myers and the building, Kim and Ryan took off for the gutted entryway of the industrial meatpacking plant. Once they reached the door, Kim glanced over her shoulder. He had disappeared.

Moonlight came through the shattered windows and turned the building haunted. If they weren't scared enough, the building escalated their terror.

Kim hurried to catch up to Ryan and tripped over the detritus covering the floor. Her leg tore open. Blood poured.

Kim, through multiple cheerleading injuries, had developed a high threshold for pain. She stifled her scream and powered through.

Ryan helped her to her feet and pointed to a dark corridor. They hurried in that direction.

Ryan and Kim navigated the lightless building, looking for a back exit. One corridor led to another and another. Soon they were trapped in a maze of hallways.

Finally, they ducked into what used to be an office. They hadn't seen Michael since they'd entered the building, and Ryan hoped he hadn't followed them inside.

They had three options, as far as they could tell: run back in the direction where they'd entered, hoping they wouldn't meet the killer; go in the opposite direction, and hope to find another way out; or wait there and see what would happen. The last option didn't sit well with either.

Everything grew quiet except for the squeal from the swinging sign outside and their frightened breathing.

Ryan gave Kim the look. It was time to move.

Ryan took some deep breaths to gather enough confidence to peek out. He tried to swallow, but he had no spit in his mouth. He squeezed Kim's hand and moved through the doorway.

A second later, a faint grunt could be heard. The sound of pain.

"Ryan?" Kim whispered.

The only response she received was more dull grunts and what sounded like an oozy mush splattering.

A stream of blood ran past the door.

And then, nothing…

Kim's survival instincts kicked in, and her eyes darted around the darkness in the room for anything she could use to defend herself when he came through the door. She could hardly see a thing, only mounds of wreckage. Kim dragged her foot over the floor, uncovering broken pieces of tile as she pushed through the cords dangling from the ceiling.

Kim's foot brushed against a piece of metal decoration. It *dinged*, and the sound resonated through the vacuous building. She expected that Michael would appear in the doorway at any moment. But he stayed hidden. Kim grabbed the object that had rang out so loudly, a brass letter holder designed to spell *Do It Now*.

Kim slipped her fingers through the lettering and held the novelty desktop instrument like a set of brass knuckles. And then she moved to the door.

Instead of carefully stepping out of the office as Ryan had done, Kim just ran. She bolted through the door and lost her footing in her boyfriend's blood.

Kim slammed into the wall and slid to the floor. She splashed in Ryan's blood as she scrambled to her feet and took off in the opposite direction to where she'd seen Ryan go. The direction that she knew would take her deeper into the building.

Low-hanging wires and busted floorboards slowed her journey, but Kim finally made it into a larger part of the facility. The kill room.

Large rusty hooks hung from above, chained to a sliding rail system. Some had fallen onto the ground. Kim found an exit barricaded by a mountain of broken machinery. The windows in the room lived twenty feet off the ground.

Total dead end.

Kim pushed the letter holder into her waistband and grabbed a fallen meat hook, which made for a sounder weapon.

Kim quietly repeated the motivational refrain

she'd used when trying out for the cheerleading squad—"Kim, you're a winner"—as she cautiously walked through the kill room back to the door through which she'd entered. She decided the only way out was to run all the way back to the entrance.

"You are gonna haul ass through the door, and you are not gonna stop until you reach the car. And then you are gonna get in that car, and you are gonna drive the fuck away from here as fast as you fucking can. Got it?" Kim strategized out loud. She nodded as if the plan had been told to her by someone else.

Just then, the rail system above her screamed nightmarishly. Kim looked up as Ryan's slashed body came flying out of the darkness, dangling hideously from one of the hooks. The pointed end ripping out of his chest. His body tearing open under the weight. Blood gushing out of him.

"*No…*" Kim wailed in disbelief.

The rail system stopped, and Ryan's lifeless body swayed for a moment before it tore free from the hook and crashed to the ground.

From the back of the room, Michael stepped into view. The moonlight breaking through the ceiling-high windows seemed to be designed specifically to let Kim see the horror of his masked face.

Kim raced back into the labyrinthian halls of the plant, clenching the meat hook in her grip, watching over her shoulder as she ran.

Kim rounded a corner and got clotheslined by a sagging cable. Her feet came off the ground, and she slammed to the floor. The metal hook in her hand came down on her leg, slicing through her flesh. Kim cried out in pain. With each passing second, the pain became less bearable.

Kim looked back. She saw no sign of him. She grabbed the hook and held it tight. Her breath moved to her nose as she prepared to remove it. Before she allowed herself to give it one more thought, Kim jerked the hook with all her strength. The metal tore open her leg as she pulled it out. The pain, blinding.

Kim grabbed the wall and pulled herself up. Her injured leg struggled to hold any weight. Kim ripped off her sweater and tied it around the wound to try and stop the bleeding. She couldn't see Michael in the darkness, but she could feel him everywhere.

Kim fell forward, crashing against the wall and sliding across it as she stumbled back through the building clumsily. She told herself not to look back. "Just keep going."

One hall after another, Kim kept going. Refusing to turn but expecting at any second to feel him behind her.

She reached the entrance and fell out of the building. The night greeted her with much more light and much more open space.

Kim lurched to the car, but as she opened the door, she realized: *Ryan had the keys.*

She broke her rule and looked back just in time to see Michael stepping out of the building. His head pivoted in her direction. And he pursued her.

Kim abandoned the car and limped across the

dirt road that cut through the trees. The path Ryan had driven to get to the secluded clearing.

Even in his deteriorating state, Michael pursued with purpose. Fluid but rigid. Ghostly but animalistic. Straddling the line between hell and earth, he was unrelenting.

She weaved through the trees. The blood streaming from her leg collected in her shoe, making her getaway even more uncomfortable.

He followed. The moonlight caught the bloody knife in his hand as he moved silently through the dark wood.

Kim ducked behind a tree. The searing pain in her leg forced her to stop. Everything else told her to give up. There would be no escape. There would be no surviving.

She could sense him drawing nearer the way you can feel an approaching storm.

"You're a winner," she whispered again as she tried to summon the last bit of willpower from within.

Kim took a step forward but nearly fell over. Her wounded leg refused to go any farther. She pushed herself back against the tree and looked up at the branches. She recalled the parallel bars her cheerleading team used at half-time during the varsity basketball tournament in her junior year. An idea formed.

"You're a winner," Kim repeated once more.

He came to the other side of the trees. In the distance, an old bridge road. Surrounding him, not much else. No sign of his prey.

His head moved right to left. Searching.

Directly above him, in the tree, Kim sat perched on a branch, her arms wrapped around the trunk. Biting her shirt to steady her breath and manage the pain.

He gazed back into the trees from where he had entered, but he remained in that spot beneath Kim as if he could smell her blood. The blood that now spilled over her shoe and trickled down the leather.

A car passed over the bridge road. Kim watched, wishing she could yell loud enough to draw their attention.

Kim watched his mask turn. Right to left. Precisely. Michael took a step forward and then reversed direction. But he didn't stray from the spot where she had hidden.

Kim carefully removed the letter holder from her waistband and held it tightly. Just in case.

Leave… leave… leave… Kim begged inside her mind.

Drip. Drip.

The blood dripped off Kim's shoe and fell onto Michael's shoulder.

He looked up. And Kim jumped.

Kim came down on Michael with the brass letter holder, surprising him with the words *Do It Now*.

Kim nailed Michael in the face. She slammed the brass weapon into his head repeatedly and did not stop until his blood surfaced through the blackened char of his awful mask.

Michael fell to his knee, dazed by Kim's aggression.

When Kim swung her weapon once more, he raised his knife and sliced open her forearm. Kim dropped the letter holder and collapsed. Her head floated as she lost more blood.

He gripped his knife. And rose.

Kim's fear brought her back to her feet and propelled her forward toward the bridge. Swaying right to left as she moved. Dizzy and struggling to maintain balance.

Michael adjusted his bloody mask and continued the hunt.

Kim screamed and waved her arms as another car passed over the bridge, but they didn't see her —or chose not to stop.

Kim neared the road. Out of breath. Hoping to get someone's attention but with no energy left to do so.

She reached the underpass and struggled up the sloped embankment. Clawing at the grass. But the light rain from earlier had turned it slick. She couldn't get a grip and slid to the ground.

Kim looked back to the woods but could no longer see him.

Her leg gave out, and she fell.

"Help..." Kim couldn't get her volume above a whimper.

Light-headed, Kim's eyes moved into the shadows of the underpass.

Kim crawled beneath the bridge, hoping to find a place to hide and nurse her injuries. Her hands splashed through the pools of blood that her lacerations created as she moved toward the entrance to a pipe hidden within the underpass.

Kim's head drifted back and forth, looking for his mask as she crawled. She saw no sign of him.

She reached the tunnel and climbed inside. Crawling through the pipe, a smile surfaced as she realized that maybe she had gotten away. Maybe she had outsmarted him. And maybe she and Allyson weren't so different. Both had survived the boogeyman's attack and lived to tell the tale. She kept moving through the darkness.

The deeper Kim got, the more constrictive the tunnel became. But a sliver of light ahead of her let her see a wider opening, and she kept going.

Kim emerged from the tunnel into a large concrete cave. Shards of faint light made it through the corroded grate above but did little to help Kim see through the darkness. Rocky tunnels led to darker places. While deep crevices eroded out of the earthen walls did not lead to an escape route, they allowed one to conceal oneself. That's what she would do.

A broken piece of steel rebar poked Kim in the back as she pushed herself into one of the crevices. Kim grabbed the steel bar and bent it back and forth until it snapped free. She held it tightly and backed up farther.

Kim's eyes stayed glued to the dim chamber. Praying for daylight, when Halloween would end.

She listened intently for the sound of his breath. But she heard nothing.

Kim's eyes fought to stay open. The blood leaving

her body encouraged them to close. Encouraged her to sleep.

Each time she blinked, her eyes stayed closed just a little longer.

And then… he passed by. Like a featureless shadow in the dimly lit chamber. Just the shape of a person and nothing more.

Tears filled Kim's eyes. Why could she not escape him? What had she done to deserve this?

She gripped the bar in her hand and silenced her cry.

He moved back nearer to the crevice hiding place, hunting. Getting closer.

Kim knew it would only be a matter of time until he turned in her direction.

He investigated the perimeter of the concrete cave. Kim held her breath. Trying desperately not to make a sound.

He stopped. Directly in front of the place she'd hidden. His back to her. His head pivoting right to left.

Kim's breath escaped her lungs in a small exhalation. Barely audible. But loud enough for him to hear.

His head turned, and Kim used the last bit of energy she had to attack.

She rushed out of the crevice and stabbed the steel bar forcefully into Michael's arm.

Both of them collapsed. Next to each other.

Kim looked at his masked face watching her. And when she moved to get away, he did not let her.

She tried to crawl, but Michael held her leg. He removed the steel bar from his arm and drove it through Kim's spine. He listened to the music it created as she took her last breath. As her bones splintered and organs burst. As the bar traveled through the entirety of her body and her blood poured out.

Michael's arm fell to his side. Deadened by the stab. He studied his victim. Watching as her blood drained. Then he grabbed Kim's lifeless body and dragged her deeper into his dark chamber.

*

Michael made the cave his home. And he rotted slowly. His injuries growing more infected. That was how Nelson found him. His arm limp like his hand. His body eroding like the insides of the cavern. Slowly becoming part of the concrete structure that encased him.

Finally reunited with his God, Nelson made good on his promise to serve him and lured someone under the bridge on the next Halloween. A hitchhiker named Meredith, who he had seen panhandling as she tried to make her way down south.

Nelson invited Meredith to his camp and fed her a bottle of Boone's. Nelson sang to her as he pulled at his beard and waited for the drink to set in.

"Trick or treat…" They could hear the voices of children drifting into their drunken evening.

Inspired by the holiday, Meredith wrapped some fabric over her head. She painted a mustache and goatee onto her face with some ash from Nelson's fire, and called herself a pirate.

"*Arrr*, got any candy?" she jokingly asked her host.

As the alcohol stunned her, Meredith wandered into her childhood memories of the holiday. How she remembered being so frightened every October 31st.

"My dad would put a mask on and run through the house, scaring my brother and me. And we'd run outside to hide. Both of us believing that monsters really did exist on Halloween."

Meredith looked at Nelson. "Why do people like to scare?"

While Meredith recounted her memories, Nelson stepped behind her and struck her with the empty bottle. Meredith went blank.

Nelson dragged her into the tunnel's entrance. Then he hunched in the shadows and waited.

From within the cave, he heard Michael approaching. And then he heard the woman's body sliding across the concrete floor within.

*

Michael gazed at his reflection in the shallow pool of glistening scum collected at the bottom of the cave as he scrubbed the bones clean.

Images of his earliest bloodshed appeared in the reflective pool. He watched them blankly.

Taking the knife from the kitchen drawer.

Kill.

Retrieving his mask at the top of the stairs.

Kill.

Entering her bedroom.

Kill.

His hand absorbing the blade as he became the weapon.

Kill.

Her skin folding as the knife sliced it open. Her color going from pink to red. The fear in her expression.

Kill.

Descending the stairs to find more.

Kill.

Walking into the dark Halloween night.

Kill.

"Michael?"

The voice that stopped him. And then removed his mask. The voice that later screamed upstairs when the body was discovered, *"What have you done?!"*

*

Michael removed the bones from the shallow pool and arranged them inside a hidden recess within the structure.

Nelson continued to feed the monster with whatever he could find. When a couple of neon-colored teenagers ducked underneath the bridge to get high and spray-paint the walls on the following Halloween, Nelson surprised them both with a metal rod. When Nelson swung his weapon and put the first one on the ground, the other friend just stood frozen in a stoned stupor, stuck on the look he saw on Nelson's face.

"You're next," Nelson told the boy as he slapped him across the face with the metal rod.

Nelson pushed both their bodies into the tunnel and listened to their screams as they woke to find the boogeyman.

Nelson smiled. "I be your Michael Myers. I be your God."

*

Allyson sat on her bed staring at the scarecrow mask she had bought Corey. She slipped it over her face to hide her tears.

She couldn't escape the thought: *Why did I push him so hard?* Allyson could not shake the image of Corey's frightened face. Or how vulnerable he looked. *Why did I push him so hard?*

Allyson turned out the lights and moved to the window. She looked through the eyeholes of his mask as she gazed out into the Haddonfield night. Standing in the same way she'd seen her mother standing at Judith's window inside the Myers' house. Wondering what it felt like in that last moment of life. And wondering where he might be.

Allyson grabbed the wedding rings hanging from her necklace and squeezed until her hand ached.

*

Drip–drip.

In the small but horrific sanctuary of fallen concrete

slabs, fat drops of contaminated water plopped from the ceiling.

The drops created a torturous rhythmic noise. Each drip brought the waking nightmare a second closer.

Two beady eyes stared into Corey's as he regained consciousness within the gothic chamber of urban decay.

> *"There's a hole in the boat*
> *And we can't keep afloat*
> *Ooo-lie-fee-ist in the sea…"*

The vagabond's song floated into the cave and rattled around Corey's head alongside the ticking clock of the dripping water.

Drip–drip.

Corey's eyes fluttered as he woke. He found a fat, greasy rat perched on his chest, investigating the features on his face. Two more crawled up his legs. Corey feverishly knocked them away. They let out high-pitched squeaks and then chattered off into the darkness.

Corey struggled to focus on the details of his location. Flashes of memory came back to him. He saw Allyson staring at him, concerned. And Mrs. Allen's wrath. He heard the laughter from the bullies. And he saw Terry pushing him over the railing…

Drip–drip.

Corey's head throbbed. He lifted it off the ground and felt queasy. He reached out his arms but could only feel the strange pools of scum surrounding him. More toxic liquids streamed in from above and slid down the walls.

Drip–drip.

Corey heard a rustling from somewhere deeper in the cave. And then footsteps. He did not wait. Corey got to his feet and stumbled into the darkness.

Drip–drip.

Corey ran through the rocky passageways. Blind and frantic for a way out. Disoriented.

Drip–drip.

Corey's panic made his breathing harsh. He wheezed as he pressed against the curved, dank walls, using them to guide his path.

He came to a wider chasm where more light came through another drainage grate above. Corey located an iron ladder fastened to the wall beneath it.

Drip–drip.

As Corey took a step forward, the ground crumbled beneath him.

He crashed into a pit of rubble and shit. Perhaps a collapsed sewer. Corey scrambled to his feet, lost in his surroundings. His feet sunk into the muddy bottom of the pit.

He reached one of the metal rungs on the wall and pulled himself up.

Moss and sludge oozed off the oxidized steel bars on the grate above him. Corey climbed to reach it.

Drip–drip.

Corey grabbed the slick grate and tried to lift it, but it wouldn't budge. He tried again, straining to budge its weight. Nothing. Corey pushed his hands against the bars. His feet bent against the rung as he put all his muscles into it.

SNAP!

The rungs broke free, and Corey plummeted back into the pit. Landing on his back.

The ground knocked the air out of his lungs. His breath turned into broken glass as he struggled to regain oxygen.

Corey crawled to one side of the rubble and attempted to ascend a slick slope to get back to where he'd begun his attempted escape.

Drip–drip.

A sharp edge of broken concrete punctured his wounded hand. He moved his hands to a duller part of a thick slab and pushed down for leverage. The slab came loose and fell forward, landing in the mush with a meaty thump.

The wall behind the slab came to life with bugs, maggots, and putrid life. Creatures that survived on the dead. They slithered through a significant collection of human remains. There were bones picked clean and bones that still had meat and hair attached.

Corey tried to get back, but his foot sunk deeper, and he fell into the recess. Into the bones and bugs. He desperately brushed the grotesque creatures off his arms and face.

Drip–drip.

Corey dug his hands into the muck until he felt something more solid, and he used it to hoist himself up and reach the lip of solid ground. He pulled himself out of the pit and moved back into the pitch-black darkness of the cave.

His heart pounded as he navigated with outstretched arms. Bumping into walls and fallen pieces of concrete.

Corey reached the clearing in which he had awoken. He hurried along the long wall toward the light coming through the end of the tunnel. His eyes glanced at the chasms along the wall. Each one revealing a deeper recess.

Corey had almost reached the light when a hand shot out from one of those crevices in the wall and caught him by the throat. His eyes widened as he saw the pale gray mask staring at him from within this opening.

Drip–drip.

Michael forced Corey's gaze into the dark eyes behind his mask. Opening his mind to the essence of pure evil.

Drip–drip.

The wall behind Michael slowly spun as Corey's head swelled. A flurry of images presented themselves in the vortex of the swirl.

Fear.

Blood.

Death.

He saw the terrified look on Jeremy's face.

He saw the blood beneath the boy's head.

He saw the death in his eyes.

The images horrified him… until they did not.

Drip–drip.

Corey trembled as he felt an electric awakening. As the fear worked to excite him. As the hate he'd ingested turned outward.

Michael's eyes stared back absently.

And Corey's eyes slowly transformed into his.

Drip–drip.

Michael's head tilted as he studied Corey's fearless expression. He squeezed Corey's throat tighter. It had no effect on Corey's demeanor, as Corey absorbed the darkness.

Michael's arm shook as he squeezed. His energy fading, he squeezed until he could hold on no more.

Michael released his grip, and Corey fell back.

For a moment, Corey remained on the ground. Examining this new feeling. A feeling that inspired a new intention.

Corey rose to his feet and looked at Michael, watching him from within the dark crevice. And then Corey turned and crawled through the tunnel.

Drip–drip.

Corey spilled out of the tunnel and hit the ground hard. The harsh daylight made it difficult to focus. Traffic screamed across the bridge overhead.

The atmospheric change confused Corey's senses, and he stumbled to his feet awkwardly.

As he moved from underneath the bridge, a man appeared before him.

Corey turned to find Nelson Christopher wearing his handmade tarp mask. With the same void in his eyes that he felt in his own.

"You seen that man in there?" Nelson barked. "He got that mask on, why he let you go?"

Corey stood bewildered. "Let go," he muttered under his breath.

"Nuh-uh." Nelson removed the pocketknife Laurie had given Corey. The one Billy had knocked out of his hand the night before.

Nelson unfolded the blade and pointed it at Corey. "Get back in that hole 'fore I cut you. You take that man mask?"

Corey pulled back, and Nelson poked Corey's chest with the tip of the knife.

"I take your face, you don't get me that man mask."

Nelson stepped closer so that Corey could see the mean in his eyes.

But Corey didn't feel fear or dread. He didn't feel anything but one single desire. *Kill.*

Corey latched onto Nelson's wrist and redirected the knife in his direction. Nelson struggled to resist, but Corey overpowered him and buried the blade deep into Nelson's chest. He twisted the knife and watched terror overtake the blackness in Nelson's eyes.

The sensation exhilarated Corey, and he pushed harder. The blade dug deeper. Corey held it firm until Nelson surrendered to it.

Nelson slid away from the knife and collapsed to the ground, dying painfully. Moaning and twitching. Blood pumping out in thick dark spurts.

Corey glanced back to the tunnel. He could feel Michael's eyes on him.

Corey's heart beat steadily. Unhurried. Staring at

the opening. And then he turned and moved back to the light.

*

Corey carefully opened the door to his home and peeked inside. He could see his momma in her bathrobe cooking a pot of Cream of Wheat on the stove.

Corey hurried by the kitchen and ran upstairs quickly to evade his momma's interrogation. But not quickly enough.

Joan's ears perked when she heard the creak of the stairs.

"Corey? Is that you? Corey?!"

Corey continued into the bathroom. Joan chased after him.

"Corey, stop and talk to your mother! Where have you been?"

Corey closed the door and quickly locked it.

Joan twisted the knob and banged on the door.

"Corey! Don't you lock the door on your mother! Don't you lock me out! What's happened?! *Where have you been?!*"

Corey ran the hot water in the sink. His clothes and body were caked in filth from Michael's lair.

When Corey saw his reflection, he saw the violence covering his body. He ripped his clothes off and bathed himself furiously in the sink. Scrubbing the blood off his face. Scrubbing the scratches and bruises. Scrubbing so hard it looked like he was trying to scrub his skin away.

Joan continued her interrogation, but her voice got lost in Corey's exhilaration and confusion.

The images of Corey's kill, running on a loop, appeared in the haze of steam rising from the faucet. The blade. The blood. The fear. The death. Over and over. Making Corey feel something he'd never felt before. New. He'd come out of the darkness of the cave reborn. His former shape disappeared behind the steam, and a new one emerged.

NEW BEGINNINGS

Allyson's disappointments from the previous night spilled into the clinic the next day when she learned that Dr. Mathis had awarded Deb the promotion Allyson had been working so hard to get. And Allyson dealt with it as she dealt with all her other disappointments: by pushing it into her gut and letting it burn.

Allyson watched Dr. Mathis strut around the office, stopping to chew the shit with the radiographers, and making bad jokes to the patients in the waiting room who were enamored with the doctor they'd seen in the corny local commercials. Dr. Mathis had arranged it so that the commercials he had filmed a couple of summers before played continuously on the TV as you entered the clinic.

"Hello, I'm Dr. Tanner Mathis, and I'd like to tell you a few things about Grantham Primary Medical Clinic. It's the place I call home…"

Deb, who didn't notice or care about Allyson's quiet rage, skipped to the reception desk and flicked Allyson's hair from over the counter.

"No hard feelings about the promotion, right?"

Deb said as she slid off the counter and tried to smell her own upper lip.

"'Course not, you deserve it," Allyson replied flatly while not looking up from the insurance forms she'd been tasked with filing.

"I thought for sure you had it in the bag. I mean, after I nearly killed Mrs. Vasquez, I feel like I'm lucky to even have a job! But then, you know, at the party when Lindsey was doing her fortune-telling stuff, she did mine, and she told me, 'good fortunes await.'" Deb smeared her lips with a greasy balm. "And I had this thought in the back of my head: *What if Dr. Mathis makes me the charge nurse*? So, I guess I manifested it, you know? Have you ever done that before? Manifested something?"

Dr. Mathis passed by and lifted his leg awkwardly, trying to discreetly remove a deep wedgie. It didn't work ultimately, so he went ahead and dug his fingers back there and gave his undies a tug.

"Hey, Ally, speaking of the party," Deb continued to annoy Allyson in her idiosyncratic ways, not least making a 'cute' abbreviated version of her name. "How'd it work out with you and the silly scarecrow after his meltdown? Oh my God, that was so embarrassing, right? I felt so bad for you. But now you can see why I was all like, what are you doing hanging out with that psycho—"

Mathis called Deb into his office before Allyson could tell her to fuck off.

Deb bounced into Mathis's office, and Allyson continued filing. She could hear the two laughing inside, and then she could feel them at his office window watching her.

Allyson grabbed the letter opener and clenched the handle. Her fury spoke to her. Suggesting things Allyson refused to hear. Allyson moved from the handle to the sharpened edge of the paper knife, and she squeezed it tight enough to feel pain. For a moment, she enjoyed the physical sensation as it took her thoughts away. Then she set it down and began filing the next stack of insurance forms.

*

Officer Frank Hawkins grabbed a donut from the complimentary tray next to the coffee station at the bank. He then spent twenty minutes catching up with Cindy Mah, his favorite teller, as he deposited his paycheck.

"You know what you should do? You should call today and let them know what happened. No, I'm serious. So they have it on record," Cindy advised Frank after he told her how the dentist had messed up one of his crowns.

Frank massaged the soreness through his cheek. "Yeah, maybe I should. The dentist is a good guy. I like his style, but, yeah, every time I bite, I get a jolt of pain. Makes me want to yell 'Help!'" Frank chuckled.

"You should totally do that!" Cindy told him. "That way, they have it on record in case it gets worse."

"That's good advice. Thanks, Cindy."

Frank had never taken to ATM banking and

preferred a personal touch, especially when it came from someone as wonderful as Cindy.

"Did you get your shower regrouted, Frank?" Cindy asked as Frank turned his attention to Joan Cunningham, who had entered the bank. Frank had worked on the Cunningham case, but he knew Joan from long before the accident.

Joan was known to call complaints in to the police station about any minor offense. If someone parked on the street too close to her house. Or if the garbage collectors accidentally knocked over her trashcan. Or the one time someone cut her off in traffic. The guys at the station joked about setting up their own Joan line. "Yeah, direct to voicemail," Frank suggested.

Even though he believed in the court's decision and Corey's innocence, Joan made Frank wonder if there might be something deeper going on in the Cunningham home.

Frank stole glances in Joan's direction, careful to avoid making eye contact. He had no idea what might happen if she recognized him. She could have started ranting like she did on the phone, or maybe she'd have puffed her chest and stormed out.

On this day, Joan appeared particularly flustered. Frank noticed how she put her reading glasses on to fill out a change slip and then forgot she had them on and searched for them all over again.

"Doggonit!" Joan slapped the counter.

When the teller told Joan where they were, Joan snapped, "Why didn't you tell me that in the first place! You let me look around like a real boob.

What's wrong with you people? What's wrong with this flipping town?!"

Then, once Joan had filled out the slip, she wadded it up and began a new one.

"Yep. Your tips worked great. Always appreciate it." Frank turned back to Cindy.

"I told you it wasn't hard. You should call me whenever you have any other renovations. I can pretty much take care of anything home-related."

"Maybe I will. Thinking about updating my ceiling fans. Right now, they look kind of sad and out of date. I like the ones they got over there in Japan. I got a book all about Japanese architecture and design. It's really stunning, some of the things they do," Frank told her as he kept part of his attention on Joan.

"Oh, that's a piece of cake. I installed all my ceiling fans seven years ago. If you're serious, I'll give you a hand," Cindy told him.

"I'll be sure to give you a ring. Good catching up, Cindy."

"Of course, Frank. It's always a pleasure."

"Sayonara," Frank told her as he walked out.

"Sayonara, Frank."

Frank sat in his car, looking at his to-do list. He crossed out *visit Cindy at the bank*, and then moved on to the fourth thing on his list: *get ingredients for croquettes*.

After his extensive physical therapy, Frank had recovered and returned to the sheriff's department, where they had offered him a desk job. For years he'd feared taking on something so pedestrian. Couldn't imagine a life more boring than being parked behind a desk full of paperwork. But once he got acclimated to a more routine lifestyle, he grew to appreciate the slower tempo. It let him get to know the fellas on a different level.

The doctors who had operated on him had been skeptical Frank would ever walk again, so when he eventually got up and walked, he promised to take advantage of his second chance at life.

The podcasts his niece Monique sent him, and his new journaling habits, helped ease his need for vengeance. He lost none of the hate for what Michael had inflicted upon his town, but it would no longer get in the way of his living.

When friends and acquaintances came across Frank after he began his post-hospital life, they all noted how he looked ten years younger.

With so much free time on his hands and the energy to take advantage of it, Frank bought himself a guitar from a pawn shop, something he'd always wanted to learn how to play. He found a guy named Bryan on YouTube who gave free tutorials, and within a couple of weeks, Bryan had taught him how to play 'Row, Row, Row Your Boat.' A month later, Frank could play 'Basket Case' by Green Day without even looking at the strings.

In addition to the self-help stuff she'd given him, Frank's niece also got him a Rosetta Stone so he could learn Japanese, a language he'd long been fascinated by. Frank became diligent about learning it, too.

He woke up every day an hour early to study the language, and then he practiced all the way to work and during his lunch break. Frank fell so hard for the language that he expanded that love into Japanese culture and the cuisine, which is what took him to the grocery store that day: Japanese croquettes filled with a delicious mixture of meats and potatoes.

Frank stood in the butcher section, grabbing a few pounds of meat from Tracy, when Laurie appeared at the end of the aisle.

Every time they'd run into one another, they promised to catch up over a cup of coffee at the diner, but neither ever followed up to cement the plans. But Frank thought about her often.

Laurie teased Frank about his large meat order, and Frank dug his toes into the linoleum and fidgeted like a nervous teenager. The same way he'd done in high school when Laurie would say "Hi."

"They're for my croquettes. I make a bunch of 'em for the guys at the station. They like them," Frank smiled and reconsidered, "or at least they tell me they like them." Frank laughed to himself. "Each Saturday, I like to cook up a big batch and take 'em up to the guys working the Sunday shift."

"Well, aren't you full of surprises?" Laurie smiled.

"Yeah, I guess so, sometimes. So are you, huh?"

Laurie looked confused by his statement. So did he.

"Am I?" she asked.

Frank and Laurie's small talk mimicked how they'd talked in the halls back in high school, without rhythm or purpose but enjoying each other's company all the same.

"Oh," Laurie remembered to tell him, "I meant to call and let you know that I started writing that book like you suggested."

"Book?" Frank pondered. "I suggested writing down your thoughts, but you're making a whole book out of it? No kidding?"

"I just thought maybe someone out there as fucked up as I used to be could learn from some of the things I did. Who knows?"

"I think that's a great project for you to be involved in. Got a title for it yet?"

"Right now, I'm calling it: *You need to learn how to use a comma, Momma.*"

Frank laughed. "It's been a few years since grade school. Go easy on yourself."

"Allyson keeps me motivated."

"That's great. Tell her to stop by and pay me a visit. I miss her smile. Always lights up a room," Frank told Laurie.

"I'll do that. I introduced her to a guy I met by chance. They've been out on a date. Corey Cunningham. I'm sure you know him."

Frank smirked at the coincidence of his earlier Joan encounter. "I'm pretty familiar. I worked his case."

"Yeah? And what's your take on him? Am I being naïve?"

"I don't think so. From everything I learned, he seemed like a good kid who was part of a tragic accident."

"That's what I thought, too."

The two fidgeted some more as they looked for other things to tell one another.

"So, what are you doing with yourself, outside of being a chef?" Laurie asked.

"Well, I'm learning to speak Japanese." Frank tried to remember the phrase he'd learned that morning. "*Shatsu o nakushita…*" He rolled it over in his head, wondering if he'd gotten it correct or not.

"Sounds like the real deal to me," Laurie told him. "What's it mean?"

Frank thought for a moment. "I lost my shirt, I think, or lost my hat. One of those two… Shoot, now I can't remember."

Laurie laughed, and Frank melted.

"I'll get there. And who knows, maybe I'll fly over for the cherry blossoms and test it out on the locals," Frank told her.

"You look good. I like seeing your face," Laurie said with a sweet smile.

Frank stuttered, "So do you. I mean, I do too. I like seeing you too."

The moment brought Laurie back to her teenage life. The fall of her senior year just before everything turned. Sitting in the bleachers during a pep rally, watching Frank and the rest of the football team goof around in the center of the gym while the cheerleaders danced behind them. Frank acted a lot shier than the rest of the guys, and Laurie thought it was cute how he'd put his hands in his letter jacket and kick his leg nervously because standing still caused him too much self-consciousness. Even though she had her heart set on Ben Tramer, Laurie always had a soft spot for Frank Hawkins.

Frank and Laurie ran out of small talk and stood there looking at each other for a couple of moments, both wanting to say so much more but not quite knowing how. So, they bid their farewells. And as they did every time they ran into each other, they promised to reach out and have a proper get-together.

*

Laurie glided out of the store in good spirits. And then she crashed into the parking lot.

"What are you smiling at?" a voice full of venom asked.

Laurie turned to find a woman glaring at her. Another woman with a gruesome scar around her neck sat in a wheelchair next to her. Sisters: Veva and Sondra.

Laurie recognized neither and assumed for a moment that she'd been mistaken for someone else.

"What'd you buy at the store today?" Veva continued.

"I'm sorry?" Laurie asked with confusion. She looked back to the woman in the wheelchair for more clarity but found none.

"No, ma'am, excuse me. I am sorry to interrupt you on your way home to your nice house. Did you buy some eggs and some ice cream for your nice house? For your normal life?" Veva sneered.

"I don't understand." Laurie could not figure out what she'd done to upset the woman.

"Oh, I know you don't. You don't understand a goddamn thing, do you? You see what he did to my sister?!"

Laurie looked back at Sondra in the wheelchair, who remained silent. Laurie focused on the scar on the woman's neck. *Michael*, Laurie thought.

"She cannot speak! And it's because of you! This is your work."

Laurie retreated. "I'm leaving. I'm sorry."

"You were her neighbor. You don't even know her name, do you?" Veva asked.

Laurie stopped.

"Do you know her name?" Veva repeated.

Laurie's eyes fell. She had no idea.

"You sent the devil into her house, *and you don't know her name!*" Veva screamed.

Laurie looked around as people in the parking lot gathered to watch.

"I'm sorry," Laurie said again.

"Quit saying you're fucking sorry!" Veva screamed. She stepped closer and put her finger in Laurie's face.

"He killed her husband, then he stabbed her in the fucking neck and took her voice away. And you just stand there saying you're sorry?! Sorry ain't gonna bring back her husband. Sorry ain't gonna give her a voice!"

"I lost my girl, my daughter…" Laurie stuttered.

"I'm her voice now! And I'm using my voice to tell you what we feel!"

Laurie nodded respectfully.

"You tempted that man. You provoked him when you should have left it alone. But you had to be a hero. 'Cause you want to be a hero. You trapped him and took it into your own hands when you should have called the police and let them do their job! You made that man angry, and he took it out on the rest of us. He went to my sister's house and took their lives! Now everybody's dead, and we're all hurting. There's blood everywhere, and it's because of you."

More spectators gathered.

Laurie backed away, muttering incoherently. "I'm sorry... I'm sorry... I'm sorry..."

"What he did to this town happened because you wanted to be a hero! But you ain't no hero, are you? Nah, you're just some woman who fucked everything up."

"We all a get a second chance now, and I'm trying to use my second—"

"'Second chance'?" Veva smirked. "Where's my sister's second chance? What about the people in the morgue? They get a second chance? Do their families get a second chance? Maybe, just maybe, you need to stop preaching and listen to somebody."

Veva stepped closer to look deep into Laurie's eyes, then she continued, "Just tell me one thing, Laurie Strode. How the fuck do you live with yourself, knowing how many lives you've destroyed?"

"Laurie?" Laurie turned to find Frank at the storefront with his grocery cart. "Everything okay?"

Laurie nodded and backed up to her truck. "She's right. She's not saying anything that isn't true."

Laurie threw her bags into the bed of the truck and climbed inside. She locked the doors and tried to compose herself.

Frank approached her window. "Are you okay?" he asked gently.

Laurie looked at the concern on his face. It brought a smile to hers.

"What was it you were saying about those cherry blossoms?"

*

Lindsey met up with Allyson for a walk around the neighborhood. It used to be a more regular thing for the two of them, but ever since Allyson started pulling doubles at the clinic, they hadn't gotten as many hangouts.

Lindsey pulled a pinner out of her wallet and ignited it. She took a deep hit, held it for her requisite ten seconds, and then slowly coughed it out.

The fallen leaves snapped beneath their feet. The gray sky hung low. Cold and heavy. Lit fireplaces filled the air with the unmistakable smell of autumn.

Lindsey apologized again for what happened at the bar.

"I just didn't even think about it. I'm sorry. He had a mask; I was in another headspace—"

"It's fine, don't worry about it," Allyson quickly replied, not wanting to relive the experience.

"I know. And I know you get plenty of advice from Laurie, and the last thing you need is me chiming in, but I just want to tell you that I have looked for meaning in everything from booze to books to men, and none of 'em made anything better. I had to find meaning on my own," Lindsey told her as she took another long pull off her joint. "I mean, come on, at the end of the day, it's all chaos…" Lindsey looked around as she considered those words. "And who knows, maybe that's why I put my faith in fate and luck. The only thing I know, *the only thing* is that we're just looking out for each other. We've all been through enough to know that, right?"

Allyson nodded.

"Life's hard enough to get through without the shit we've had to deal with. I just don't want you running into something that's going to swallow you up or make your life any more difficult."

"I appreciate your concern." Allyson feigned thankfulness.

"Laurie changed because she believes in change, and she's not wrong. Nobody is cemented to who they used to be, and she's an incredible example, but she had to go through the work to change. You know that."

"I know, I was there," Allyson replied curtly, wanting to get off the subject.

"I'll stop. I'm just telling you this because I love you. And because I've been down some dark paths. I'd much rather talk to you about something other than men."

Allyson laughed. "Then let's talk about something other than men, please."

Lindsey relit her joint. "What's the word on your promotion? Mathis said anything yet?"

Allyson shook her head. She didn't feel like going into that either.

Just then, a car screamed by. Going at least fifty.

"Hey, asshole! Slow the fuck down! This is a neighborhood!" Lindsey yelled.

The car screeched to a stop. Allyson and Lindsey stopped. Allyson anxiously, Lindsey angrily.

"What is this?" Lindsey said as she prepared herself for an encounter.

The car idled long enough to raise concern. Then the window came down. An arm extended. And a middle finger rose to flip them both off. Then it sped away.

"What are we still doing in this town?" Lindsey asked.

Allyson watched the car speed away. "It's been telling us to leave for years."

Lindsey and Allyson rounded the corner, and a block later, they came upon the charred remains of another car parked on the side of the road. Police tape sloppily wrapped around it. Most of it spilling into the street and fluttering in the wind.

"Seriously. What's anybody still doing here? Somebody should just burn it down and start back over from scratch," Lindsey suggested.

Allyson looked at the unkempt streets and yards. The *FOR SALE* signs that had been implanted for so long that the landscape and elements had overtaken them.

"Think Grandma would ever leave?" Allyson asked.

"I don't think she'd know what to do somewhere else."

"And what happens if we leave and she's all by herself?" Allyson asked.

Lindsey got it. "Fair enough."

Lindsey and Allyson continued their walk. "Sometimes, I wonder if *he* turned us into this, or did we do it on our own?" Lindsey pondered. "I always think I've moved on, but as soon as Halloween gets close, I just want to run away."

Lindsey noticed a penny on the ground. "There's some luck right there. Better grab it."

"You don't want it?" Allyson asked.

Lindsey pulled her keychain out and showed Allyson her penny pendant attached.

"Found it heads up on the way to school on Halloween morning, 1978." Lindsey smiled, recalling that moment. "See a penny, pick it up. Stalker rolls into Haddonfield and tries to kill you… good-fucking-luck."

Allyson grabbed the penny. She rubbed it against her pants to clean it and then stuck it in her pocket.

*

Corey moved through Prevo Auto Body Shop with purpose. Cleaned up and with a penetrating gaze.

"Corey, where you been?" Ronald called out

from the office. "Your mom's been calling all day."

Corey ignored him and continued toward his motorcycle, pausing only to grab a leather jacket off the hook.

"Oy, Corey, that's Simmons's coat," Atilla called out.

Corey ignored him, too, as he mounted his motorcycle and kick-started it.

The motorcycle roared ferociously.

Corey revved the gas. The engine became the only noise in the shop.

And then he exploded out of the auto yard.

*

After Corey scrubbed himself clean at home, he had raced by Joan, who tried desperately to get more information about where he had been.

"Corey, come back here!" she ordered as he ran downstairs and out the door.

"Corey!!" Joan clutched her chest as she opened the door. "You're killing me!"

Usually her histrionics worked, but this time it had no effect on Corey.

Joan looked out, but Corey had already disappeared.

Joan stormed upstairs, worried about his disturbing behavior. She threw open his dresser drawers, looking for clues to tell her more about the change in his demeanor.

On the dresser, Joan found Corey's phone and unlocked it. There she discovered missed calls and text messages from a girl named Allyson. *Where are you?* being the common theme.

"Who is this Allyson?" Joan barked at Ronald over the phone.

"That's one of Corey's friends," Ronald answered.

"You've met her?"

"She came up here yesterday to deliver his bicycle. She works at the clinic. I think she's Laurie Strode's granddaughter."

"Laurie Strode?!" Joan snapped.

"She seems like a sweet girl. I think they're just friends."

"Oh, you do, do you? A girl? A girl that he didn't tell me about?"

"He probably just wanted to see where things went before he introduced you to her," Ronald meekly suggested.

"Ronald, my baby boy was missing. No phone calls, no nothing! So quit acting so flipping calm!"

Joan hung up the phone and looked at the messages again.

"I don't like secrets!" she screamed into the empty room.

Joan stormed into the bathroom and retrieved Corey's filthy clothes. She shoved them into her face to smell them and recoiled. "Disgusting!"

Joan investigated closer. The redder splotches grabbed her focus. And her heart raced as she considered the awful implications.

"Leave my boy alone!" Joan yelled through the house as she carried his things to the laundry room.

"He's my boy!" she shrieked as she shoved his clothes into the washer and started the cycle.

"It's not a joke!" Joan told her rabbits as she left the house to run her errands.

Joan slapped her purse against her car as she got in. She saw her neighbor across the street watching, and waved her away. "Go on and get out of here! There's nothing to see. Got it?!"

*

Joan bounced off the curb stop in the parking lot of the bank.

Inside, she didn't calm down.

After losing her glasses on her face, Joan got frazzled trying to fill out a slip and wrote Corey's name instead of her own. She snapped at the teller several times, and then when she left, she backed her car out so wildly that she rear-ended a parked car.

"You shouldn't have parked so close!" Joan yelled at the empty car. She left without leaving a note.

Next, Joan sped to Hobby Home to see if they'd gotten their Christmas ornaments yet. She wanted to get first dibs on any rabbit-themed paraphernalia. Her mind remained a thunderstorm of activity which caused her to run through two red lights and nearly hit a jogger.

Joan burst through the doors of Hobby Home, and the employees who'd had the misfortune of dealing with her during past visits quickly turned their heads to avoid eye contact.

Joan marched down each aisle, sneering at the

Halloween merchandise. Growing angrier each time she passed another nasty bit of Halloween décor. When she reached the end of the third aisle and looked at the plush pumpkins stuffed onto the shelf, she grabbed one and threw it on the ground.

"Excuse me," Joan snapped at a teenage employee. "Some of us in this town don't care for goblins and death and all of this *Halloween*!" Joan waved her hands around all the Halloween merchandise. "Some of us want rabbits, not monsters!"

"I'll, um, tell the manager then," the employee told her, uncertain of what protocol to follow.

"For some of us, Halloween is bad business! Not good business! Got it?!"

"Yes, ma'am," the employee told Joan, hoping to defuse the situation.

"Very bad business!" Joan said as she stormed out. "I want rabbits!"

*

Joan drove erratically toward Prevo to give Ronald a dressing down for keeping Corey's girlfriend a secret. As she approached the shop, Corey flew by on his motorcycle.

"*Corey!*" she screamed as she reached her head out the window. The action caused her to veer off the road.

Joan's car jumped the curb into the carpet warehouse parking lot and crashed into a pylon that wedged itself under her car.

"*Corey!!*" Joan yelled as she tried to reverse off the pylon. The car wouldn't move.

Joan jumped out and looked down the road. She could no longer see her baby boy.

*

Corey ripped toward the bridge road where he'd emerged earlier. Fearless. Nothing mattered at that moment but getting to Allyson.

The wind beat against his bruised and swollen face. But Corey felt nothing but the thrill of becoming something new. A confidence overtook him that he'd never felt before.

*

Laurie sat in her living room, knitting. Knitting had become one of the many arts and crafts projects, along with pumpkin carving and baking, that Laurie used to take her back to a life she remembered before Halloween 1978.

Veva's verbal assault had managed to strike every single vulnerable nerve, and it surprised Laurie how quickly her strong façade came tumbling down when it got hit in the right place. She assumed she'd built herself up to withstand such a blow, but it became pretty evident that she had not.

Lindsey could tell something had happened as soon as she and Allyson came back inside after their walk, and she noticed Laurie's tense posture. Over the years, Lindsey had become adept at reading Laurie's behavior.

"What is it?" Lindsey said as she sat with Laurie in the living room.

Laurie smiled. "What is what?"

"Don't give me that shit. I know something's up. You've got a terrible poker face. All your emotions come right through your skin."

Laurie continued knitting.

"You know, you can't keep things bottled up. You gotta talk about it," Lindsey told her.

Laurie stopped and looked at Lindsey. "New beginnings, after old shit, is a real bitch."

"Tell me about it," Lindsey laughed.

Laurie smirked. "I got rattled today. And I... I just worry that... I might not be..." Laurie looked at her knitting needle and touched the point. "What happens if I can't control it this time? Where will I end up?"

Lindsey shoved some bubble gum in her mouth. "Then you come to me."

"I was being watched and didn't even notice," Laurie told Lindsey.

"What are you talking about?"

"Maybe my instincts are all wrong. I keep thinking that they are there to keep me safe, but maybe they are there to keep me crazy. Or maybe I'm just paranoid. I don't know anymore."

"You know what's true and what's not. Don't start second-guessing yourself. Who warned everyone about Michael? You knew that he'd get out again, you knew what he'd do, and nobody believed you. You, out of everybody, need to trust your instincts."

"My instincts ruined so many lives. And then I tried to move on like it had never happened."

"You didn't ruin anyone's life. Michael did. You're here like me. And you can choose life or death. Karen is dead. She doesn't have a choice. But we do, and we need to honor all the people that can't take the choice. It's your move. Take the choice."

"Take the choice," Laurie repeated and smiled. "That's good. That's a good one."

"I think so, too." Lindsey lifted her sleeve to reveal the phrase tattooed on her arm. Laurie smiled.

"Thanks for listening, Lindsey."

"Of course, that's what we do. Are you sure you're—"

"I'll be fine," Laurie told her.

"I know you will." Lindsey got up and grabbed her purse. "I gotta go. You know where to find me if you need anything."

*

Laurie sat at her computer with an apprehension building inside her that she hadn't felt in years. Anxiety created by her encounter with Veva in the parking lot, or perhaps something more. Something in the air. Halloween approaching. The memories resurfacing. Or worse yet, the sense that she might be falling back into the void she'd spent years climbing out of.

I still have the gun Frank Hawkins gave me when we were in the hospital.

Laurie reread the sentence. Then she removed the key hidden in the doll that sat crammed in between her carved pumpkins on the mantle.

Laurie unlocked a compartment inside her desk and removed the .38 handgun Hawkins had given her. She studied it carefully. Her fingers wrapped around the handle. It felt so natural in her hand. Like it belonged there.

The only weapon I still have in the house. The one I could not get rid of. Why?

Laurie checked the loaded chamber. Holding the weapon brought her some bit of comfort. And she considered holding it until the bad feelings left her body.

"Sometimes you are going to feel uncomfortable," Laurie reminded herself of the work she'd done in therapy.

Laurie laid the gun down and continued typing.

Sometimes I'm left wondering: did Frank give it to me for protection or a quick way out if I need one?

"...forprotectionoraquickwayout?" Laurie quietly muttered as she looked back to the gun. Living in the world proved to be much more complicated than the reclusive life Laurie had constructed out in the middle of nowhere. Back when she had little time for anything or anybody not connected to Michael Myers. That house and that way of life became the mask she wore to protect herself. She knew how to be scared and how to be ready. But ever since that house had burned and he'd gotten away, Laurie had been living life maskless and exposed. And every once in a while, she became painfully aware that people could see her.

Laurie put the gun back and locked the cabinet. She sighed as she held the key and sat in the discomfort.

Laurie tucked the key back into the doll's pants and then looked at the grinning expression on her pumpkin. The one that looked to be mocking her. Laurie flipped it off. "Fuck you," she said, smiling as she returned to her computer and deleted the last line she'd written.

A strange sensation came over Laurie. An instinct. Something that told her she was being watched.

"Sometimes you are going to feel uncomfortable," Laurie reminded herself again. And then she glanced out the window and found Corey Cunningham, partly obscured by the shrubs in the yard below, staring up at her.

Corey's intense gaze pushed her back into the seat. And it filled her with the same uneasiness she had experienced the first time she'd encountered Myers. The first time she saw him watching her. This was not discomfort. This was fear. And Laurie shook.

"Allyson!" she called out. When she looked back to the window, Corey had vanished.

Laurie raced downstairs and out of the house. She looked to the bushes where he had just been, but he wasn't there.

Laurie moved to the sidewalk and looked to the end of her block but couldn't see him anywhere. Then she turned. And there he was. Watching her from behind. As if he'd been there the entire time. With that same unsettling stare. With those same eyes she'd seen behind Michael's mask.

Laurie didn't pay attention to his banged-up face or his bruises. She only stared at his eyes.

"What are you doing?" Laurie asked, not able to hide her unease.

"I'm waiting for Allyson." Corey's voice cut the air like a knife. Not the soft-spoken way he talked when Laurie took him to the clinic. "I didn't mean to scare you," Corey told her.

Laurie didn't buy his apology. Her gaze remained on his eyes.

"What's happened?" she whispered.

The end of Corey's mouth crept up into a subtle grin.

"Corey?!" Allyson said as she came out of the house. Corey's grin vanished.

Allyson got caught off guard by the tension between Corey and Laurie.

"Is everything okay?"

Corey's eyes lingered on Laurie's for a few more moments. Then he turned to Allyson. His expression transformed into something softer. Something more vulnerable. Laurie watched him change before her eyes.

Corey showed Allyson his bruises.

"I got jumped. On the way home last night. These guys…"

Corey turned back to Laurie. She saw that his eyes had returned to their normal shape.

"It was those kids that were messing with me at the gas station," he told Laurie. "I tried to stand up for myself. Like you told me to do. And they…"

Believing she'd misunderstood the entire encounter, Laurie sank.

Allyson looked to Laurie for clarification. She didn't get any.

"I just want to talk to you," Corey told Allyson. "To say I'm sorry. There's no excuse for how I left."

Allyson studied his injuries. Her nursing reflexes kicked in, and she worried that some of his cuts might get infected.

"Did you clean these?" she asked as she touched his wounded face gently.

"I want to take a walk with you. Would you take a walk with me?" Corey asked.

Allyson hesitated. But then agreed.

"Let's go."

Allyson stepped off the porch, and Corey turned back to Laurie as they walked away. Laurie saw that the blackness in his eyes had returned.

*

The sense of being stared at is a powerful thing.

The first time I noticed the shape, it was just a man in a mask watching me from the distance. My introduction to pure evil. And I barely noticed. Had I known that it would eventually take over my life, I probably would have looked a little harder.

He was already watching when I dropped off the key at the Myers' house that morning. That I am certain of. From there, he followed me to school.

As I sat in the classroom, I could feel the darkness of his eyes from across the street and then through my bedroom window later that afternoon.

It left a feeling I could not articulate but one that I now understand. It was the presence of evil. That is what evil feels like when it nears. And I will never forget that feeling.

Tommy had tried to warn me all that morning. As he told me about the boogeyman. And I played the responsible adult by telling him there was no such thing as the boogeyman.

But he knew. Before anyone else besides Dr. Loomis, he knew.

I would give anything to go back and relive the banal disappointments that occupied so much of my thoughts back then. Like Ben Tramer. How I lost hours dreaming that we were meant for each other. That one day, we'd be married and have a big family with lots of children. That we'd live in the red-brick house my dad was selling... My innocence.

Everything was so simple... so perfectly mundane. Until he arrived.

I spent years living in his darkness. Trying to forget. Trying to prepare for his return. And in the process, I lost everything close to me.

I thought if I could defend myself against it, then it couldn't get me. If I could protect everyone around me, then it couldn't hurt me. I kept it alive in my thoughts, and it took everything away from me.

But the first time I saw him, it was just a man in a mask watching me from the distance...

Laurie's fingers rested on the keyboard, analyzing her encounter with Corey and doing everything she could to not lose her shit.

Laurie grabbed her phone and texted Lindsey:

Did Allyson mention anything about Corey during your walk? My instincts are killing me.

*

Several blocks down the road, Corey led Allyson toward Lampkin Lane. The street where the Myers' house once stood.

Allyson's heart raced as they neared, and when Corey turned down the street, Allyson stopped.

Allyson stared at the street sign. In the distance, she could see the garden creeping into the street.

"You all right?" Corey asked.

Allyson nodded.

"Don't be afraid. I'm here. Come on," Corey told her.

Allyson apprehensively followed Corey.

Allyson could smell the stink of rotting flowers as they got closer to the garden.

The long, barren branches from the dying trees reached out with crooked menace. The tall weeds swayed back and forth.

"We can cut through here," Corey told Allyson as he entered the garden.

Allyson followed silently. Trying to shut off her worry.

Allyson stepped over beer cans, cigarette butts, and other litter that had made the garden its home. She looked at the imposing wrought-iron sign that lived at the entrance. The one that read 'Love Lives Today'. Like everything else in the garden, the fixture stood unnaturally. Bent by the elements.

Vines curled around the post and twisted through the letters like they were strangling it and bringing it to hell.

On the plot of land where evil lived, life struggled to grow.

Some asshole had impaled a pumpkin onto one of the lampposts, and as the lights came on, so did the pumpkin. The light seeped out of the broken cracks of the ribbed skin and cast curious shapes across the garden.

The landscape completely overtook the path, so Corey made his own route.

Allyson held herself tightly in a protective gesture as she followed.

Corey turned back and took her hand as he led her forward.

Allyson looked up to where Judith Myers's window would have been. The last place she'd seen her mother. The swelling emotion choked her, and she diverted her eyes away from the memory.

They passed by the fountain where the photos of the victims had been applied to the rim.

The more aggressive, angrier vegetation broke through the fiberglass bottom of the fountain and snaked over the lip, but Allyson could make out some of the images through the erosion and decay. Tommy Doyle. Lonnie Elam. Cameron Elam.

Corey pushed through the wilder shrubs blocking the path.

The thin branches lightly cut Allyson's arms. Trying to keep her out. Telling her to go back home.

Allyson preferred the physical pain to the emotional stuff running through her mind, so she let the branches slice her skin without flinching.

In a dead clearing, Corey stopped.

"What are you doing? Where are you taking me?" Allyson asked.

Corey looked deeply into her eyes. "I killed someone."

Hearing those words caused Allyson to shudder. Standing in the place where she'd witnessed so much death made the feeling worse.

"I know you did. But it was an accident."

"I want to take you somewhere. I want to show you something," Corey told her.

Corey stepped closer. He looked deeper. His gaze penetrated right through her.

And then Corey walked toward the fallen gate on the chain-link fence that stood at the back end of the garden.

*

A thirty-minute walk later, Corey and Allyson approached the Allen house. Like everything else they'd passed along the way, the Allen house looked gray, dull, and lifeless.

Corey came through the window and helped Allyson inside.

The dust and cobwebs and the small amount of furniture left behind made Allyson incredibly uncomfortable.

"Are you sure it's okay for us to be in here?"

Allyson asked. But when she saw the paper planes scattered over the piano, she didn't require an answer.

Allyson struck a note on the piano, and it resonated eerily through the large empty rooms. Allyson found more paper planes on the floors as they walked through the home. Some fresher than others. Some that had not been yellowed by time.

Allyson lost sight of Corey and wandered through the house to find him. She could sense the heartbreak everywhere she went. And each room seemed to be crying louder than the previous.

Allyson found Corey crouching over the bloodstain left by Jeremy.

Corey looked at the blood through a new lens. His emergence from the cave had made him view things differently. Before then, Corey always regarded the incident as nothing more than an awful accident. Pure bad luck. A curse. But when he looked up to the railing where Jeremy had fallen, he considered something new. That maybe he *was* a killer. Just like they all said he was. And he'd been the only one not to see it. Maybe the killer inside him had been there the whole time, waiting for the right time to appear. And now he was here.

"Have you ever made a paper plane?" Corey asked as he left the stain and walked to the impressive staircase. "It's harder than you'd think."

Corey ascended the stairs slowly. Allyson followed.

"I mean, to make a good one. It looks simple, but everything has to be perfect for it to fly. And it's hard to be perfect." Corey looked back to Allyson. "I was never supposed to be a babysitter," Corey said as he picked a paper plane off the ground and launched it through the air.

Corey wanted to tell her everything he'd experienced inside and outside the cave, but he worried it might frighten her away. So he masked his confession. "I just wanted it to be a good night. That's all. Just a good night. Because everything that had led up to that point had been good. But then it all went bad."

Allyson continued following Corey up the stairs.

"Because people can be cruel. And they play jokes. And deep down, they hate you. They all just hate you."

Corey reached the attic door and pushed it open.

"That's when I realized I was trapped. I couldn't get out. And I was scared." Corey put his hand where the lock used to be.

"But I didn't die," Corey continued. He looked over the railing. Allyson joined him.

"He did. And his blood was on my hands."

Corey looked back to Allyson.

Moved by his openness, Allyson gently put her hand on his as they looked at the stain below. She felt compelled to open up as well.

"I know what it feels like," Allyson admitted.

Surprised by the admissions, Corey turned, wanting to know more.

"I do," Allyson continued. "Because I wanted to kill him so bad, I could not see anything else. And

Mom told me not to go. But I didn't listen. He killed my dad, and he needed to die. And I was the one who was gonna do it. And then Mr. Elam told me to stay. But I didn't listen. And he killed them. He killed them all."

Allyson kept her eyes on the stain below.

"Had I not gone, my mother wouldn't have gone to find me. But she did." Allyson took a deep breath as she tried to finish. "And because of me, she's dead."

Allyson looked at Corey as tears swelled. "So, I know what it's like to have someone's blood on your hands. I do."

Allyson fell into Corey's eyes. And he held her there. And then he moved closer.

Their lips brushed softly at first, and then they pushed harder. Their first kiss at the violent place where Corey's life had changed.

Allyson wrapped her hands around his head and pulled him closer. Everything stirred inside her. Coming to life. She desperately wanted to rip off her old skin and climb into something new.

*

Laurie sat at her desk, staring at the photo of Michael Myers's arrest from 1978. Pulling it closer to study his eyes. To figure out what she'd seen in Corey's.

She'd tried so hard to put the darkness behind her, but somehow it had managed to find her. Again.

Laurie's phone buzzed. *Lindsey.*

Laurie answered.

"Hey, what are you doing?" Lindsey asked.

"I'm just staring at Michael Myers. What about you?"

"Come up here. There's someone I want you to meet."

Laurie looked at the time. It was getting late.

"It's not too late. Come here now," Lindsey said, appearing to have read Laurie's mind.

*

Corey and Allyson came out of the Allen house. Night had fallen and the darkness made Corey's face look almost pale gray as he walked to the side of the house.

Corey's motorcycle sat parked by the curb. He climbed on.

"Wait, is this yours?" Allyson asked, confused by its presence.

Corey mounted it.

"You parked it here and walked to my house?"

Corey smiled. "Get on."

Allyson stood there hesitantly. Remembering how frightening the last experience had been.

"This time, you can ride on the back. You don't have to drive it. I can do that." Corey smiled.

"I need a helmet." Allyson remained reluctant.

"No, you don't. Not with me."

Corey kickstarted the motorcycle and revved the engine.

"Trust me," he told Allyson. "I won't let anything happen to you."

Corey's new confidence made Allyson feel protected. And even though she still had doubts, she climbed onto the back of the motorcycle and wrapped her arms around him.

Corey pulled the throttle, and the two took off into the night.

Allyson held on as Corey raced through the upscale neighborhood. She pressed her body against his and watched over his shoulder as the road unfolded. The thrill awakened her senses and made her feel as alive as she'd felt dancing with him the night before. A feeling she did not want to lose.

"Where are you taking me?" Allyson yelled as Corey sped toward the bridge road.

Corey turned off the road and onto the gravel path that led to the underpass. There he idled, looking at the darkness beneath the bridge. Wanting to confess more. Wanting to show Allyson everything he'd discovered.

Allyson sat uneasily. Something down there didn't feel right.

The vagabond's tent glowed, revealing a silhouetted shape inside.

Corey stared at the opening to the tunnel. Sensing the eyes within, watching.

Corey looked over to his shoulder at Allyson. He could see her worry.

"What are we doing down here?" Allyson asked.

"I don't know," Corey told her. And then he switched gears. "I'm hungry! I could eat everything! What about you? Are you hungry?"

"I am so fucking hungry! Let's get out of here!" Allyson yelled back.

Corey turned the bike around and roared forward, spraying dirt and gravel in his wake.

*

A diner left over from the early sixties sat on the edge of the highway. A time capsule to a bygone era. The sort of place you used to find in small towns throughout America. A place that felt innocent. Where you could fall in love, get into a rumble, spin some records, and have some pie. In Haddonfield, the diner was a relic of a time nobody could remember.

Inside, Corey pounded a double bacon chili cheeseburger, a large order of fries, two milkshakes, and a beer. Allyson couldn't help but laugh at how ravenously he ate.

"You look like you haven't eaten in months," Allyson told him.

Corey looked up with a smile. "I feel like I've never eaten in my life. I'm starving."

This new confident side of Corey gave him a dark charisma that Allyson felt drawn to. This was not the same helpless guy who'd come to her with a wounded hand. This was a guy who could do something.

"What happened to you?" Allyson asked curiously.

"I finally decided to let go," Corey told her as he shoved a fistful of fries into his mouth.

Allyson took one of Corey's fries and ate it. She could still feel the road rumbling beneath her. As if she'd never climbed off that motorcycle. And it felt incredible.

"Can I ask you something?" Corey asked as he finished his second milkshake.

"Yeah?"

"Why are you still here?"

The question caught Allyson off guard.

"I mean, why do you stay in Haddonfield?" Corey clarified.

Allyson thought about it for a minute. "I don't know. Sometimes it feels like a curse to be here."

"Tell me about it," Corey responded with a devilish grin.

Allyson continued, "It's not just the big things, either. It's the small things too. And whatever I do, it never seems to work out. Like, I do the work; Deb gets the promotion. I kiss the doctor's ass; he treats me like shit."

"You try to do the right thing, but everything you touch falls apart?" Corey asked, understanding exactly what she meant.

Allyson nodded as she got lost in that question. "And sometimes, I feel trapped. But, I don't know if I even could leave."

"Sure you can. And we should." Corey pulled her back to him.

Allyson sighed. "If it were only that easy."

"Is it not?" Corey asked. "Because when I look around, I don't see anything here except for you and death. That's it," Corey said with an intensity that overwhelmed her.

"Yeah, well, it's my home," Allyson replied tersely, relating entirely to everything he just told her but feeling powerless to do anything about it.

Allyson moved the straw through her soda and spun some of the ice cubes. "Can I be honest, though?" Allyson asked.

"Of course," Corey encouraged.

"Ever since everything happened, I sometimes find myself thinking…" Allyson leaned closer to quietly tell him. "What I really want to do… is burn it all to the ground and get the fuck away from here and never look back," Allyson admitted. She'd had those feelings inside for years and never dreamed of telling them to anyone.

Corey slapped his hand on the table. "Hey. Me too!" he replied excitedly. "So, why don't we? Why don't we burn this entire place down and get the fuck away from here?"

"Because we are civilized." Allyson smiled.

"No," Corey replied.

"No?"

"That's just a mask we wear. And I want to take mine off. Cause I'm tired of always doing the right thing. I'm tired of trying to be perfect when everybody else just says fuck it. And something tells me that you might be tired too."

Allyson smirked. "Maybe I am. I don't know."

Corey sensed her reluctance. She wasn't sold.

"You ask me what I think? Why you can't leave?"

"Yeah, tell me what you think?"

"I think all that stuff messed your grandma up so

bad that she's the reason you can't leave. Because she won't let you go. Not as long as she's alive."

"If you could have seen her after everything happened. She was bad before that night, but after… you're right, she lost her mind. But she got sober, she got into therapy, and she's better, but I still get scared thinking about what might happen if she was all alone again. If I left her."

"So, you gotta stay here? To protect her from herself? You're not her granddaughter. You're her babysitter."

"You don't understand. She used to live in a cage. Her finger was always on the trigger, ready to blow everything away."

"And now she keeps you in her shadow."

"That's not true," Allyson responded, wondering if it were in fact true.

"I don't know, you tell me. Are you living Laurie Strode's story or your own? 'Cause I see you in front of me. Not her."

Corey's words excited Allyson. To hear the things she'd thought about over the years but never knew how to express provoked her in a way she enjoyed. He was right. It was just them. Nobody else mattered. Not in Haddonfield.

Allyson pulled the cherry out of her soda, popped it into her mouth, and dropped the stem on the table. Corey grabbed the stem and carefully tied it in a knot.

"I'm sorry I lost my head at that bar," Corey told her. "Walking out on you was a huge mistake, and I said fucked-up things. And I promise you right here and right now that I will never walk out on you again."

A grin snaked across Corey's face. "And you say the word. You tell me you want to burn it—"

Corey looked up and saw Doug Mulaney approaching with a beer buzz in his step. Corey instantly flashed back to the night Doug arrested him. Even while in shock, Corey remembered how Doug had indicted him before anything had been investigated.

"You're guilty, you son of a bitch, and you're gonna pay for what you've done," Doug whispered into Corey's ear as he put a fist into Corey's ribs before handcuffing him outside of the Allen home. "Fucking psycho, you'll be lucky to make it to the station alive. I might just put a bullet through your head right fucking now. Tell 'em you came at me, and I had no choice but to put you in the ground. How'd that be?"

The Mulaney clan consisted of either rule-enforcers or rule-breakers, and Doug had landed firmly in the middle of both. Doug's father, Conrad, an officer in the Haddonfield Police Department up until a few years before, had pushed his boys into his line of work. Doug decided to go all in.

"Twice in one week, pretty cool," Doug said as he arrived at their table.

Allyson turned to find him. *Shit.* She sank in her seat. Behind Doug, she saw his police posse. Joe Grillo, Joe Ross, and the others. All of 'em looking at her with some bit of suspicion. All but Elvis Ross, Joe Ross's father, who stood at the jukebox on the other side of the diner watching. He had a different, more compassionate expression on his face. The only one.

Doug smiled and showed all his teeth. He didn't acknowledge the guy sitting across from Allyson.

"You said you were gonna call. You were gonna call me, but you didn't." Doug adjusted his look to one that appeared more inquisitive. "I do something wrong?" Doug leaned close enough for Allyson to smell the Budweiser on his breath.

"I'm with someone." Allyson timidly admitted.

"Oh. Oops. Forgive the intrusion." Doug gave the slightest glance to Corey but not enough to recognize him.

"It's Joe Grillo's birthday," Doug refused to leave, "and Joe Ross made a sponge cake. You should head over for a slice after you're finished with your little—"

"I'm good right now. I'm with—"

"All right, well, if you change your mind, it's dairy-free frosting. Cashew cream cheese or something, Old Elvis turned vegan over the summer—"

"Hey. She said she's good," Corey said with an aggressive tone. "We're both good. So, go on. Get out of here."

Doug feigned concern. "Hey, buddy, is there a problem?" Then he recognized Corey's face. And the recognition hurt. Allyson had rejected Doug for Corey Cunningham.

"Allyson," Doug said with disbelief. "What are you doing?"

Allyson kept her eyes on Corey. Doug moved

in closer. His lips touched the tips of her hair. His whispers made her skin crawl.

"Do you call Mr. Aggravated Manslaughter in the night when you can't sleep? When you see the boogeyman in your nightmares."

Allyson squirmed and moved away from his intimidations.

"Does he make you feel safe when you're certain Michael Myers is watching—"

Corey shot up. Within half a second, Corey stood an inch from Doug's face. Their heads almost touching. Dead-eye fucking serious.

"Get the fuck out of here," Corey told him without an ounce of trepidation.

Doug looked into Corey's eyes and watched them turn black. Doug's eyes remained fixed. So did Corey's. Who would flinch first?

"Corey, let's get out of here," Allyson told him quietly.

The intense blackness in Corey's eyes proved too much, and Doug broke the staring contest. He raised his hands in mock surrender.

"Uncle," he sarcastically told Corey. "Just playin' around." Then he turned to Allyson. "I'll see you around, little lady."

Doug returned to his party.

"Joe Grillo! Happy birthday!"

Corey's eyes stayed on him.

Allyson watched as Doug sat with his buddies and told them what had happened. Each of their heads turned one by one in Corey and Allyson's direction.

Elvis Ross put his hand on Doug's shoulder to calm him down, and he glanced at Allyson. His eyes seemed to be apologizing for his younger friend's behavior. The only one in the group who appeared remotely sympathetic. He had always been kind to Allyson, but it did little to change her mood.

"Come on, let's get out of here," Allyson said as she turned back to Corey. "I'll light the match."

Corey grinned and looked back to Doug Mulaney. His eyes said one thing: *You're fucking dead.*

ELVIS ROSS

Velkovsky's, Halloween Night, 1982

Back when Velkovsky's was mainly a cop bar, Frank Hawkins nursed a seltzer water with a group of officer buddies who were sucking down cans of beer. Frank had been working up the nerve to approach Laurie, who'd come in alone just a minute earlier. Frank had never developed a taste for alcohol, but he'd have loved to have had some liquid courage flowing through his veins to give him enough nerve to tell Laurie all the things he wished to tell her.

Laurie stood at the other end of the bar and ordered three double Scotches. She downed one there and took the other two to an empty booth, where she proceeded to down them in quick succession. Laurie's eyes anxiously moved around the bar, waiting for someone to join her.

Laurie looked achingly beautiful beneath the neon light of the sign hanging in the window. Frank just thought she was the sweetest, brightest, and most beautiful girl in all of Haddonfield. And Frank wanted nothing more than to heal her heartbreak, which you could see in every look she gave. Any time you saw Laurie's eyes after *that* night, you could also see her pain.

Laurie finished her third drink, and Frank worried what might happen in her intoxicated state.

He decided to approach and make sure she was all right. But just before reaching her booth, all the words he wanted to tell her got tangled up in his head, and Frank retreated to the bathroom to arrange them into something more coherent.

Frank stood in front of the cracked mirror of the bathroom, staring at his nervous expression. He wet his hands and patted down a few unruly strands of hair that crossed his part line. Then he practiced, "Hey, there, Laurie, how've you been? It's been a while, hasn't it?" Frank smirked. "'*Hasn't it*?' Get real, man."

Frank shook it off and began again. "Laurie, it's good to see you. How are you holding up? Are you doin' all right?"

"Oh, Frank, I've been waiting for this moment for years. Kiss me, you big ole stud." A faux-femme voice teased from within a bathroom stall. A second later, the door swung open, and Elvis Ross rolled out laughing his butt off.

"I was just messing around. I knew you were in there, Elvis," Frank said with a humiliated chuckle.

Elvis Ross shoved his way past Frank to get in front of the mirror. He dragged a comb across his jet-black head of hair and then ran it down his sideburns and handlebar mustache.

"You want some tips, Casanova? Study the master," Elvis Ross advised him.

"Oh, you're the master now? Is that right?" Frank joked; his cheeks were bright red with embarrassment. He prayed Elvis Ross wouldn't tell the fellas what he'd heard.

Frank watched Elvis strut out of the bathroom, envious of his swagger.

Elvis might have been beer-bloated and always stunk of cheap cologne, but he never seemed to have a problem finding female company. He'd been fortunate enough to be born without any self-doubt, which gave him plenty of fuel for his conquests.

Frank had been cursed with the heart of a romantic and wanted love more than fun. Wouldn't have turned fun down if it had said, '*Hey, Frank, good to meet you,*' but Frank's primary motivator was love. Especially when it came to Laurie Strode.

Frank splashed some water on his face to mute his blushed cheeks, and then he took a deep breath and left the bathroom.

Frank reentered the bar and found Elvis sitting with Laurie. Elvis had his arm draped over Laurie's shoulder, and he had his big grin pointed right at Frank. Frank could read Elvis's mind: *Better luck next time, partner.*

Elvis whispered something into Laurie's ear, then they slid out of the booth and headed for the door.

Laurie stumbled as the alcohol took effect. "Easy there," Elvis Ross joked. "Want to get you back to my place in one piece."

Frank gave Laurie a smile as they passed by. Laurie barely noticed.

"Laurie, you—" Frank tried to see if she needed help.

"Don't worry, Frank," Elvis said, "I'll take good care of her."

Frank walked to the window and watched as Elvis and Laurie climbed into Elvis's tan Monte Carlo with the blood-red interior.

Elvis saw Frank watching and decided to rub a little extra shit in Frank's face by kissing Laurie. When he finished, he gave Frank another toothy grin and a patronizing salute.

Frank backed away from the window and rejoined the guys at the bar. He ordered another seltzer and tried to forget about Laurie.

*

Laurie had spent each Halloween since 1978 in some form of inebriated state. *Just make it go away*, she'd repeat in her mind as she swallowed her mother's painkillers or drank a fifth of Scotch or both.

But that Halloween night in 1982, Laurie had bigger plans than just drinking until she couldn't remember anything that had happened.

Laurie sat at Elvis's bent Formica table in his double-wide trailer situated amongst the dozen other double-wides, drinking cheap Chablis out of a dixie cup. Elvis's place smelled of soured beer and stale cigarillo smoke, not an altogether unfamiliar fragrance in 1982.

After his nana passed on, Elvis classed up his home with the antiques he'd inherited from her.

Still-life paintings of bountiful fruit bowls hung on the wood-paneled walls next to oil drip lamps and cherub sculptures. Nana's tattered recliner sat awkwardly between Elvis's hi-fi stereo system and refrigerator. The chair had so many miles that you'd just about sink to the carpet if you sat on it, which is exactly what Elvis did when he plopped down.

Laurie ran her fingers across his nana's ceramic prayer hands. *Maybe that would work*, she smirked.

Elvis poured another splash of Chablis into Laurie's cup, then he lit a cigarillo off the one already in his mouth.

Elvis looked mildly embarrassed about the messy state of his home. The bed hadn't been made, dishes climbed out of the sink and ran across his countertops, and his dirty laundry was strewn over his recliner. He tossed some of his socks and shirts behind the seat, and he hid a few dirt footprints on the carpet with his feet, hoping she would overlook the trail. Usually, he didn't think about those things when he brought a woman back to his place, but with Laurie, he felt different. She seemed like she deserved better, and he had never had the desire to clean up until Laurie Strode came inside his house. Then he wished it looked pristine. Elvis tried to push those thoughts to the back of his mind and proceed with the reasons he'd brought her to his home in the first place.

Laurie slammed the rest of her Chablis like it was the Scotch she preferred and then looked at Elvis with surrender. "Okay, I'm ready."

Elvis's grin twisted, unable to get past the bleakness in Laurie's declaration.

"Why don't you go on in there and get comfortable, darling. I'll be there in just a minute," Elvis told her.

Laurie disappeared into his bedroom. He could hear her undressing and getting into his bed. But Elvis remained on the recliner. He couldn't bring himself to get out of it. He'd been with women in all matter of situations, but never one who had to numb herself so severely just to lie down with him. Elvis closed his eyes, and on his nana's old chair, he fell asleep.

About a quarter to three, Elvis woke to a nudge against his arm. His eyes strained to open, and when they did, he found Laurie standing over him, gripping one of his kitchen knives with both hands.

"What the hell?" Elvis sprung up. "What's gotten into you?"

"Have you ever seen him?" Laurie asked in a near-hypnotized state.

"Have I seen who?" As Elvis became more awake, he became more frightened. Laurie seemed like she'd become possessed. The look in her eyes sent chills up and down his spine.

"Michael Myers," Laurie answered coldly.

"No. They caught that lunatic two years before I joined the force," Elvis told her as he wiped the drool off his chin and pushed himself farther back into his seat.

"I want you to kill him." Laurie offered him the knife.

"You're just drunk. Or out of your mind."

"I want him dead. That's why I'm here. That's why I came to your home." Laurie put the knife in his hand.

Elvis could see by her expression that she meant it. He took the knife and set it down on the table. Laurie instantly grabbed it and pushed it back to him. "Take it."

"What do you want me to do with this, huh?" Elvis's voice cracked as he held the knife. "Walk into Smith's Grove and stab him?"

"No." Laurie shook her head. "I want you to walk into Smith's Grove and cut his fucking head off."

"Well, I ain't doin' that, so just get it out of your mind, all right?" Elvis said.

"Dr. Loomis is right, but nobody will listen to him," Laurie said as tears filled her eyes. "Michael isn't a man. Michael is evil, and he needs to die before he kills again."

Elvis sat frozen by her intensity. "Shit, if you want to do it so bad, go do it yourself. I won't stop you," Elvis told her.

"You don't think I've tried?" Laurie replied.

Laurie's hands shook as she became overwhelmed with emotion. "I close my eyes, and there he is. Watching me. Wherever I am, he's right there. And he will always be there until he's dead. And I just want to know… why won't anybody help me kill him? Why does he have to be all mine?"

Laurie's vulnerability shook Elvis and made him realize she hadn't lost her mind at all. She had every right to be as upset as she was. He remembered hearing the shocking stories of that night. And he couldn't imagine what he'd have turned out like had he experienced them too.

"Get dressed. I'll take you home," Elvis told her gently.

Candlelit jack-o-lanterns adorned the porches in Laurie's neighborhood. 'Eye in the Sky' by The Alan Parsons Project played at a low volume inside Elvis's Monte Carlo. Laurie stared out the window, watching the houses pass by.

"Here," Laurie told him as they reached a small home.

Laurie got out without saying a word.

"Good night, Laurie. See ya around," Elvis told her.

Laurie closed the door and looked through the window. "As long as he's alive, nobody is safe. Because he will kill again. And you could've stopped it. Just remember that when more blood is spilled, and more people are dead."

Elvis nodded and then drove off.

In his rearview, Elvis saw Laurie cross the street from the house where he'd left her and continue down the block.

Elvis pulled a U-turn and headed back in that direction to see where she was going.

He came to a stop alongside a parked car and watched Laurie walk up to a small apartment complex.

Why did she tell me to drop her off somewhere else? he wondered, not understanding Laurie's protective strategy.

"Go on home, Elvis," Elvis heard Frank Hawkins tell him.

Elvis turned, surprised to find Frank sitting in the parked car next to his.

"I got it from here," Frank told him.

"Frank, what the hell you doing parked outside her place? You bein' a creep?" Elvis asked.

"I'm just making sure she got home safe. That's all."

"Of course she did. I brought her back."

Both men watched her walk up the stairs to the only unit not decorated in Halloween fun. The lights were already on inside her apartment before she entered. Laurie never turned them out.

"What that woman went through... Hell, I wouldn't wish that on anybody," Elvis said with some newfound empathy.

Frank silently agreed.

"All right, Frank. See ya Monday."

Frank nodded, and Elvis drove away.

Frank stayed parked there until the sun came up. Not once did he see Laurie's lights go out.

LOOK AGAIN

Elvis came to mind as soon as Laurie stepped into Velkovsky's. Ever since getting sober, Laurie made it a rule not to visit bars—especially not Velkovsky's, where she'd clocked so much time during the early eighties—but she made an exception for Lindsey.

"Did you call me to tell me that I'm not losing my mind?"

"That's exactly why I called." Lindsey turned to the man sitting at the end of the bar, flipping through her stack of Tarot cards. "Hey, Roger, I want you to meet a good friend of mine. This is Laurie Strode."

Roger Allen, Jeremy's father, turned to meet Laurie. His eyes sat lower than they once had. Almost as if the features on his face had fallen under the weight of the loss.

"Laurie. Roger Allen, good to make your acquaintance." Roger, a little drunk, showed Lindsey the moon card in his hand.

"Lindsey, this one mean I won the moon?" Mr. Allen asked with his trademark charisma.

Lindsey turned to Laurie. "I think you need to hear this."

"I'm all ears," Laurie told her.

"Hey, Roger, tell Laurie what you told me about Corey Cunningham. He's been seeing someone close to Laurie, and we've been concerned."

Mr. Allen sighed and set the moon card back on the deck.

"I was telling Lindz, here—you don't mind if I call you Lindz, do you?"

"Under normal circumstances, I'd probably break your nose, but tonight, it's allowed," Lindsey told him as she poured herself a glass of wine and settled in.

Mr. Allen looked at Laurie. She recognized the grief in his eyes. "I hate to even... My wife, ex-wife now, Theresa, was so certain about him. I'm the one who had doubts. Doubts, I suppose, that ended up breaking up our marriage, but that's a whole other ballgame." Mr. Allen shook it off and took a swig of his beer. "You know... everything is one way until it's not. And then it's hard to remember what it used to be."

"I know exactly what you mean," Laurie told him.

The two shared a look.

"I can see that you do." Roger rolled the end of his bottle around the bar. "Even with my doubts, I spent every day during the trial hoping they'd give him a guilty verdict so I could move on. 'Cause there's no closure when something like that happens. And you think hearing the word 'guilty' might give you some. Well, it didn't happen, and I didn't move on."

Mr. Allen finished his beer, and Lindsey handed him a fresh one.

Mr. Allen folded his cocktail napkin into a paper airplane and continued. "I always liked him. Corey. He was a good kid. Sweet. Some kids, you can tell they're assholes, but Corey, Corey was sensitive, he cared about things, and I just couldn't imagine he'd be capable of hurting anyone, much less my…" Mr. Allen cleared his throat as emotion surfaced. "My son." Mr. Allen used his beer to push the emotion back down. He then gave the women a smile, resorting to the tricks he utilized in the corporate world to mask his feelings.

"So, I started following him. I followed him everywhere. Mostly he just stayed at home. He had weekly trips to a psychiatrist for a while, but that was it. And this went on for months. Me watching him. Waiting for him to show me something. Hoping he'd show me something. But he never did. And I'd think, *give it up, Roger. What the hell are you doing? You're never gonna get an answer*. But I kept going because I didn't know what else to do. Hell, sometimes I'd forget why I was even following him around. It just became what I did."

Mr. Allen drank most of his new beer and wiped his mouth with his paper plane.

"But I never saw anything. And I actually started feeling sorry for him. Seeing the way people in this town avoided him or how they made faces behind his back. If I'm honest, it made me angry. It pissed me off to see the way they treated him. I felt like they took my despair and Theresa's despair and used it for their own. But I kept following him around because I had nothing else. Nothing. No son. No wife."

Mr. Allen turned his attention directly to Laurie. "And then this morning, I'm driving home, and I see him walking down the side of the road. And I think I'm gonna give him a ride. I am going to put this misery to bed right now. So, I pull up next to him, and he looks at me, and it's not him. At least, not the same kid who used to mow my lawn. Not in his eyes. And he doesn't say anything. He just stares at me. And I don't know what it was but…" Mr. Allen slowly tore the plane he'd built in half. "It made the hairs on the back of my neck stand up. I felt like I was in danger, so I got the hell out of there. But I feel like I finally got my answer. I do." Mr. Allen looked to Laurie and Lindsey. "That kid who used to mow our lawns didn't kill my son. I know that for sure. But the guy I saw on the side of the road, he'd have done it without blinking an eye."

Lindsey looked to Laurie. "You got to talk to Allyson."

*

Corey devoured the road on his motorcycle with Allyson behind him, holding on. Allyson rested her head against Corey's back and watched the landscape turn into a blur. She gripped the bike with her legs as they flew through the night. She wasn't ready for it to end, and the closer they got to her house, the more she wanted the night to last forever.

Corey's intense gaze moved to the rearview and clocked the headlights in the distance behind them. Headlights that had been there since they'd left the diner.

Corey pulled to a stop in front of Allyson's house. Allyson climbed off and tried to convince him to come inside with only her look. She felt too alive to kill the night right then. She grabbed Corey and kissed him passionately. Ready to strip everything off and show him what she felt.

Corey broke the embrace. His eyes moved to the mirror and then back to Allyson.

"Another night," he told her.

Allyson kissed him again, unable to persuade him to stay.

Allyson walked inside and lingered by the door as the emotion radiated through her. The details of her suburban prison threatened to undo her love buzz, and she hurried upstairs to get away.

She hurried by Laurie's office, filled with reminders of the past. All she wanted to do was get to someplace where the past wasn't suffocating her.

Allyson paced back and forth across her bedroom, stopping at the window, hoping he'd return. She had no idea where to put the energy from the night, so she climbed into bed, pulled the covers over her head, and screamed at the top of her lungs.

*

As soon as Corey pulled away from the house, the headlights he'd been watching in his rearview pulled onto the street and followed him.

Doug Mulaney beamed with excitement as he pursued Corey. It had been quite some time since he'd roughed anybody up, and he was looking forward to mixing it up with this little piece of shit. He just needed to find the right time to attack.

On the radio, Willy the Kid detonated the L.A. Guns jam 'Rip and Tear', a song Doug remembered from his youth. A song that never failed to pump his guts. Doug cranked the volume, gripped the wheel, and stepped on the gas.

Doug saw Corey's motorcycle veer off onto the gravel road beneath the overpass as he approached the bridge. Doug killed his headlights, eased off the gas, and followed him below. Doug stopped under the bridge and climbed out with his Maglite. He twirled his keys like a gunslinger and attached them to a key clip on his belt.

Doug saw Corey's motorcycle parked next to a glowing tent. Random junk scattered around. A shopping cart. Aluminum cans. Human feces.

"You want to play games with me?" Doug asked as he fired his light on. "All right then, son, let's play some games." *Hell yeah*, Doug smiled with cocky confidence. This was gonna be fucking fun.

Doug saw the silhouette seated inside the tent and smirked. *Dumbass thinks he's hidden.*

Doug put out his light and approached, ninja-like. The silhouette inside didn't move an inch.

Doug grinned as he reached the tent. Ready to surprise. Then he grabbed the door flap and yanked it open.

Nelson Christopher's dead body spilled out before him. His face carved hideously like a smiling pumpkin. His clothes caked in his blood.

"Jesus Christ!" Doug stumbled back.

Before Doug could process what he'd seen, Corey jumped him from behind. Corey wrapped his jacket around Doug's throat and pulled him back. Doug wrestled out of Corey's hold and landed a shot across Corey's chin.

Corey jumped up and bolted for the tunnel's opening. Doug chased after.

"I'll teach you about running away from me, you little bitch," Doug said as he crawled into the opening.

Doug's flashlight lit the cramped passageway, but Corey had already disappeared inside.

"Goddamn." Doug grimaced as he got a whiff of the foul odor inside the tunnel.

"You shit yourself?" Doug yelled, trying to build his confidence through some intimidation. "If you didn't, you will when I get ahold of you."

Doug had more bulk than Corey, and navigating the constrictive dimensions of the tunnel proved much more challenging.

Corey whistled from within. Taunting. "*Dooooug…*" Doug could hear him laughing.

"You little motherfucker, I'm gonna kick your ass double for that!"

The death-like stench inside the cave made it hard to breathe. It caused Doug to spit up some of his beer and that sponge cake Joe Ross had made. "Fuck me," he whispered under his breath as he wiped the regurgitations off his shirt.

Debris fell over him from above as he moved through the tight space, which seemed to be getting tighter the deeper he got.

Doug's hands and knees splashed through the thick gunk collected along the bottom of the tunnel. Two rats bolted by Doug and made him reconsider the pursuit. But he'd come too far to let Corey out of this one.

Fuck. Doug's Maglite went out, and suddenly he found himself navigating in complete darkness. He opened his eyes wider, trying to see anything. But he couldn't. He stuck his hands out and waved them blindly.

Corey made pig noises from inside the darkness. The tunnel made Corey's voice sound like he was all around Doug.

"Come on, you little shit, quit fucking around," Doug whispered, terrified. All he heard back was the echo of his voice which traveled from one end of the tunnel to the other.

Doug could feel the tunnel pushing against his back as he moved farther inside. He crouched lower to get through it and eventually had to get down on his stomach to pull himself forward.

Claustrophobia set in, and worries rose when Doug considered the idea that maybe Corey had intentionally lured him in to get him trapped. And what then?

"You're gonna die in here…" Corey whispered. The words reverberated through the tunnel and through Doug's mind.

Doug's heart pounded angrily. Furious that Corey had put it in this situation. It beat so intensely that Doug felt like it might crack his ribs.

The shallow layer of rotten waste sitting on the bottom of the tunnel splashed against his chin and kissed his lips. Doug spit it out. *Fuck this.*

Doug decided to turn back, get out of there, and wait for Corey on the other side. He'd give the psycho a few extra licks for the trouble he'd caused.

But when Doug tried to turn around, the cramped space refused him such movement.

More debris spilled down on Doug as he struggled to reposition. It made him fear that his rustling would cause the tunnel to cave in on him.

Doug paused and reconsidered his options, but he didn't see any besides proceeding forward and hoping he'd soon find another exit.

He crawled forward cautiously.

His Maglite created loud booms throughout the tunnel each time it hit the ground.

Boom… boom… boom…

The noise amplified his fear. Like a ticking bomb about to blow.

Boom… boom… boom…

Alerting his opponent that he was nearing.

Doug splashed through the muck toward an exit

he could not see. His breath turned shallow as he realized Corey would likely be waiting for him on the other side. Ready to surprise.

Boom… boom… boom…

Doug desperately tried to gain control of his breath. "Come on, get it together, you weak piece of shit." Doug muttered to himself the things he'd heard his dad say when anyone let him down.

The stench inside the cave became more rank the deeper Doug got.

Doug had grown up deer hunting and was intimately familiar with the smell of death, but this was the equivalent of crawling inside a decomposing animal. The repugnant odor caused him to throw up again.

Doug slid over his vomit and continued forward. His hand reached out, and he found there was no more tunnel left.

Doug couldn't catch himself in time as he came out of the tunnel. He crashed into the wider chamber.

The impact from the crash jostled Doug's Maglite, and it fired back on. The beam landed on a wall. Doug got to his feet and stumbled over some rocks as he retrieved his flashlight and took in this new larger space. Doug moved the Maglite around the disgusting perimeter. Past the chasms dug into the walls. The crevices and cracks all around the cave. The rusty grate above. The pathways leading to more darkness. The slimy residue creeping down the cavern walls to form toxic puddles on the ground.

Doug's light landed on a shape near the wall. Twisted and abstract. Hunched over so he couldn't make out what it was.

At first, Doug mistook the shape for some ratty fabric draped over a fallen rock. At least, that's what made the most sense in his excited state.

But then the shape rose. And turned. And Doug saw the monster clearly.

"Michael…" Doug said as his breath disappeared.

The shape tilted his head as he studied the terrified cop. Then he moved forward.

Doug stumbled back across the uneven ground. He glanced over his shoulder to the tunnel. Wondering if he had enough time to turn around and crawl through. He did not.

Michael caught Doug by the throat to take him to hell.

Michael pulled him closer so that his black eyes could consume Doug's terror.

Doug struck Michael with his Maglite. The flashlight bounced off Michael's shoulder, and Doug lost his grip. The light hit the ground spinning, creating a disorienting effect, illuminating the two in brief flashes.

Doug grabbed Michael's moldering torso and threw Michael back into the darkness.

He frantically grabbed for his flashlight and cast the beam across the cave. But Michael had vanished.

Doug jerked his flashlight in every direction but could not find the killer.

He pointed the light at the cramped tunnel he'd

fallen from. His mind strategized: *Get through the tunnel, get out, and call in the posse to raze this hellhole.*

Doug's light cut through the darkness and caught the fat drops of awful liquid that dripped into the cave. The drops splashed against his neck and turned his skin cold.

Just as Doug made it to the tunnel, he sensed something next to him and turned his light to find Corey watching him with a disturbing grin from a deep crevice within the wall.

"What the fuck?"

Michael surprised Doug from behind and wrapped his arm around Doug's neck. Doug lost his grip on the flashlight, and it rolled across the ground as he fought Michael's hold.

Michael held him in place. Slowly cutting off Doug's oxygen.

Corey watched as Michael reached his hand into a hole in the wall and grabbed the handle of his rusty knife. A beam of light caught the glint of the blade.

Doug's fear surged and he slammed the crown of his head into Michael's mask.

Michael collapsed to the ground and Doug raced to grab his flashlight. But Corey jumped out from the crevice and reached it first.

Corey met Doug's face with the heavy Maglite and split open Doug's scalp. A sheet of blood rained down his face.

Shaken, Doug's knees buckled, and he slumped to the ground. The pain hadn't yet been realized, but Doug could taste the blood running across his lips.

The concussive effect disrupted Doug's balance. He grabbed the wall and pulled himself upright, but he grew dizzy and toppled back over.

Corey turned to Michael lying on the ground and ordered him to, "*Get up! Kill him!*"

Michael's bones snapped as he attempted to rise.

Doug wobbled to his feet, and Corey spun around and cracked him again with the flashlight. Doug's legs turned to jelly, and he fell back.

Corey hurried behind Doug and held him up as Doug tried to shake off the dizziness that overtook him.

"*Get up!*" Corey screamed at Michael again.

Michael stood, unstable but gripping his knife forcefully. Slowly coming back to form.

Corey watched with morbid amusement. Alive with anticipation as Michael neared.

"*Do it!*" Corey screamed.

Michael raised his knife and sliced Doug Mulaney's stomach wide open.

Doug fell back onto Corey, and they hit the ground.

Michael crouched and raised his knife. This time, with more strength, he jammed it into Doug's chest.

Michael pulled the knife out and stabbed him again. And again. And again. Growing stronger with each strike.

Corey laughed maniacally as he felt Doug's life leave his body. As the blood cascaded out of the man and across the floor.

Michael withdrew the knife. His head tilted to consider the death before him. His body crackled as his posture resituated itself.

Corey watched as Michael slowly returned to the evil shape he'd once embodied. Perfectly upright and still. A cold, killing machine. Corey had brought him back to life.

Corey hurried out of the tunnel. Behind him, he could see Michael watching from within. No longer restricted to the chamber, the shape had fully woken.

Corey couldn't believe the powerful energy coursing through his veins. He didn't know where to put it, but he knew it had to go somewhere or else he'd explode.

*

Allyson moved from her bedroom to the living room and back to the bedroom. Her charged night with Corey made it impossible to sit still or get comfortable.

Allyson opened her computer and put on one of Lindsey's playlists. Then she proceeded to skip past each of the songs as she couldn't focus her attention on any one of them.

She peeked through the curtains and saw that Laurie's truck wasn't in the driveway. It was late, and she still hadn't come home. Under normal circumstances, that would have caused some concern, but Allyson had way too much on her mind to give it any thought.

Allyson understood that the first moments of a new relationship were always filled with excitement and nervousness. She'd experienced it with both Cameron and Doug. She'd even experienced it with Brendan in seventh grade when he asked her to homecoming. But what she felt with Corey was something new. It was bigger and more overpowering. And if it weren't for the incredibly short amount of time they'd been together, Allyson would have called it love. But her rational mind wouldn't accept that as a possibility. She barely knew him, yet she couldn't get enough of him.

Allyson scrutinized the scarecrow mask on her dresser and then turned to the window. She looked for Corey, but she couldn't see anything but the night. Typically, she'd have closed the curtains for fear of anyone possibly watching her. But at that moment, she didn't care who saw.

Allyson stepped into the kitchen and dug through the cabinet for chamomile tea. She put the kettle on and sat by the stove, waiting to hear the water whistle.

She anxiously picked at her nails and cuticles as she sat waiting. The action made her recall the 'Itsy-Bitsy Spider' routine she'd learned in kindergarten.

Inspired by the memory, Allyson made L-shapes with both hands and pressed her fingers together. Then she rotated them, pantomiming the movement of her finger-spider crawling up the waterspout. She hummed the song quietly to herself, remembering the more innocent years of her life.

Allyson jumped as the whistle from the kettle blew. She hurried to turn off the stove.

A second later, somebody knocked.

Allyson approached cautiously. Through the

stained-glass window feature on the door, Allyson could see a shape, but she couldn't make out anything more.

"Who is it?" Allyson called out.

"It's me," Corey announced through the door. "Can I come in?"

Allyson opened the door, and Corey rushed by her with fresh wounds on his face.

"I don't know what's happening to me," he said as he moved into the living room.

Corey's agitated state worried Allyson, but she didn't feel the need to inquire about his cuts or the dirt covering his clothes. She knew. She'd seen the look in his eye when Doug had come to the table. Corey had gone back to the diner, and he and Doug had gotten into it.

"Are you okay?" Allyson asked. It was the only thing she needed to know.

Corey didn't answer. He paced erratically back and forth across the living room. He pulled at his skin, wanting to tear it off.

Allyson led him to the couch and sat him down. She knelt before him and gently touched a bruise on his cheek.

"Does it hurt?" she asked softly.

Allyson's skin felt so soft and comforting that Corey melted under her touch.

"No," Corey replied. And then he smiled. "It doesn't hurt at all."

Allyson moved closer. She placed his hand on her shoulder while she studied his new injuries.

Corey slowly slid his hand up from her shoulder and across her throat, caressing it with his fingers. Allyson leaned closer, pressing her neck into his hand, wanting to feel every sensation. Wanting to be a part of his darkness. Her breath quietly strained as she pushed herself deeper into his grip.

"I need you," Corey whispered as he slid his hand up from her throat and onto her face. He traced Allyson's lips with his thumb.

Allyson swayed gently against his hand and stared into his eyes. Slowly losing herself.

Allyson opened her mouth and accepted Corey's thumb. She circled it with her tongue. And then she pulled her head back and bit the tip of his finger.

Corey shuddered. Then grinned.

"Does that hurt?" Allyson whispered.

"Not at all."

Allyson bit harder. Corey smiled wider.

"Anything?" she asked. Her breath full of passion.

Corey shook his head.

"Okay, let's go." Allyson grabbed Corey and kissed him brutally. Wanting to get inside. She grabbed his neck with both hands and pressed her fingers into his skin until it changed color.

Allyson brought her mouth to Corey's ear and ran her tongue around its shape.

Corey put his hand on her back and pulled her closer. Allyson's breath deepened. She quietly moaned and then took his earlobe between her teeth and bit down.

Corey flinched.

"What about that?" she whispered.

"I don't feel anything," he told her. She moved back to his lips. Their faces smashed together as the moment escalated.

Allyson held Corey's wounded hand in hers. She pushed her thumb into the stitches beneath his bandage.

Corey moaned softly. The pain bringing him closer to ecstasy. "Harder," he implored.

Allyson pushed harder.

"More," Corey encouraged.

Allyson bit her lip as she increased the pressure. She didn't stop pushing until blood surfaced.

The sensation overwhelmed them, and both felt a near-orgasmic release as the blood raced up and soaked through the gauze. Turning the white red.

Allyson moved to straddle him. She ground her body into his. She pushed her face into his. She put her look into his.

Outside of the house, Laurie pulled into the driveway. When she got out of the truck, she saw the two through the window on full display.

Laurie watched her granddaughter grab Corey's hair and pull him back as she attacked. And then she watched Allyson tell him, "I need you now."

Allyson climbed off Corey and took his hand. Then she led him upstairs.

Laurie remained motionless outside. Knowing that Allyson was slipping away and unsure what to do about it.

As Allyson and Corey walked up the stairs, Corey

turned his head in Laurie's direction. She could feel his stare.

In the distance, something else lingered behind Laurie. Watching. Breathing. Laurie felt it.

When Laurie turned, she saw nothing but a dark and quiet neighborhood. The leaves on the trees rustled in the breeze. A dog barked in a yard several houses down. A porch windchime jangled. Laurie looked at the rotting jack-o'lantern decaying on her porch, and then she moved her look to Corey's motorcycle. She sensed something deep in her psyche. An evil presence arriving.

*

Laurie sat in her office, sinking into a pit of growing paranoia. Intuiting an approaching nightmare. Wanting to bust through Allyson's door to stop her granddaughter from going too far with the guy she'd brought into her life, but restraining herself from doing so. And all the while questioning her feelings. How much was fueled by obsession? By Michael? And how much came from her worry that Allyson might leave her?

"Take the choice." She quietly whispered the advice that Lindsey had told her.

*

"Do you judge me?" Allyson whispered as she lay in bed next to Corey.

Corey shook his head. "No. You can tell me anything."

Allyson stared at Corey, wanting to do just that but not knowing how. She'd spent years keeping everything bottled up. Corey made her want to let it all out.

"Everyone looks at me like I have it so put together. But it's bullshit. Almost every day, I feel like I'm on a tightrope where, any second, I could fall off."

Allyson rested her head on Corey's bare chest. She listened to his heart.

"I've had dreams." Allyson continued with trepidation, admitting something she had never even thought about telling anyone. "Nightmares, where I wake up in bed, and I'm covered in blood. But it's not mine. It's not my blood. And I get up, and I see the knife. It's next to me on my nightstand. The knife I used to stab Michael…" Allyson smirked. "The one that Grandma now keeps in the drawer and uses to cut apples…" Allyson closed her eyes as she concentrated on the memories from her nightmare. "The knife is covered in blood. And I call out. I call for Grandma, but she doesn't respond. So, I walk to her room. I push open the door… and there she is. Dead. Stabbed to death on the floor. Her blood is everywhere. And somehow I know that I'm the one who did it."

Allyson opened her eyes and looked into Corey's.

"But the scary thing is… that's not the nightmare. The nightmare is that I feel nothing. Nothing at all."

Allyson considered those words and asked Corey again, "Now do you judge me?"

Corey again shook his head. "No. I understand you."

Corey wrapped his arms around Allyson and held her tightly.

*

Corey twirled his scarecrow mask around his finger as he watched Allyson sleep. He peeked through the eyeholes to see if it made him see Allyson differently. Then he quietly climbed out of bed and got dressed.

He leaned over and kissed Allyson's forehead.

"I gotta go," he whispered.

Allyson's eyes fluttered as she woke. And she smiled. "Will I see you later? After work?" she asked.

"Yeah. You will." Corey smiled as he left her room with the mask in his hand.

Corey snuck downstairs quietly. Then he came across the kitchen threshold and found Laurie standing behind her kitchen island, in the dark, watching him. As if she'd been watching him through the walls.

"Do you know how many people get killed on motorcycles every year?" Laurie asked.

Corey smiled. "I don't think about it."

"I think about it. Especially when my granddaughter is sitting on the back of yours. A lot of people die. And many more get hurt. Just FYI."

"Don't worry. I won't let anything happen to her. *She's* gonna be safe." Corey's words could have been taken as either a guarantee or a threat. Laurie wasn't quite sure.

Corey started to leave and then stopped. "Laurie?"

Laurie's eyes stayed on his.

"How did you survive?" Corey asked sincerely. "When everybody else died?"

"Do you really want to know?" she asked.

Corey nodded.

"Fine, then I'll tell you... I got lucky."

Corey laughed. "Lucky. Right."

"And I hope you're lucky too," Laurie added.

Corey smiled and crossed his fingers. "So do I, Laurie."

Corey turned back to the door. "Okay. I'll see you soon."

Again, his words sounded foreboding. And Laurie stepped to the window and watched as he got onto his motorcycle and drove away.

*

Joan poured half a box of detergent into the washing machine. As she dumped another round of laundry into the machine, she noticed that Corey's shirt and pants were again covered in grime. The same filthy condition as they'd been the previous morning. The bloodstains had darkened to the point of abstraction.

"Corey, open up!" Joan ordered as she tried to get into his room. He had locked the door. "We do not lock doors in this house. You know the rules! Why are you breaking them?"

Joan heard the bedsprings recoil as Corey sat up and approached.

Corey barely opened the door. He spoke to Joan through the crack.

"Your clothes are filthy, again! Tell your mother where you went last night."

Corey stared at his momma but said nothing.

"Were you with that girl? Huh? The one you text with? Allyson? Is that where you were?"

Corey remained silent.

"Say something! Say something to your mother, who waits on you hand and foot. The one person who takes care of you and keeps you safe. The *only* person who cares about you."

"You keep me safe, Momma?" Corey shot back. "Then where have you been?"

Joan didn't pursue her line of questioning any further. "When you are gone, I worry. I worry so much. And your mother does not like to worry."

Corey nodded and closed the door in her face. She could hear the lock click inside. Before she could say something, Ronald called upstairs, "Joan, someone is at the door to see you." Ronald had come home for lunch instead of hitting a drive-thru.

"Who is it?" Joan barked as she came downstairs and set the clean laundry on the kitchen table.

"It's Laurie Strode," Ronald told her as he used oven mitts to carry his piping hot box of Lean Cuisine to the TV tray in the living room, where *Judge Judy* played on the television.

"Laurie Strode? What the heck does she want?"

"She wants to talk to you," Ronald told her.

Joan approached the door and found Laurie standing in the small entryway.

"Yeah? What the heck do you want?" Joan had no patience for Laurie Strode.

"Hi," Laurie greeted her warmly. "I was wondering if I could have a word with you."

"About what?" Joan snapped.

"About your son."

"Corey?" Joan looked Laurie up and down before begrudgingly letting her in.

Laurie moved into the living room. The smell of Pine-Sol, microwaved alfredo, and old carpet hung in the room.

Joan stepped into the kitchen and poured a cup of vanilla strawberry tea. She offered Laurie nothing. Then she returned to the dining room and folded the clothes from the basket. She kept her back to Laurie, refusing to acknowledge her presence any more than she had to.

Laurie's eyes discreetly searched the home, careful to not call attention to her suspicions. But outside of Ronald watching *Judge Judy* and the bizarre collection of rabbit figurines crammed into the curiosa cabinet, nothing stood out to Laurie.

Laurie picked up one of the rabbit sculptures and looked it over. Joan heard it slide off the cabinet, and she tensed. She had strict rules about her figurines, and grabbing one from the shelf was a clear violation. Joan snorted in protest.

Ronald choked on his lunch and rocked in his chair back and forth until he dislodged the obstruction and cleared his airway.

"What is it you want to know about Corey?" Joan

asked as she made a stack of Corey's briefs and placed them in Laurie's view. Laurie wondered if she'd done it intentionally. "Has he done something bad? I don't understand why *you're* here," Joan added.

"He's seeing my granddaughter," Laurie said, averting her eyes from Corey's underwear.

"I know that. You don't think I know that already? *Sheesh.*"

Laurie continued, "Well, I introduced them, and I just wanted to meet you and introduce myself."

"I know who you are. Everybody in Haddonfield knows who you are."

Laurie tried to maintain a calm disposition, but Joan made it difficult.

"Your granddaughter should be so lucky to be with a boy like Corey. He's handsome, he's sensitive, I don't like when he stays out all night with girls," she put a little extra attitude on the word *girls*, "but he can do what he wants," Joan said as she grew angrier about the intrusion.

"It's just that I want to make sure he's got the right support," Laurie told her sympathetically. "There's a good therapist I've talked to. She did wonders for me, and I know that he's had… difficulties. I'm just afraid of how they might manifest. What if he hurts someone he loves?"

"Loves? Now they're in love?" Joan snapped. "What do you know, Ms. Strode?! What the heck are you even talking about?"

Laurie sighed and regrouped. "I'm talking about your son, Mrs. Cunningham."

Joan made a mocking smile, and her face bobbed up and down spastically, unable to control her escalating wrath.

"You know what, Ms. Strode? This town turned against my boy after that terrible accident with the Allen boy. And in any other situation, they would have felt for him and let him heal. They would have supported and cared for him, but because *your* boogeyman disappeared, they needed a new one, and they turned on Corey. You are a part of this, and I don't very much like you entering my home and picking up my things! Got it?"

Laurie carefully put the figurine down. "Got it."

"And now I think it's for you to leave."

Laurie looked at Ronald in the next room. His attention remained on the TV. He hadn't given the slightest acknowledgement to their argument.

"I said, I think it's time for you to leave," Joan repeated.

Laurie sensed something and turned to the staircase. When she turned back, Corey appeared beside Joan. Staring at Laurie with his black eyes.

"So nice to see you again, Laurie," Corey said coldly. His sudden and unnerving appearance startled Laurie.

She moved to the door to get away. "It was nice to see you too," Laurie whispered.

Laurie left the home, and in a fit of rage, Joan grabbed the rabbit figurine from the shelf and smashed it on the ground.

"Look what you made me do!" Joan screamed out.

Laurie stood on the porch for a moment, collecting herself. Feeling more certain about her suspicions.

She crossed the lawn to her truck and looked back to the house. The downstairs windows had an unnatural darkness to them. But Laurie could see one thing through the glass. Corey. Watching her from inside the house. His chest moved in and out as he breathed heavily. He lifted the silly scarecrow mask and gazed at her through the eyeholes.

Laurie acknowledged his presence, and then she got into her truck and drove the fuck away from there.

Corey remained at the window as Laurie disappeared from his view. He didn't move. Not even when Joan passed by with his fresh laundry.

"I don't approve. Can you hear me? I don't approve of any of this one little bit, buster."

Corey's eyes stayed outside the window. Upstairs he could hear Joan slamming his dresser drawers as she put his clothes away.

"Are you listening to your mother? I don't want you seeing that girl!" Joan screamed from his room.

Corey stayed silent at the window. Watching.

Joan stomped back downstairs and saw the scarecrow mask in his hand. "What the heck is this? Trick-or-treats?" Joan snatched it from his hand and dropped it in the kitchen trash. "Not in this house!"

Joan crossed back to the table and yelled at Ronald, "Ronald, get to work!"

"Okay, Joan," Ronald replied and climbed out of his chair.

"Corey, I don't know what's gotten into you, but

I do not like it," Joan yelled while folding Ronald's laundry. "All this secrecy. Sneaking behind your mother's back. Locking me out. This is not the way I raised you. Laurie Strode." Joan blew a raspberry. "Oh boy."

"Joan, I will see you when I'm home from work," Ronald said as he grabbed his keys. Joan didn't respond.

"You are supposed to tell your mother everything. *Everything!*"

Joan marched back to the window where Corey stood. "What the heck are you doing there at the window? What are you looking at? What's gotten into you? Say something! Is this behavior because of that girl? Is that it?"

Corey remained frozen in place.

Joan looked at his hand and saw the blood on the bandage.

"Corey, come away from that window and let me clean your injury."

Joan went back to the laundry.

"Corey, I am speaking to you!" she yelled again. She shook her head and huffed, "This is very disappointing. I am very disappointed in this behavior."

Corey didn't hear her words. He just stood in place at the window. As if hypnotically drawn there. Feeling an uncontrollable intention swelling inside him. An intention so dark and so violent that it would not let him move until he'd adequately disguised his humanity.

Corey remained in that position until the sun lowered and the moon rose. Then he removed the mask from the trash and left the house.

*

Laurie stood at the window in her office. Watching too. Waiting for Allyson's return home from the clinic.

She sat down at her computer and skimmed through her draft. *Violence. Evil. Death.* On every page, one of those three words appeared. Three names appeared just as frequently and caught her attention each time: *Karen, Allyson,* and *Michael.*

How do you get away from evil once it enters your life?

Laurie typed, hoping the answer would present itself.

When it frightens you, it holds you hostage.

Laurie considered the thought, but it brought her no more resolution.

*

Allyson heard Deb laughing with Mathis inside his office as she restocked the supplies in the exam room. Allyson's responsibilities became more menial after Mathis gave Deb the promotion.

"Hi, I'm Dr. Tanner Mathis, and I'd like to tell you a few things about Grantham Primary Medical Clinic. It's the place I call home…" Allyson passed by the TV as she hurried to the reception desk to answer the phone.

"Grantham Primary Medical Clinic, this is Allyson," Allyson answered. She could see Mathis and Deb through the cracked slits of the blinds in his office. Deb stood behind the doctor massaging his shoulders.

"Well, you definitely want to come in and let us take a look so we can make sure it's not infected," Allyson told the caller, who'd been bitten by some kind of bug and their skin had discolored. "Those infections can spread through the rest of your system, so it's better to get ahead of it, just to be safe. It might be nothing, but you never know."

Allyson headed downstairs, where she stood at the vending machine debating whether to eat a potato chip and granola bar dinner or just skip it.

Allyson had never taken to her job as a nurse. As soon as Mathis hired her, nothing inside Grantham ever fit right. She never found a rhythm and always felt out of place. But she'd persevered because she had nothing else to do and nowhere else to go. And because she thought becoming a nurse would help heal her own scars. But as she stood at the vending machine, looking at her reflection in the glass, Allyson wanted to be anywhere but inside that building.

Allyson opened the door to get some fresh air. The night was chilly, and her scrubs did little to keep her warm. She wrapped her arms around her body and held herself.

Allyson's eyes drifted across the parking lot aimlessly, not situating themselves on any one thing.

She looked at Mathis's Porsche parked across three spots, away from the handful of other cars.

Something didn't sit right with Allyson. Even though she couldn't see anyone, Allyson had the unsettling feeling of being watched. Her eyes studied the lot again. She saw nothing, which made the feeling more unsettling.

Allyson hurried back inside and watched the parking lot through the glass door. She homed in on the shadows and the places one could hide, but still didn't see anybody.

*

"You're fucking him, aren't you?" Deb asked Allyson regarding Corey as she picked up her things before her shift ended.

Allyson didn't engage and continued filing.

"I mean, it's so fucking weird when you think about it." Deb didn't require an engaged audience to perform, she just needed an audience. "It's like the perfect Haddonfield romance, you know what I mean? A cute young girl falls for local psycho. I mean, imagine if Laurie Strode had fucking fallen in love with Michael Myers. Can you imagine? If they were together? But nope. She wasn't having it. She decided to trap him in her basement and light the fucking house on fire. Badass bitch."

"What's your problem, Deb? Am I here or not? Seriously, do you ever shut your goddamn mouth?" The words exploded out of Allyson and caught Deb off guard.

Deb stood confused like a deer in the headlights. She'd never seen that side of Allyson. And after a moment, she decided that Allyson must have been joking and broke into a laughing fit.

"I know, right? I know I talk too much. I just get so excited about all that boogeyman bullshit!"

Dr. Mathis came out of his office arguing on the phone about a fantasy football trade. Mathis was the league commissioner, and he ran his group in the same ego-driven way he ran the clinic.

Dr. Mathis bluntly handed Allyson some paperwork without acknowledging her. The papers slid out from the folder and scattered across the floor. Deb hurried after Mathis while Allyson collected the loose paperwork.

Allyson waited until Dr. Mathis and Deb had left the building, and then she slammed the folder against the ground violently, wanting to destroy everything inside it. Her knuckles cracked against the floor as her rage took control. The force brutally ripped the papers and bruised her knuckles. Allyson wanted to kill it all.

Once her furious eruption had settled, Allyson looked at the destruction. Breathing heavily. Then she collected herself, straightened the paperwork, and set it down on the desk.

Allyson stepped to the window, where she saw Deb and Dr. Mathis heading to his car.

Again, Allyson felt the sensation of being watched. But this time, she needed to be seen.

From across the parking lot, Corey sat on his motorcycle, watching Allyson through the window.

Then he turned his focus to Deb and Dr. Mathis. Dr. Mathis ended his phone call and handed his dry cleaning for Deb to carry as he unlocked the door.

Deb took his clothes and jumped into his Porsche. "This car is soooo cool!" she screamed. "You have to go fast, okay? I love to go fast."

"You came to the right guy," Dr. Mathis said as he began the process of getting into the driver's seat. Dr. Mathis had difficulty getting into such a small car, but he never once considered getting something more pragmatic. His car represented everything he believed he was.

Dr. Mathis gripped the roof with one hand and swung himself inside. The car bounced mightily under his weight.

"All right, my lady, let's go fast."

Dr. Mathis revved the gas, but then he limply proceeded at a slow and safe speed out of the parking lot. Deb tried to keep the moment exciting by screaming, but it didn't really work.

Allyson returned to her desk, where she saw a text from Laurie: Hey, just checking in. I'd like to discuss some things when you get home.

The last thing Allyson was in the mood for was another Laurie discussion. Allyson put her phone away and looked at the clock. Time to count down the seconds until she could leave.

Outside, she heard a motorcycle driving away. It sounded like Corey's. Allyson hurried to the window but got there too late to see anyone.

Deb turned the radio dial away from Dr. Mathis's preset oldies station and cranked the volume when she heard Marteen's 'Freak'.

"Do you mind?" she asked after the fact.

"No, do yo thang, girl," Dr. Mathis replied, desperately trying to sound young but coming off painfully out of touch.

Deb rolled down the window and sang the lyrics to the passing cars. She threw up white girl versions of gang signs as she danced in her seat.

Dr. Mathis licked his lips as he watched Deb's chest bounce up and down in the seat. He had curbed his libido ever since sexual inappropriateness became the national topic, but he was very much looking forward to getting back in the saddle with one of his young nurses. But the volume was a bit much, so he turned it down.

"Boner killer," Deb joked.

"No, not at all. Dr. Mathis loves a party. I just want to hear you."

Deb smiled and put her hand on his leg. "You are such a gentleman, Dr. Mathis. And I'm looking forward to your examination this evening."

Dr. Mathis grinned with lustful excitement.

Corey flew by them on his motorcycle but neither noticed.

*

Deb's eyes grew wide as she stepped into Dr. Mathis's mid-century spectacle. His home looked like a tackier version of one of Frank Lloyd Wright's creations. A retro stone wall stretched along the living room filled with space-age furniture, surrounded by floor-to-ceiling glass sliding doors with gold trim. Those sliding doors wrapped around the entire U-shaped design of the home.

"Holy shit!" Deb said as Dr. Mathis turned on the lights and she saw the pool in a courtyard. "Your house is *so* rich," Deb said as she looked at the abstract poster art on the walls and the teak furniture.

"Yeah, I know," Dr. Mathis replied as he removed a bottle of wine from his rack and grabbed a corkscrew. "It's pretty cool to be a doctor," Mathis said with a wry smile.

"Alexa, play 'Tell Me with Your Eyes' by Rob Galbraith." Modern music might not have been Mathis's favorite, but he adored the soft, sexy rock-and-roll stylings of Rob Galbraith.

Deb gazed through the glass doors at Dr. Mathis's outrageous courtyard.

"Maybe when we're done, we can take a dip. Have some fun in the pool, too. It's heated," he told her as he grooved nearer.

Deb pushed her derriere against his pelvis. Dr. Mathis fully inflated.

"Oh, hello," Deb said with a coy smile, feeling his erection.

"Oops, did *you* do that?" Dr. Mathis jokingly replied as he gently brushed Deb's hair to the side and lightly tickled her neck with his tongue. A chill went down Deb's spine, and she trembled. Dr. Mathis mistook her discomfort for arousal, and he turned her around to face him. He breathed deeply through his nose.

Dr. Mathis held Deb's shoulders and massaged. "I've been waiting for this all day. You looked so fucking hot at the office. I got a bottle of Au Bon Climat just for you. It's my favorite wine, and I *do not* just give it to anyone."

"You make me feel so special," Deb whispered breathily as she grabbed Mathis between the legs. The moment caught him off guard, and he sprung up on his toes.

Deb giggled.

Dr. Mathis came back to the ground and kissed her. His breath was hot and stale. *Like an attic,* Deb thought.

"I'm gonna take you to the fucking moon tonight," Dr. Mathis told her as he got more aroused.

Deb smiled and kissed him again. This time she deposited her spearmint gum into his mouth to brighten the old attic up a bit.

Dr. Mathis smiled and chomped away.

"Why don't you go get clean before we get started. Bedroom's down the hall. Keep the shower hot, and I'll meet you in there."

Deb smiled and began the journey to his room. She soaked up the gaudy details of his house as she walked down the hall. Masculine sculptures of eagles and lions made of bronze and brass could be seen everywhere. A wall had been dedicated to framed photos featuring Dr. Mathis shaking hands with minor celebrities, like state representatives, low-seeded tennis pros, and local news teams. Two of his bookshelves were filled with copies of the book he'd written.

Deb tried to imagine a life with Dr. Mathis. She wondered if she'd get a Porsche too. She could see herself on Christmas morning, sitting with Dr. Mathis in that awesome living room. Drinking cherry mimosas. He'd tell her, "You have one more gift. It's parked out front." Deb would hurry outside to discover her brand new car, topped with a bow. Then they'd drive it to the airport for a first-class flight to Cozumel.

"It would beat the hell out of my shitty efficiency where I don't even have a parking spot," Deb said as she fell out of her fantasy.

Dr. Mathis's bedroom smelled like money. That's what Deb thought when she came through the door. A fragrant mix of wood, citrus, and musk. Sort of how her grandfather's room smelled. Deb moved away from that thought as quickly as it surfaced.

Deb found a box with a ribbon tied around it. She read the note attached: *For Deb, congratulations on your promotion.*

Charmed, Deb untied the ribbon and opened the gift. Inside she found a beautiful silk kimono.

Deb pulled off her scrubs and tossed them over a chair. She put the new robe on. The silk felt incredible against her skin.

Deb turned the shower on and stood at the mirror while the water heated up. She heard what sounded like a dull thud outside the room but didn't think much of it. A muffled noise that followed drew her attention.

Deb stepped closer to the door and heard a bottle shatter outside.

"Dr. Mathis?"

Deb quickly turned off the water.

"Dr. Mathis? Is everything okay?"

Deb carefully pulled open the bathroom door and peeked out.

The lights were off throughout the house, but the music kept playing.

"Dr. Mathis?" Deb yelled over the music, growing more uneasy.

Deb moved slowly through the bedroom to the glass door, where she could see the glowing flames coming from the rock firepit sitting in a cozy nook in the outdoor space.

Deb opened the sliding door and stepped outside. By the firepit, Dr. Mathis had arranged some tarts and cheeses and flowers. Deb saw a broken bottle of wine on the ground. No Dr. Mathis anywhere.

"Dr. Mathis—" she called out again, "—Alexa! Music off!"

The music stopped, and Deb heard a rustling behind her, but nothing distinctive enough to tell her what it was.

Deb approached the firepit and flipped the light switch on the wall.

The outdoor lights came on, and Deb turned.

Against the wall, she found a nightmare in progress.

Dr. Mathis lay outstretched over the grass with the dry-cleaning bag wrapped over his face. A shape held him from behind, repeatedly jamming the corkscrew into his head. Blood sprayed inside the plastic bag, and Mathis's features distorted horrifically as he gasped for air. His blood filled the bag.

The shape behind Dr. Mathis lifted his head.

Deb screamed when she saw the silly scarecrow mask looking at her. She raced back to the bedroom.

Corey threw Dr. Mathis across the grass and chased after Deb.

Deb slammed the sliding doors just as Corey reached her. The doors bounced off Corey's wounded hand, and he jerked it back.

Deb quickly shut the doors again and locked them.

Corey banged against the glass and yanked the handle.

Deb flipped him off victoriously and screamed through the glass, "I'm calling the police, you fucking psycho!"

Deb raced to her phone. But just as she reached it, Michael Myers appeared before her.

Michael grabbed Deb's face and carried her to the wall.

Corey watched through the door, studying Michael's methods as he slowly unwrapped the bandage on his hand to let the blood run out.

Michael lifted Deb off the ground. Then he raised his knife and impaled her so deep through her chest that the blade stuck into the wall and held her in place. There she hung like a macabre installation. Life fading quickly from her eyes. Michael observed his work curiously.

Corey pressed against the door. Watching closely. Learning from his master.

Deb's head fell toward Corey as he removed his mask. The last thing she saw before she stopped breathing was Corey Cunningham's excited face.

*

Corey looked at his injured hand as he waited outside Allyson's home. The stitches had torn open, and Corey clenched and unclenched his hand, ripping his wound open even more.

Corey stared up to Laurie's window. She hadn't yet gotten home, but he kept his eyes on her empty room.

For the remaining hour of her shift, Allyson could only think about Corey. And the second she heard his motorcycle pull up, she came to life.

Allyson raced out of her home in a fresh change of clothes. She kissed Corey excitedly and jumped onto the back of the motorcycle.

"Where are you taking me?"

"Away from here," Corey said as he saw Laurie's truck approaching.

Allyson smiled and held on.

Corey turned the throttle, and the motorcycle blasted down the road.

Laurie pulled into the driveway just in time to see the light on the back of the motorcycle disappear as they turned the corner. She heard the engine screaming as they raced into the night.

*

The motor whirred at full throttle as Corey and Allyson flew down the road. The wind lifted their hair and threw it behind them violently. Turning them into wild monsters of the night. The dashed stripes on the black asphalt became one long seamless ribbon.

"Do you trust me?" Corey screamed over his shoulder. Needing to know for certain how far she was willing to go with him.

"What?!" Allyson yelled back as she pressed closer.

"Do you trust me?" Corey yelled again.

"Yes!" Allyson shouted. "Yes, I trust you!"

Corey killed his headlight, and the bike shot down the road through total darkness.

Allyson clenched her eyes and grabbed Corey tightly.

"What are you doing?!" Allyson screamed.

"Trust me!" Corey yelled.

Corey gripped the handles as the motorcycle ripped across the road.

This is how you disappear, Allyson told herself.

"I won't let anything happen to you," Corey promised.

Allyson opened her eyes to the darkness. The ground shook as the bike shot through the night. She forced herself to loosen her grip.

When two cars raced past them, Allyson let go. Her eyes opened, and her arms shot into the air. Allyson screamed excitedly. The thrill electrified her as she embraced this darkness. As she disappeared completely to become a new shape.

"Faster!" Allyson screamed, never wanting to go back.

Corey leaned forward and barreled down the road toward the radio tower flashing in the distance.

*

Corey led Allyson to the side of the radio station, where they came to a ladder fixed to the building.

Corey grabbed a rung and climbed. Allyson followed him up to the rooftop.

Allyson stared at the lights glimmering above Haddonfield. Haddonfield looked like a graveyard on the ground, but on the roof with Corey, where she couldn't see the memories, it didn't look as bad. Standing above it all, Haddonfield even looked kind of beautiful.

Corey gazed up to the looming radio tower.

"I used to come here every day after the accident, and I'd sit for hours looking at the tower. Wanting to go back to a time when things weren't so bad. I thought, maybe... maybe if I climbed all the way to the top of the tower, I could see my old life before everything changed. Sort of like a beacon to what used to be. Maybe it would take me back to that place."

Allyson clenched the rings on her necklace. She understood. "I have something like that too. Some nights I squeeze these so hard, thinking that if I can squeeze them hard enough, then maybe I can remember what things used to feel like."

Corey looked her in the eye. "But now, it's

different. Because now I know. If I had never killed Jeremy, I never would have known you."

Allyson understood those words to be true, but she had no idea what to do with them.

"So, now I look up at that tower, thinking about that old life, and I don't give a shit about it. I want to destroy it, and I don't want to ever think about it again. I only want you."

Corey looked over Haddonfield. He didn't see the beauty Allyson saw. He saw only a prison.

Corey shifted. "I gotta get out of here. Because if I stick around... I don't know... I don't know what'll happen," Corey told her as a crooked smile emerged on his face. "I just know it won't be good."

"You have me. I'm here."

"I don't even think *you* can stop this," Corey told her.

"Stop what?"

Corey smirked. "Eventually, the boogeyman's gotta die, right?"

"Don't talk like that," Allyson told him as she pulled at his hair. She played it bravely, but inside she worried what would happen if she lost him. What if she couldn't protect him? And what if somebody did finally do something to him? She knew he needed to get away. And she did too.

Allyson grabbed Corey's unbandaged hand and held it as she studied his injury. The color had turned greenish-yellow, and a spider-like web of red veins spread out from the broken stitches and stretched across his palm.

"I think you're getting infected."

Corey took his hand back and grabbed Allyson's. He scratched at the nail polish on her finger with his thumbnail and quietly sang the vagabond's song:

> *"There's a hole in the boat*
> *And we can't keep afloat*
> *Ooo-lie-fee-ist in the sea*
> *Nail my hands to the door*
> *And my knees to the floor*
> *To stop that water till we reach the floor…"*

Corey looked at Allyson. "Do you ever feel separate from yourself? Like you're watching yourself do something, but *you* aren't really there?"

"That's been my life up until I met you." Allyson rubbed her hands together as if creating heat.

"What's that?" Corey asked curiously.

"My mom taught me this thing to protect myself." Allyson explained. "Any time you feel like you're losing yourself or something bad is trying to get in, you're supposed to do this."

"You're supposed to rub your hands together?"

"No, I'm creating a ball of positive energy in my hands." Allyson pantomimed an invisible ball in her hands. "Then you sculpt it, making it super strong. And once you can feel it in your hands, really feel it—" Allyson brought one hand close to her chest and pushed the other hand out, "—you use that good energy to push away everything negative and keep your soul protected."

Corey laughed. "Magic tricks? I like magic tricks." Then he clapped his hands and sloppily recreated Allyson's therapeutic ritual.

Allyson slapped his hurt hand. "Don't make fun."

"Ow!" Corey laughed and shook off the pain. "Now you're infected."

Allyson tucked her arms into her shirt to warm up. The same way she had as a little girl.

Corey took off his jacket and placed it over her shoulders.

"Did it ever work?" Corey asked. "That magic trick?"

Allyson smiled and shook her head. "No. But it gave me hope."

"Hope that what? You'd be okay?"

"Hope that I could survive anything that came my way."

"Immortality, right?"

"Something like that."

Corey looked over the town. "I'm serious. Let's go right now. Let's find a place where nobody knows us. Where it's just you and me."

"And fuck everything else?" Allyson said with a coy smile.

Corey jumped to his feet and raised his arms excitedly. "*Yes!*"

Corey straddled the ledge on the side of the building. "'Cause I'm not all right here. Allyson, I am not all right," Corey laughed.

"Hey, come away from there." Allyson worried he might fall.

"Are you all right, Allyson?"

Allyson shook her head. "Not at all."

"Then, what the fuck are we doing?" Corey smiled, and then he dropped off the side of the building.

"*Corey!*" Allyson screamed as she hurried to the edge. There she found Corey looking up at her from the top of the marquee that stuck out from the building. Still grinning.

"You don't have enough bandages to keep me together," Corey told her.

"You scared the shit out of me!" Allyson yelled. "Get back up here!"

"I can't," Corey shouted up to her as he grabbed onto the edge of the marquee and dangled. "It's too late. I'm already falling."

"What are you doing? Corey, *don't!*" Allyson screamed.

Corey looked at the ground below. At least fifteen feet from where he hung. Then he looked back up at Allyson.

With a big smile, Corey told her, "I'm so tired of hanging on. And I'm just not that interested in immortality."

Corey released his grip and fell.

Allyson heard his body smack painfully against the concrete.

Frantically, Allyson leaned further over the ledge and saw Corey on his back, laughing. Watching her.

"You are out of your mind!" Allyson couldn't restrain her smile. "You are a—"

"Psycho?" Corey finished her statement. Then he

sat up at a perfect ninety-degree angle. "But Allyson…
it doesn't hurt."

Allyson grabbed hold of the ladder as the radio
station door flew open. Willy the Kid stormed outside.

"Hey! What's up out here?"

Willy the Kid had gotten used to such disturbances.
It was usually just kids fucking around, but every
once in a while, a disgruntled listener would show
up at the station to raise hell. Those people mostly
banged on the door and yelled some shit, and Willy
rarely had to deal with them one-on-one. Usually,
Susan, the assistant station manager who sat up front
keeping things moving and answering calls, dealt
with that stuff, but it was her night off, so Willy was a
little extra on edge being all alone at the station.

"I'm talking to you." Willy felt in his pocket for
his taser. *Shit*. He'd left it on his desk inside.

"This is private property. Not safe to be up there,
doin' whatever it is you're doin'. You hear me? So go
on. Get out of here," Willy demanded.

Corey rose. The shadow along the building hid
his face. And then he stepped forward.

Willy recognized his face.

"Oh shit, would you look at that? Corey
Cunningham," Willy said with a chuckle.

Willy had followed the Cunningham case close
enough to know that Corey wasn't a guy to be
frightened about. Corey's timid demeanor during
the trial made Willy believe that if Corey had acted
violently toward Jeremy, which he sincerely doubted,
he'd only done it because Jeremy was a kid he could

overpower. "No way that dude could ever step to me," Willy would tell his friends at the bar as they discussed the case. Even though Willy was the biggest perpetrator of the more extreme Corey Cunningham conspiracy theories, he believed none of them. But he loved to stoke a fire, and when his ratings started climbing, Willy leaned into his narrative.

"So, the local psycho decided to pay me a visit? What an honor. Now, why don't you get outta here, you ugly motherfucker."

Corey stepped closer.

"Man, I'm fucking serious as a heart attack. You take one step closer, I'm gonna fuck your face up!"

"*Stop it!*" Allyson yelled as she raced in between them. "You stop it too," she told Corey.

Allyson looked back at Willy. "We're leaving. Go back inside."

"Hey, pretty thing." Willy recognized Allyson immediately. "I don't think you know who you're talking to, but I know who I'm talking to."

Willy put on a creep's smile, and his voice dipped back into DJ cadence. "Why don't you leave this loser and come play with me in my booth? I'm sure my listeners would love to hear the Laurie Strode story from someone who lived it. Maybe you can tell us how she teased a man with brain damage until he snapped." Willy smirked. "Look at you. Now you want to make a name for yourself, huh? Using this psycho here to get your own headline. All right, I see you. All-y-son. You teasing him too? Trying to get him to snap like Michael?"

Allyson looked to Corey, who stood perfectly still. Eyes black. Face expressionless.

"What kind of a vulture are you to feed on people's misery. To make it a game?" Allyson's voice got louder.

"I'm the kind of vulture people crave, baby," Willy said as he ran his hands across his chest sexually.

"You're sick. That's what you are. And one day, you'll pay for the bullshit you've stirred." Allyson grew angrier.

"Oh, I'm paid now, Ally-son. And I'm everywhere, baby. They got my billboards up and down this town. People can't get enough of Willy the Kid because once you turn me on, you can't turn me off. I'm in your ear like a song that won't leave. That you hear every day…" Willy looked at Corey. "Even when I'm not there… boo."

Corey remained still with a hard stare.

"Bullshit. All you do is scare people," Allyson told him.

"So do you." Willy chuckled and turned away. "See you around, Corey Cunningham. See you around too, Little Laurie."

Willy reentered the station and locked the door behind him.

Allyson turned back to Corey. "You're right. Let's do it. I don't want to be in Haddonfield anymore. I want to be with you."

Allyson took Corey in her arms. He leaned over her shoulder and looked to the distance behind her. And he smiled when he saw Laurie Strode watching them from inside her truck. Corey raised his hand and inconspicuously acknowledged her. Allyson never noticed.

*

The pitch-black night fell over the two-lane road as Laurie followed the red taillight on Corey's motorcycle. The blackness spilled into Laurie's truck, swallowing her slowly as she replayed that initial introduction between Corey and Allyson. Her doing. And now it would be up to her to stop it.

The road growled angrily beneath Laurie's truck as she accelerated. Her hands strangled the wheel. Her eyes refused to let go of the motorcycle.

*

Corey rolled to a stop in front of Allyson's home as Laurie pulled into the drive.

"What are you gonna tell her?" Corey asked.

"I don't know. I'll figure it out."

Corey grabbed Allyson and kissed her. He kept one eye open to make sure Laurie saw. She did.

Laurie went inside and stood at the window, waiting for Allyson to come in.

Allyson climbed off the bike, and Corey rode away.

Allyson turned back to Laurie at the window. She could smell an argument coming. She could sense Laurie's tension. And rather than confront it right then, Allyson got into her car.

Laurie rushed outside as Allyson started the engine.

"Hey, I want to talk!" Laurie shouted as Allyson drove away.

*

Allyson drove the streets aimlessly. She noticed even more despair than she typically did. The patina of death covered homes, fell off storefronts, and weathered people's expressions everywhere she turned.

Streetlights barely provided enough illumination to see through the darkness of Haddonfield. It was always dark in Haddonfield, but it seemed much darker on this night.

When Allyson stopped at an intersection, she spotted the masked face of Michael Myers painted onto the brick wall of a deserted building. The building's windows had been punched out some time ago, and nobody cared enough to replace them or board them up.

Allyson drove by the park where Marion, Marcus, and Vanessa had been slain four years earlier. The place she tried to avoid. All the playground equipment had been removed, and now the park was nothing more than an empty lot. Still, Allyson could see their dead bodies, arranged grotesquely as if the violence hadn't been enough for Michael. Allyson would never shake those images.

A gang of rats scurried across the street and into the gutter as Allyson drove past Dr. Mathis's house. She saw his Porsche parked outside but had no idea what horrors were tucked away inside.

Allyson pulled up to the cemetery. Judging from the green grass and litter-free landscape, the cemetery appeared to be the only place in Haddonfield anyone cared about.

Allyson rounded the perimeter to the shorter wall in the back and scaled it. After her parents had been killed, Allyson spent a lot of time at their gravesites, thinking that being close to them would help ease her pain. When it didn't, she quit coming.

She navigated the sprawling cemetery. So many graves. Haddonfield contained more dead bodies than live ones.

Allyson reached her parents' plot and found fresh flowers and the scarf Laurie had spent the week knitting. Allyson had no idea Laurie had been there too. She sat down and touched the scarf. Then she pressed it against her face.

The emotion took Allyson back to when Laurie was so fragile and scared and hid far away from everyone else. Back when her parents and everyone Allyson knew wanted nothing to do with Laurie's paranoia. Back when Allyson felt so much sympathy for a woman who simply wanted to protect the people she loved.

Allyson lay down between her parents' headstones and tried to find some stars. None broke through the heavy clouds of blackness covering Haddonfield. She clutched her parents' wedding rings on her necklace, wishing that her beacon would take her back to that time before everything had turned.

Allyson rubbed her hands together in the gesture

her mom taught her brought one hand to her chest and pushed the other one to the sky. *Don't make it hurt so bad*, she silently prayed.

*

"*Get in here this instant!*" Joan screamed from atop her floral-print throne in the living room when Corey came through the door.

Corey stepped into the room and found Joan's anger waiting for him. Ronald disappeared into the shadows behind her, drinking a beer and keeping his lips zipped.

"Now you're driving a motorcycle?" Joan berated. "A *motorcycle*?!"

Corey said nothing. He just stood there. Watching.

"Ronald? Did you know about this?!" Joan yelled behind her.

Ronald lowered his eyes and sipped his beer. He wasn't about to say a word.

Joan jumped from her seat and flew to Corey. She sniffed his clothes and face aggressively. Her face soured.

"I can smell her. I can smell that tramp on you. She's taking you away from me, isn't she? That's where you go at night? You want to leave your mother all alone?! What's happened to my baby boy? *What have they done to you?*"

Corey's eyes turned black. The look caused Joan to gasp, and she slapped him hard across the face, trying to remove it.

"If you want to go, then get out of this house!"

Corey turned to leave—

"No!" Joan snatched him and kissed him hard on the lips.

"You're killing your mother!" Joan wept and removed a wadded tissue from her brassiere to dab her tears as she fled the room, leaving Ronald and Corey alone.

"I hope you find love," Ronald told Corey in a whisper.

*

Corey stood in the darkness of the Cunningham kitchen with a knife in his grip.

"You just sit there, and you encourage him! You encourage him to leave me!"

Corey could hear Joan yelling at Ronald upstairs.

"I am dying. I am dying because of you! You are supposed to support me, not wage war against me!"

Corey held the blade until the yelling stopped. Then, he ascended the stairs.

He stood motionless in the doorway of Joan and Ronald's bedroom. Watching them sleep. An evil intention boiling inside. He could feel something else taking control. Something he couldn't stop. His hand tensed around the handle of the knife.

He forced himself back to his room. Then he positioned himself in front of the window and stared into the blackness outside. He squeezed the knife tighter and closed his eyes, hoping he could disappear into that blackness. His hand eased its grip on the handle and inched down to the blade.

When he felt the knife's sharp edge touching his wound, Corey winced. He clenched his hand and pushed the blade into his palm. He squeezed until he could feel the sharp edge breaking open the skin. He squeezed and felt the blood stream out. An electric current of pain buzzed. Ice cold and burning hot all at once.

He dropped the knife and lifted his hands. Rubbed them together, as Allyson had shown him. He put his clean hand against his chest and pushed his bloody hand against the glass, attempting to keep his intention from getting closer. It did nothing but leave a bloody handprint on his window.

Corey fled the house. When he fired up his motorcycle, Joan appeared in her bedroom window, yelling and banging against it to get Corey's attention. But Corey couldn't hear her over the roar of the engine.

He raced back to Allyson's house. If anyone could save him, it would be her.

*

Corey parked down the street away from Allyson's house to not draw Laurie's attention, but he saw Laurie sitting on the porch, waiting, as he approached.

He quickly hid behind a tree across the street.

But Laurie saw him. And after a moment, Corey heard her say, "You think I don't see you. But I see everything."

Corey didn't move.

"So, are you gonna hide there all night, watching me? Or are you gonna make me come to you?"

Corey remained quiet.

Laurie rocked back in her chair, tapping the edge of her seat against the wall to create a musical *thump thump thump*.

When Corey didn't present himself, Laurie got up from her chair and approached.

She crossed the street. Her boots made the same *thump thump thump* against the asphalt.

As she neared, Laurie heard his motorcycle engine rumbling in the distance. When she looked behind the tree, Corey was gone.

*

Corey burst through the window of the Allen house and stormed upstairs to the attic, where he kicked the door off the hinges. In a fit of ferocious rage, Corey destroyed the attic. He jammed a knife into the walls and splintered the wood. He dug his fingers into the cracks and pulled the planks loose. He grabbed the fallen boards and smashed them against the walls. He wanted to destroy the entire home. He wanted, so badly, for it all to go away.

Out of breath and covered in dust and tears, Corey stood hunched over the third-floor railing, staring at the bloodstain on the floor below. Knowing that he could never make it go away. And knowing he could never go back to how things were before.

Corey lifted a leg over the banister and then brought the other over.

He grabbed onto the handrail and leaned back as he always did, hoping that he'd wake up somewhere different if he let go.

Corey held the railing and let his feet drop off the edge. His fingers struggled to support his weight. And when the strain became so extreme that he could no longer manage, Corey finally let go.

The fall flattened him, and he looked up to the stairs. The same place where Jeremy had fallen. But Corey survived. And the emotional turmoil churning inside caused his expressions to alternate between elation and despair. Back and forth from a silly smile like the scarecrow mask he'd worn, to a frown that made his features violent.

HALLOWEEN

Corey's eyes opened to a *thump thump thump*. He had fallen asleep on the stain of blood. His head pounded painfully. Everything else on his body ached terribly. His body could no longer contain the shape he'd become.

"So, nice to see you," he heard Laurie announce from the shadows.

Corey glanced over his shoulder and found Laurie sitting behind him, rocking gently, tapping against the wall with her chair. She had one of his paper planes in her hand and tossed it in his direction.

Corey stared up to the attic. *What was she doing there? And how much had she seen?*

"You know, there are two kinds of evil in the world," Laurie explained. "There is the evil that exists as an external force and threatens our well-being. An evil we can survive through understanding and awareness. And there is the other kind of evil that lives inside our hearts like an infection. A more dangerous evil because we might not even know we are infected. And that the infection is what is motivating our actions."

Corey slowly turned to face Laurie. "What's your point? Am I a bad person? Are you? Is this what you saw that day at the gas station. When you... rescued me?"

Laurie laughed at his naivete and attempt to out-intimidate her. This was a game he could not win.

Corey parroted her laugh and then killed it.

"We're both fucked up," Laurie answered, "and capable of... things. The real question is, do we let it out or lock it up?"

Leave me alone, repeated in Corey's head as his violent intentions became more evident in his blackening eyes.

Laurie had spent all night watching Corey. Through the window and then in the chair that she now tapped against the wall. Making herself a promise. This Halloween, she would not let anything happen to Allyson.

"I want to help you. Let me help you or find help for you."

Corey rose and stared. The shadow from the stairs hid his expression, but his posture told Laurie how he felt about her presence in the house.

"Allyson isn't equipped for this relationship. I don't want to see her get hurt," Laurie told him.

"I think it's you who's not equipped, Laurie. I see through it. Your bravado. Your bullshit. I *see* you, even when you think nobody's there."

The tension between the two became almost unbearable.

"I'm only gonna say this once... stay away from Allyson—"

"You started it!" Corey exploded. "You brought me in! You invited me!" Corey breathed heavily. Overcome with emotion. Chest heaving. "And he said to me, 'I hope you find love.' And I found it. And you can hate me all you want, but *you're* the one to blame. 'Cause you go, 'you wanna do it, or you want me to?'"

Laurie put the legs of her chair back on the ground. Corey's sentiment gave her pause, but it did not change her agenda.

Corey turned his attention to a spider slinking up a web on the staircase. He approached curiously and watched intently. "People are afraid to live in this house. And you're afraid of being alone. When Allyson leaves you, just know you'll always have Michael."

Corey watched the spider more closely. As it weaved toward a fly that had gotten trapped in its web. The spider inched nearer and then, with lightning speed, it attacked and buried its fangs into the fly. The spider released its venom, then wrapped the fly in silk and waited for it to die. Corey smiled as he watched nature play out before him. Without looking away from the spider, Corey told Laurie, "You say I'm the problem, but it's you. And if you really wanted to help Allyson, you'd put a bullet through your head and let Allyson leave with me." Corey laughed. "But you miss the fight, don't you? And you pray that Michael comes back for you.

'Cause who are you without the boogeyman?" Corey smirked. "A psycho? Or a freakshow?"

Laurie remained silent.

Corey ran his finger through the web, breaking it apart. The spider dangled from a thread of silk. Corey cupped it in his hand and then squished it in his grip.

"If I can't have her, you can't either," Corey threatened. When he turned back to Laurie, she had disappeared.

Corey ran to the window and looked through the curtains. He didn't see Laurie anywhere.

Corey's body distended viciously as he could no longer stop his violence. He gripped a fire poker and beat the exposed strings of the piano. Sparks erupted as the metal struck the strings.

Clang! Clang! Clang!

The discordant notes screamed through the house and inside Corey's head.

Clang! Clang! Clang!

*

Allyson got home at dawn. Laurie had not yet returned.

Allyson walked through the quiet home and up the stairs to get ready for work. She looked into Laurie's office and recognized a box sitting on the couch by the coffee table. The same box of mementos that her mother kept in the hall closet back in their old home. Allyson never had much interest in digging through it when everything was good. When she had her parents, friends, and her life hadn't yet rearranged itself into what it would soon become, Allyson had no use in revisiting the good old days.

Allyson rifled through the memories inside. There were a few photos from her mom's and dad's childhoods that must have not been good enough to make it into the photo albums Karen kept on their bookshelf. There were no photos of Laurie in the box. Most photographs of Laurie existed pre-1978. The ones taken after were off-center snapshots Karen had snapped inside Laurie's compound as Laurie tried to dodge the lens.

Buried at the bottom of the box, beneath Allyson's field day prizes, fifth-grade soccer trophies, and her high school leadership plaque, Allyson found a bundle of birthday cards from Laurie that she'd never seen before. Half were opened, and half were unopened.

Allyson read one of the open cards.

Hey kiddo,
Happy birthday!
Hope you are enjoying the second grade. I had a dream last night, and it caused me great worry. I told your mom, but she got mad and hung up on me. She will not tell you the things I know. But I need you to know that there are two sides to everything. There's what your mom tells you, and there's the truth. And the truth is this, just because your mom doesn't believe in the boogeyman does not mean he's not real.

Always be prepared for his return. Because, Allyson, until he is killed, he will always come back. I promise.
Love, Laurie.

Allyson opened another card and found a similar message from Laurie.

Karen had done what she could to shield Allyson from Laurie's hysteria until Allyson was old enough to understand it. That's when her mother allowed Laurie back into their lives, but only from a distance. Of course, it did not stop Laurie's frantic midnight phone calls or pre-dawn intrusions to make sure they were prepared. It did not stop Laurie from secretly meeting with Allyson after school or anywhere she knew Karen wouldn't be.

Allyson thumbed through the cards, knowing why her mom had kept them hidden.

She's out of her mind, Allyson told herself as she put on her scrubs.

Allyson examined the details of her room, feeling no connection to any of them. Ready to say goodbye to it all.

This is how I turn normal, Allyson's thoughts repeated.

*

Allyson drove to work deliriously, having not slept the entire night. Things moved dreamlike past her window. Scattered trick-or-treaters went from home to home in broad daylight, searching for candy. Daylight trick-or-treating had become a more common Halloween sight in Haddonfield since the Michael Myers massacre. Many believed the boogeyman only existed after the sun went down.

Halloween decorations hung lazily on storefronts, not for any festive reason but just because that's what you did, even in a town like Haddonfield. It seemed like everybody in Haddonfield had turned into a zombie, mindlessly moving in one direction because they didn't know how to go any other way. Trying to ignore the bloody history that poisoned the soil. The history that you could smell from miles away. You could not escape the ominous dread that came with Halloween in Haddonfield each year. But still, people tried.

Allyson pulled into the parking lot at the clinic ten minutes late, but she didn't see Dr. Mathis's car, so she knew she wouldn't have to hear anything about it.

On her way in, Allyson noticed a bird picking at some food. She didn't think much about it until she got closer and realized that the bird's meal was the fresh carcass of a flattened squirrel. The bird picked at the squirrel's head and pulled long strings of red meat out of its body. Even the animal world seemed more vicious on Halloween.

Allyson walked into a total shitshow when she entered the clinic. The phone rang off the hook, disgruntled patients clamored in the waiting room, and the nurses scrambled to keep up with the unusually crazy afternoon.

"Happy Halloween," Epstein, the stoned nurse, sarcastically told Allyson as he strolled into the exam room. "It's gonna be a fun one."

Allyson put her purse down and looked at the check-in list.

"Yeah, it's fun today," Stephanie, the newest receptionist, said as she picked up the phone.

"What happened?" Allyson asked.

"Dr. Mathis is MIA, and so is Deb. Nobody can get ahold of them. Lydia thinks they eloped." Stephanie unmuted the phone. "Grantham Primary Medical Clinic, can you hold, please?"

Allyson took over the intake. She was nowhere near as rattled as the other nurses frantically trying to attend to the stranded patients filling the waiting room. Not because Allyson had a cooler head or could handle the pressure any better, but because she just didn't care anymore. And each time another patient snapped at her, she cared a little less. All she could think about was Corey and their new world—

"Allyson, line three," Stephanie told her as another call came in.

Allyson picked up the phone. "This is Allyson, how—"

"Allyson—"

Allyson immediately detected the distress in Corey's voice. "What is it?"

"I need to see you."

"Now?"

"Tonight. Meet me at nine o'clock. At the diner."

"What's the matter?"

"It's your grandmother. We have to leave, Allyson. We have to leave tonight."

"What? What did she do?"

Corey paused, breathing on the other end.

"What did she do?"

"She threatened me."

"What?"

"She wants me dead."

Corey hung up.

"Corey? Corey?"

Allyson tried his number, but he didn't pick up.

*

The person at the center of Allyson's new world blasted down the road on his motorcycle, a blur of fury. Riding so fast, the landscape transformed into straight lines that shot past his face at warp speed. Corey leaned forward and pushed the bike as fast it could go.

Corey skidded onto the gravel road leading to the underpass and shut the bike down. He dismounted and moved to the festering entrance of the tunnel where he'd been transformed.

He crawled toward Michael's chamber. Ready to confront the monster.

Within the rotten sanctuary, Corey found Michael standing against the wall. Watching.

Corey stepped closer. And then he charged.

"What did you do to me?" Corey screamed as he grabbed Michael.

"What did you do to me?! Say *something*!" Corey

cried as his rage boiled up through his veiny, sinewed, red face.

Michael wrapped his hands around Corey's throat and pushed him back. Corey fought the hold as he stared into his black eyes. This time they had no power over him.

Corey slammed Michael to the ground. He grabbed Michael's head and banged it against the concrete floor repeatedly. Over and over until Michael's hands let go.

Corey took the mask and ripped it off Michael's head.

Corey stumbled back, staring at the unmasked Michael Myers. His breath trembling.

"What did you do to me?" Corey whispered.

Corey looked at the mask.

And his breathing slowed.

A frightening calm came over him.

"And what are you gonna do now?" Corey asked with growing conviction.

*

"Terry!" Terry's dad barked as he opened the door to his son's bedroom and found him playing video games with his deadbeat friends.

Billy quickly hid the painkillers he'd stolen from his mom. Stacy stashed her weed behind the console. Margo, who wasn't doing anything, still looked away.

"You left the goddamn back gate open again," Mr. Tramer yelled.

"No, I didn't, Dad." Terry glanced around the room at his friends. None of them made eye contact with him.

"Don't call me a liar! And if I have to tell you again, there's gonna be hell to pay."

"Yes, sir."

Robert Tramer looked with contempt at the losers sitting in his house. *How did this idiot become my son?* he thought as he stared at the boy, whom he did not want to claim as his own.

Robert had such high hopes for Terry, but Terry let him down at every turn. Robert had dreamed that Terry would end up a great man. Instead, he got a scrawny, unmotivated, and awkward dweeb, which is how Robert most often described Terry when telling anyone about his son. And, when Robert thought it couldn't get any worse, Terry went and joined the high school band.

Before Robert and his wife Erin moved to Buffalo, Robert had been a linebacker on the Haddonfield High football team in the early nineties, and he couldn't have been more embarrassed by his son's course in life. *Drumline, you gotta be fucking kidding me.*

Erin, who divorced Robert when Terry turned three, had since remarried and lived in South Beach with two new children. Terry rarely saw her, and she had little interest in seeing him. Robert and Terry moved back to Haddonfield, so Robert could take over his father Ben's used car dealership. So, it was just the two of them in the house. The father who despised his son and the son who feared his father.

"And hold it down in here. This is my house, not yours. Remember that," Robert ordered.

"Yes, sir," Terry answered timidly. His father never failed to put the fear of God in him.

Robert slammed the door, and they all could hear him muttering in the kitchen, "Shit for brains," Robert's go-to insult.

"Your dad's so mean." Stacy spelled out the obvious as she gathered her weed.

"Facts," Billy seconded as he grabbed his pills.

Terry played it off that he wasn't embarrassed by the dressing-down by taking it out on his friends.

"You left the back gate open," Terry accused Margo, "I told you to close it."

"Shit, Terry, I didn't mean to. I thought I closed it," Margo replied.

"It's just a gate, like what's the big deal?" Stacy asked. "Your dad needs some anger management. Getting that upset will put him in the grave early."

"He's just very particular about the way he runs the house," Terry explained.

"Terry gets a beating if he doesn't do the dishes properly," Billy joked.

"Shut the fuck up, Billy," Terry snapped.

"What are we gonna do tonight?" Stacy asked. "I don't want to sit in your bedroom all night long worrying that your dad's gonna bust in and start some more shit."

"It's Halloween. We gotta do something," Margo said.

Billy removed the fake license he thought he'd

lost. "Get some beers and go to the warehouses? Eat these pills, put some masks on, and raise a little hell, know what I mean?"

Terry looked at Stacy. "If we get fucked up, can I spend the night at your house?"

"Nah, my mom's still pissed at you for ruining the couch. And she said she can't trust the things you say."

"Your mom's a bitch," Terry sneered.

"Fuck you. Maybe next time, don't spill Kool-Aid on her furniture," Stacy retorted.

"You can stay at my house," Margo offered. "I mean, everybody can if you want, my sister went to Niagara Falls with some dude for the week, so I got the apartment to myself."

"And now you tell us?" Terry smirked. "Sometimes, Margo, I think you might have shit for brains," Terry repeated his dad's insult.

Margo flipped him off. "Fuck you, I'm offering up my home."

"Hold it down in there!" Robert shouted from the kitchen.

"All right," Terry decided, "we're gonna go get some beers and then we're gonna go to Margo's. That's the plan."

Robert sat at the kitchen table with his legs propped up on a chair, watching CNBC and slurping a bowl of soggy Wheaties.

"Where do you think you are going?" Robert asked without looking at the gang as they walked toward the door.

"We're just going over to go to Billy's house to work on our group project. I might stay the night if that's okay."

"Not on a school night," Robert denied the request.

"But we're gonna work on our project until late, and I can just go to school from Billy's—"

"What did I just tell you?" Robert glared.

"Yes, sir," Terry politely responded.

"Be home no later than ten," Robert ordered.

"Yes, sir."

As Terry turned to leave, Robert stopped him. "Hold on. Let me see your eyes."

"Why?"

"Don't make me ask twice," Robert told him.

The drumline stood in nervous anticipation as Robert pulled Terry close and investigated his eyes as if keenly aware that Terry was up to no good. Then he let him go.

"Ten o'clock," Robert told him again.

"Yes, sir."

"And I better not find a scratch on the LeBaron, or it's your ass."

"Yes, sir."

Robert slurped up the milk from the bowl and refilled it with fresh Wheaties as the drumline hurried out of the house.

"Don't slam the door!" Robert shouted as Billy slammed the door.

Billy laughed as they ran to the car. "Yo, I slammed that shit."

"Yeah, and I'm gonna get yelled at now," Terry told Billy.

Across the street, Corey sat on his motorcycle, watching the drumline as they spilled out of the house and ran toward the LeBaron.

The drumline jumped in and drove away.

*

Underneath the bridge, Michael emerged. Maskless. Halloween night fell over him. The distorted features of his face remained mostly obscured by the darkness of the night.

Michael stepped out from the underpass. Cars passed him by without notice. The crowd at Bernie's Soft Serve across the street appeared oblivious to his presence.

The man who ruled Haddonfield proceeded through it anonymously.

Michael walked alongside the small river that ran parallel to the road. The moon allowed him enough light to see his reflection in the shallow stream. He gazed at the image. Then he pushed his hand into the water, and the ripples took his face away.

Michael's head turned from right to left.

The neighborhoods in Haddonfield rested in the distance. And Michael continued toward them.

*

"Turn it down. You're gonna blow the speakers," Terry yelled at Stacy when she reached up and cranked the volume on the car's stereo.

"Your dad's giving you a complex," Stacy replied. "You're gonna need to find a psychiatrist, or else you're gonna mess other people up too."

"Hurt people hurt people," Margo whispered in the back seat. It was something she'd heard her Aunt Jamie say over the years, but nobody paid her comment any attention, least of all Billy, who had already dosed and slid comfortably into his painkiller high.

Terry carefully parked his car at the Quickie-Go gas station, and the gang jumped out.

"Who's got money?" Terry asked.

They all looked at him blankly.

"You guys are not good friends," Terry told them, knowing they expected him to pay again. Then they headed in to ransack the store for beer and treats.

Billy let his hand float over the shelf of sour candies. Drool spilled out of his mouth and ran down his shirt as he considered which variety to get.

"Tonight's gonna be a good night," Stacy said as she bumped into him. "We gonna get fuuucked up."

Billy could only manage a small laugh. "Facts."

The gang burst out of the convenience store with arms full of malt liquor and Sour Patch Kids. They reached the car, and one by one, they stopped and turned to Terry. Something bad had happened.

"Oh shit, Terry," Margo said in disbelief.

"What is it?" Terry asked as he hurried to see the damage.

Psycho had been carved into the paint on the hood of the LeBaron.

"Your dad's gonna murder you," Margo added.

A motorcycle revved its engine at the pump. Stacy looked over and recognized the rider.

"Holy shit, it's him," she told the others.

Terry looked up as Corey blasted out of the parking lot and took off down the street.

"He's dead. Get in!" Terry ordered.

The drumline jumped into the LeBaron, and Terry took off after him.

*

Ronald hid in his office at Prevo, watching *Hard Target* on his laptop. He dipped some Ruffles into a freshly made bowl of sour cream and onion dip and sipped the rest of his Mountain Dew Code Red like a fine wine.

When Corey didn't come home, Joan went berserk and lashed out at Ronald.

"Why did you let him run out on me?" Joan screamed as she stormed through the house.

"I was asleep," Ronald told her as he played on his phone and tried to stay out of her way.

"You are always asleep!"

Joan ordered Ronald to find her boy. And she warned him not to come home until he did or else there'd be hell to pay.

But instead of combing the streets of Haddonfield, Ronald drove to the auto shop for an impromptu movie night. He didn't have any desire to find Corey. In fact, he hoped Corey wouldn't return. Ronald prayed the kid had gotten out of town and had already begun a new life somewhere else. A town where the looks weren't so condemning and his mother's control not so restrictive.

Ronald's phone buzzed. Joan was calling again.

*

Terry pressed down the gas as he chased Corey across the bridge road. Stacy screamed for Terry to go faster. Billy giggled with stoned excitement as he drummed on the dashboard with his drumsticks. A collection of droogs thirsty for violence.

Corey turned a couple of hundred yards down the road from Terry.

"He disappeared," Billy said with astonishment.

"He just turned, dumbass," Terry said as he hung a left where Corey had turned.

Terry didn't see Corey, but he saw the Prevo Auto Body Shop in the distance. "That's where he's going."

Terry cut his lights as he drove down the dirt road to the shop and pulled through the open gate.

"Anybody see him?" Terry asked as they climbed out.

"There's his bike," Margo pointed to Corey's motorcycle sitting at the entrance to the open garage. She could see a light inside the adjoining office. "I think he's inside."

"Little chickenshit asshole. Hiding in there like a little bitch," Terry replied as he looked around for what to do next. He noticed Stacy standing by a long chain rope and came up with an idea.

"Hey, Billy, back up the car. And don't mess it up," Terry whispered as he tossed the keys. Billy stood in a stoned stupor, operating on a five-second delay. The keys hit him in the chest and fell to the ground, and then, *one… two… three… four… five*, Billy raised his hands to catch them.

Billy grabbed the keys and walked to the car.

"Give me a hand," Terry told Stacy as he carried the chain to Corey's motorcycle.

"What are we gonna do, Terry?" Margo asked nervously.

"You're gonna stay out of the way. Me and Stacy are gonna strap this chain to his bike, hook it to my car, and drag it until there's nothing left."

"Stacy and I, loser," Margo corrected his grammar.

Billy's arm dangled out of the car, holding his drumstick as he inserted the key. He gazed at the rows of broken cars before him. "I need to get my own car," Billy muttered, inspired by the sea of automobiles. "And when I do, I'm gonna drive it so fast that nobody will ever see me. Facts," Billy added. Then he felt something tug at the drumstick. He assumed it was Terry.

"I'm goin', hold on," Billy said as he reached to turn the key.

The drumstick was then yanked from his hand. Billy turned to find Corey's shape wearing his Prevo denim jumpsuit standing at the door.

Terry and Stacy weaved the chain through the motorcycle frame and waited for Billy to back up the car… Billy did not.

"Billy, now," Terry whispered as he waved his hands to get Billy's attention.

It failed to work.

"I always gotta do everything myself," Terry said as he hurried to his car.

"Billy, let's go, man, come on," Terry said when he approached the driver's side. "We gonna do this or what?"

Billy did not respond. His head leaned strangely against the steering wheel.

Terry grabbed Billy by the collar and pulled him upright. That's when he discovered the drumstick sticking out of his eyeball. Tears of blood streamed down Billy's dead cheek.

"Oh fuck, man!" Terry said, falling back. "Oh fuck, oh my God!"

"What is it?" Margo called out as she and Stacy left the bike to see what had happened.

"Billy's dead!"

"What?" Neither Stacy nor Margo understood.

"He's dead! Somebody killed Billy!"

Just then, an engine growled. Two headlights fired up. The tow truck facing Stacy and Margo came to terrifying life. Growling angrily.

"*Run!*" Stacy screamed as she took off for the gate.

Margo came into view of the truck. "Who's that?"

Before she got an answer, the truck peeled out and blasted toward her. Creating a cloud of dust and terror.

Stacy reached the gate, but someone had locked them in.

"Shit!" Stacy yelled as she scaled the fence. Margo was close behind.

The truck raced toward them. Growing meaner. Shaking the ground as it approached. Its headlights burning through the girls.

Terry watched from a distance. Unable to stop any of it.

Stacy reached the other side as Margo climbed frantically. She lost her footing halfway up and scrambled to regain her position.

"Hurry, Margo!" Stacy screamed.

Margo reached the top of the gate and swung her legs over.

"Margo, hurry!"

Too late. The tow truck arrived explosively.

Stacy jumped out of the way. Margo clung to the other side. And the tow truck plowed right through the chain-link fence, taking Margo with it.

The truck broke to a stop. Idling. With Margo pinned underneath within the folds of the fence, clinging to life.

Stacy ran to help her. She screamed in horror when she saw Margo's bloody condition.

Stacy frantically searched for a way to pull her friend free. She grabbed the fence and tried to move it. Margo cried out in agony. The broken ends of the steel fence impaled Margo's skin and kept her trapped.

The truck door squealed as it opened, and then two boots landed on the dirt. Stacy desperately jerked at the fence again, but she couldn't pull it off Margo.

"Hurry, Stacy!" Margo pled.

"I can't get it. I'll go find Terry."

"Don't leave me!"

Stacy saw no sign of the driver as she stood. But Margo did.

"Stacy, look out!" Margo yelled.

Before Stacy could turn, she felt something strange pressing against her back forcefully. And then her breath disappeared as blood rushed up and filled her throat. She looked down and saw her sweatshirt extending unnaturally as the sharpened edge of a wrecking bar exited her stomach, bringing Stacy's guts with it.

Inside the office, Ronald yanked the headphones out of his ears, uncertain if the loud noise he heard had come from Van Damme blowing up the truck in the movie or if it had happened in real life out in his yard. He listened intently. Whatever the crash was, it pushed Ronald back in his chair. And before he'd recovered, he got an even bigger scare when Terry appeared in the window banging against the glass.

"Good God!" Ronald screamed.

"Help! He's out here!" Terry yelled.

"Who's out there?" Ronald asked as he pulled himself out of his chair.

Ronald looked through the window and saw the tow truck parked over the broken gate.

"He's gonna kill us all!" Terry screamed desperately.

Ronald hurried to let Terry inside.

"He ran over Margo. And Billy's... He killed Billy too," Terry stammered as he entered the office.

Ronald rushed through the door connecting the office to the garage. Terry followed.

Pumped up by the John Woo action film, Ronald flipped on the garage lights and headed for the gun locker against the wall. He grabbed a .357 revolver and handed Terry a lever-action .30-30.

"You know how to use this?" Ronald asked.

Terry looked at the weapon with confusion. He'd never held a gun in his life.

"It's loaded. Stay here. If he comes for you, just pull the trigger. Got it?"

Terry nodded.

Ronald moved through the open garage door into the auto yard with his gun drawn. Eyes scanning detail.

Terry remained at the entrance. His head darting right to left, finger on the trigger, terrified. Suddenly, the garage lights went out.

Terry spun around, waving his gun blindly.

"Who's there?"

Terry received no answer.

For moments, silence. And Terry shook harder.

"Hello?" Terry's voice cracked.

A metal pipe slammed to the ground behind Terry and rolled toward him. Terry did not wait for the killer to attack. He bolted out of the garage.

Ronald heard a pained cry from the tow truck, and he stumbled back when he found Margo pinned beneath.

"Oh, good Lord." Ronald fell to his knees and assessed her wounds. This wasn't good at all.

"Please... don't let me die," Margo begged.

"No, no, no, we're gonna do everything we can to get you help," Ronald told her. "Who did this to you?" he asked.

"Him," Margo said, pointing across the street.

Ronald turned to find Corey twenty feet away on the other side of the fence, pulling Michael's mask over his head.

"Corey?" he muttered in disbelief.

Terry ran toward Ronald and the truck, glancing over his shoulder to make sure he wasn't being followed. Then he saw the monster in the pale gray mask lit by the tow truck's headlights, staring in his direction. Terry stopped and raised the scope to his eye. He lined him up in the crosshairs. His nervousness gave way to adrenaline.

"I got you now, you fuckin' psycho," Terry declared.

Ronald turned back and saw Terry aiming the gun at Corey. He jumped up to stop him— "No! Wait!"

KA-BOOM!

Terry blew a hole through Ronald's head. Blood splattered across the truck and covered Margo.

"Oh fuck," Terry whimpered, terrified by what he'd done. "Oh my God. Oh my God. Oh my God."

Ronald fell back, revealing that the psycho had disappeared.

Terry stood, momentarily frozen in shock. His eyes glued to where he'd just seen Corey standing.

"Terry, help me!" Margo cried out.

Terry cautiously approached. He found more death before he reached her.

Stacy sat against the tree with the wrecking bar jutting out of her chest. A pool of blood shimmered beneath her.

"Margo?" Terry's voice broke as he reached her. The blood pouring out of her head intermingled with her red hair. Streams of it joined the bloody lake swelling beneath Ronald.

Everywhere Terry turned, he saw blood.

Terry's hands shook furiously as he investigated the fence, but he saw no way to free Margo. Every time he pulled on it, Margo screamed louder.

"Where's Stacy?" Margo asked.

"She's… dead…" Terry stuttered.

"Oh shit, Terry," Margo looked at him. "You're dead too."

Terry turned to meet his killer.

Corey snatched the gun from Terry's hand and slammed it into Terry's head with stunning force.

Upon impact, Terry's brain went blank. Corey threw him to the ground.

Terry's eyes rolled in his head as Corey retrieved the cutting torch from the back of the truck.

Corey twisted the nozzle on the tank, ignited the flame with a striker, and brought it to Terry's face.

The torch brought Terry back to awareness as Corey inserted the tool into Terry's mouth and lit him on fire.

Margo watched helplessly as Terry's face bubbled and melted. As the flames burned through his cheeks and turned his head into a ball of fire. Corey burned him until there was nothing left. Then he stepped over Terry's scorched face and looked down at Margo, trapped in the fence.

Margo knew he would not let her live, and with her last breath, she yelled, "They were all right about you! You're nothing but a fucking psycho!"

Corey raised his leg and held his boot over her face long enough to draw out her fear. Then he stomped Margo's head with crushing force. Corey stomped until her skull cracked open and her brains sprayed out. Corey didn't stop until her head had turned into a mushy pie of viscera and bone.

*

Allyson sat parked in front of her house, watching Laurie through the living room window. Seething with rage. Wanting to run inside and scream and wanting to avoid Laurie altogether.

As soon as she saw Laurie move upstairs, Allyson hurried in.

Allyson quickly changed out of her scrubs and grabbed two dusty suitcases from her closet. She blindly shoved all her clothes into the baggage and then ran downstairs.

Allyson grabbed Corey's leather jacket from the hall closet and slipped it on. When she turned to the door, she found Laurie blocking the exit.

"You're leaving? With Corey?" Laurie asked with disbelief. "You can't do this. I can't let you."

"Yeah? Tell me, Laurie, why the fuck can't I?" Allyson had fire in her eyes.

"Because I care about you, and I have very serious concerns about him." Laurie was surprised by Allyson's anger.

Allyson couldn't believe the fucking gall. "Oh, do you?" Allyson asked mockingly. "Is this a suspicion or paranoia, intuition… an inkling? Does Laurie Strode have another inkling?"

"Yeah. I do. You want to hear it?"

"No."

"I think he's capable of real harm," Laurie answered anyway.

"That right? That's why you're stalking him? That's why you're threatening him?"

"No. I'm doing that because I am trying to protect you."

"What did you say to him? *Tell me!*"

"Baby, you have to believe me—"

"*What did you say to him?*" Allyson screamed.

"I said he's down a dark path, and he needs help."

"What makes you think Corey is any more dangerous than you?"

Allyson grabbed her bags and moved to the door. Laurie followed.

"Because I've seen the exact same thing in Corey's eyes that I saw in—"

Allyson stopped and turned. She put her finger in Laurie's face. "Don't you dare fucking say 'Michael Myers!'"

"It's true. You have to believe me."

"Michael Myers lives because you keep him alive! Why can't you see that? You pretend you've moved on, but it's bullshit! You sit in that office writing about him. Staring at his photos. Thinking about him. You're obsessed with Michael like he's some sort of game, and you won't rest until you've finished it or everyone is as crazy as you. I have to get out of here before you, and this town, kill the one person that actually makes me feel something good."

Angry tears rolled down Allyson's face.

"You have to believe me." Laurie's voice softened. "Please."

"What have you *ever* done to protect me?! My parents are *dead*! My friends are *dead*! And now you're telling me this is for my protection? *You're* the one that's capable of harm! And I have to get the fuck away from you 'cause I'm scared of what you might do next."

Laurie put her hand on Allyson's suitcase and gently tugged it.

"You have to believe me."

"I spent too many years believing you."

Allyson jerked the bag from Laurie's hand and opened the door.

"Please, baby, don't let the darkness take you," Laurie begged.

"Maybe one day you'll find out where I've gone," Allyson said as she stormed out.

Laurie stood in the doorway, devastated.

Allyson started the car and drove away without turning back.

Laurie remained in the doorway and stayed there long after Allyson left her sight.

*

"The witching hour is nearly upon us. And call me crazy, Haddonfield. But I think the boogeyman is tuning in…" Willy the Kid announced as he began his broadcast that Halloween evening. He'd spent the past several months planning a big *War of the Worlds*-style prank on Haddonfield where he'd act like Michael Myers had returned and was out terrorizing the citizens. Susan, the assistant manager, warned him not to, but Willy never took her concerns seriously.

Not that it mattered, though, because Willy never got further than thinking about it. A week before Halloween, he knew he needed to start writing out a script, but then he got stoned and forgot about it, and now here it was: Halloween. Oh well.

Willy had gone through that same idea with the same results ever since 2019, but he'd forgotten about those other attempts.

Sitting in the booth that Halloween night, Willy promised himself: *Next Halloween, we are gonna turn up the volume in Haddonfield, and Willy the Kid's gonna become a fucking legend.*

Willy put on 'Surfin' Dead' by The Cramps and ducked outside to burn another joint.

The thin alley next to WURG filled with a cloud of marijuana smoke as Willy texted Susan about the takeout order she'd gone to pick up: Xtra hot mustard for my crispy egg rolls!

Willy sent the message and then noticed the shape of someone in the distance across the street. Still. They were too far away to make Willy confident it was even a person. Could have been a fencepost or signpost of some sort. A strange-shaped shadow. Could have been anything.

Willy acknowledged the shape with a nod, but he received no response.

"Fuck this," Willy muttered and quickly went back inside, where he texted Susan again.

Willy peered through the glass door, but he no longer saw the mysterious figure.

*

Susan sat next to an antique gumball machine half-full of dull-colored, mostly broken spheres in the two-seat lobby of Yummy House, waiting to pick up Willy's order. Her phone dinged for the fifth time in seven minutes. Another message from Willy: And hurry up! Susan rolled her eyes and stashed her phone.

"Six months..." Susan whispered to herself. "Six months."

When Brent, the station manager, hired Susan, he assured her that she would gain the experience necessary to run a station, something Susan had been working toward since she started in radio years before. But seven years later, the only thing Susan had learned to do was schedule Willy's acupuncture appointments, deal with the angry callers, and pick up his Chinese takeout from Yummy House.

Susan decided that she would give it six more

months, and if things hadn't changed by then, she'd pack up and set sail for new waters.

"Do you want any extra hot mustard for the crispy egg rolls?" the waiter asked as she handed Susan the order.

Susan looked back at the phone and then answered, "No. I think we're good."

On the way to the station, Susan stopped at her apartment to grab some mid-shift Advil. It had become a routine of hers a couple of months into taking the job.

Susan's neighbors had hung a string of paper ghosts above their door, and it gave her a tinge of sad nostalgia as she remembered doing those sorts of arts and crafts as a child. A childhood that now seemed so far away.

Hal, Susan's black Chihuahua, yipped and jumped on her leg as she came through the door.

"Just here for a second, Hal. I'm not off work yet," Susan told him as she hurried to her nightstand, where she kept her headache medicine. Many mornings it was the first thing she put in her body.

Susan swallowed the pills dry and noticed that the leaves on the small fern plant sitting on her dresser had browned and wilted. It made her angry that she'd let it go. When she'd bought it, she had promised herself that she would take good care of it, and now it looked as bad as she felt.

"Goddammit," she muttered.

Hal ran in and licked her ankles.

"Not you, sweetie. Not you."

Susan took the plant to the bathroom to water it in the sink.

Her phone *dinged* again, and when she reached for it, Susan lost her grip on the plant. The terracotta planter smashed into bits on the ground, and dirt went everywhere.

"No!" Susan yelled.

She looked at the mess and then to her phone. Another Willy text: Yo, you left yet? You're killing me. I'm hungrier than I've ever been in my entire life!

Susan's gaze moved to her reflection in the mirror. She studied the forty-one-year-old woman staring back at her. The woman who lived in a cramped one-bedroom apartment with a dog and two hundred seventy-eight dollars in her checking account. She couldn't escape the feeling that she hadn't done anything with her life, and now it was halfway over.

And then, on cue, the lightbulb in the bathroom flickered and died. Susan started to cry.

"How do you start over?" she asked as she dabbed the tears away. "Fuck." Susan got angry at her tears. She hated to cry.

Hal ran in and peed on the mess covering the floor. "Thanks, Hal," Susan laughed through her tears.

Susan carried Hal out of the bathroom and gave him a kiss goodbye.

Willy's inane blather poured out of her car radio.

"Michael, is that you lurking out there in the dark? Watching Willy the Kid as he guides Haddonfield through another Halloween? Don't think I don't see you, you old boogeyman. And don't think I'm not prepared. You might be a stone-cold killer, but you have not seen what Willy the Kid is capable of. And you don't want to, either."

Susan spun the dial past Willy's show and stopped on Dolly Parton's 'Nine to Five'. And as she listened to Dolly sing about working and dreaming, Susan made a decision.

"Fuck six months. I'm quitting tonight."

*

Allyson passed by Susan's WURG van as she pulled into the diner to wait for Corey. He had not yet arrived.

Allyson sat down and ordered a coffee. She looked at the time.

The door chimed. Allyson turned. No Corey.

Buzz… buzz…

Allyson's phone vibrated across the table. Laurie was calling. Allyson sent it to voicemail and kept waiting.

*

Susan entered the station and saw Willy's *ON AIR* sign lit up, so she sat at her desk and considered what she would say when she told Willy that she had decided to quit.

As Susan brainstormed various ideas, mainly the *take this job and shove it* variety, she grabbed her scissors and started cutting out the same paper ghosts she'd seen hanging above her neighbors' door.

She could hear Willy through the walls. "The hotline is open, and we're taking requests. Songs for the resurrection. What's gonna draw out the monster? Give us something to scream about! Caller, you're on the air."

Susan continued her craft project and fantasized about where she'd go after leaving the station. *Anywhere*, she kept repeating in her head. Just that thought was enough to bring a smile to her face.

Susan heard Willy howling from inside the booth as he played Paul Chiten's 'Transylvania 6-5000'. The *on-air* sign went out, and Willy yelled, "Where's that Yummy House, Susan!"

All right, let's do this, Susan told herself as she prepared to tell him sayonara. She grabbed the food and then dropped the container of fortune cookies.

Susan reached down and picked them up off the floor. When she stood back up, she found Corey in the Myers mask standing before her.

"Um... can I help you?"

Susan looked down and saw a bloody wrecking bar in his hand.

"Please, don't," Susan quietly begged.

He stepped toward her. She had little time to scream.

*

Inside the booth, Willy flipped through his favorite vintage *Hustler* magazine. The one he'd used as a young teenager to enter the world of orgasms. It had withered substantially with age and use, but Willy still got a kick out of it.

The door swung open.

"It's about time, Susan! Did you go to Yummy House or freaking China?"

Willy spun around to find Corey standing in the doorway, holding Susan's scissors.

"What the fuck do you want?" Willy tried to look past the shape and into the station to see if he could find Susan. He wanted to believe this was some sort of prank, but he couldn't convince himself.

Willy reached back and quickly toggled the *ON AIR* switch as he strategized a way out of this potential nightmare.

"This is private property, man. You are breaking and entering. You don't want to go to jail, you'll leave right now," Willy told him nervously.

Corey did not move.

Willy sprung to his feet and threw his chair to create an obstacle. Then, he turned to the microphone and screamed, "*Helllp!* He's in the station! Michael Myers is here to kill me! This ain't no joke!"

Corey tossed Willy's chair out of the way and attacked. He grabbed the back of Willy's head and smashed it into the controls on his desk, breaking open the casing as well as Willy's face.

He brought Willy back up. Willy's head hung limp, dazed by the impact. Corey put Willy's tongue between the blades of his scissors. Then he clamped them closed. The scissors sliced right through Willy's tongue, and it flopped down onto the spinning turntable and caused a distorted loop.

Corey passed by Susan's body attached to the wall on the way out. Impaled by the wrecking bar. The string of paper ghosts she'd cut out hung above her to create a morbid tableau. An homage to his teacher.

*

Allyson ordered another refill as she watched the late-night crowd come into the diner. She was on her third cup. "Come on, Corey, where are you?" Allyson whispered. The coffee didn't help her growing anxiety.

A motorcycle pulled up outside. Allyson watched the door with anticipation. Instead of Corey, a lawyer in a midlife crisis entered. Allyson looked at her phone as another call from Laurie came through.

Corey was over an hour late, and Allyson still had not heard a word from him. She left the diner to go find him.

On the way to his house, Allyson's mind jumped from one possibility to another to explain why he hadn't shown up and why he wasn't answering his phone.

"*Helllp!* He's in the station! Michael Myers is here to kill me! This ain't no joke!" Allyson turned the dial past Willy's screams and stopped when she heard 'Halloween' by the Dead Kennedys. The same song she and Corey had danced to. Listening to it at that moment created a more ominous tension than it had that night at Velkovsky's, and it made Allyson feel as if she was moving toward something dreadful. Allyson turned the radio off.

*

Joan sat on her loveseat with the lamp pulled close as she carefully dabbed superglue onto the rabbit figurine she had broken after Laurie's visit.

Joan had about an entire vat of cold cream slathered over her face, which hung off her chin like a yogurt goatee.

She had turned out the porch light to keep the trick-or-treaters away, but it didn't stop them from knocking.

"Go away! We don't celebrate Halloween in this house!" Joan cried out.

The kids who trick-or-treated in the Cunningham neighborhood were of the more feral variety. Miscreants dressed in makeshift costumes of sloppy makeup, dirty sweatpants, and whatever else they could find to disguise their appearance. Their parents were nowhere to be found, and they roamed the streets like a wild pack of hyenas scavenging for candy and chanting nasty Halloween rhymes.

Joan looked at her phone. Still no word from Corey or Ronald. She tried both their numbers and got their voicemails. Joan slammed the phone down on the side table.

Outside, an even more foul group of trick-or-treaters arrived with mischief on their minds.

"*Trick or treat, smell our feet, give us something good to eat, if you cheat, and retreat, you will turn into dead meat,*" they chanted in unison as they rapped their filthy knuckles against Joan's darkened door.

"We don't got any sweets for you little shitheads! *Go away!*"

The trick-or-treaters heard Joan's muffled admonishments, and when she did not bring them treats, they took their aggressions out on the home. Paper bags of dog shit were catapulted into the air and crashed against the door. Rolls of toilet paper unspooled as they soared over the trees in the yard. The children bayed dreadfully as they pounded the door and continued their evil chants.

"*Go away!!*" Joan's screams devolved into a nasty choking fit that caused her body to convulse horrifically.

"*Go away, you nasty children!*" Joan's choking made her voice hellish.

The back door opened.

"Ronald? Corey? Is that you?!" Joan coughed.

A shape moved through the kitchen in search of the mask that had been taken from him. He watched the woman from inside the dark kitchen.

Kill.

He removed a knife from the kitchen drawer and proceeded forward.

The children's chanting grew louder and uglier. Like devilish battle cries. Thrilled to destroy. The bags of dog poop were ignited. Sacks of flour exploded. Silly string sprayed everywhere.

"Ronald? Corey? Who's there?! I'm speaking to you!" Joan screeched.

The children kicked the door and punched the windows. They hurled rocks at the walls and carved profanities into the trees. The chaos grew feverish and upsetting.

Joan turned to meet the evil. "Help! *Hellllp!*"

He raised his knife, and Joan's voice went soft. "No..."

Joan grabbed the pillow from her chair to defend herself.

Feathers exploded, pluming into the air and covering Joan's face as he slashed the pillow.

And when there was nothing left of the pillow, he brought the blade down on her. First, her hands. Then her face. And then her body.

Joan's skin peeled back as the knife sliced her open. Blood spewed across her face and mixed with her cold cream to give her a nightmarish Kabuki appearance as she fell back into her curiosa cabinet and smashed through the glass doors. The shattered reflection distorted his unmasked face as Joan's rabbit figurines erupted. Firecrackers detonated across the lawn as the pack of trick-or-treaters finalized their pranks. The bright explosions lit the windows as Joan quivered on the floor. As blood gushed out from her fatal wounds, Joan made one last guttural plea. "Please... don't hurt my boy..."

Michael raised his knife to finish the job, but the light left Joan's eyes. He dropped the knife to his side and looked at the rabbit figurines covered in her blood. He crushed several with his boot before leaving the home.

The trick-or-treaters had left to spread more trouble, and Michael moved into their destruction. Then he crossed the street and continued his hunt.

*

"It's me. I just want another chance to explain... I love you..." Laurie hung up the phone and returned to the box of mementos in her office that Allyson had gone through earlier. She put the unanswered cards to Allyson back inside and folded the lid closed.

Downstairs, Laurie looked at the clock and checked it against her watch. As if she expected something to happen soon.

Lightning struck outside. She could smell a storm coming.

Laurie drifted to her stereo and skimmed through the records. She decided on *Led Zeppelin IV*, and she cranked the volume to the max level.

As the record spun and 'Black Dog' shook the house, Laurie moved into the kitchen, where she retrieved a dusty bottle of Scotch and a rocks glass.

*

At Velkovsky's, Frank Hawkins sat on a stool, nervously tuning his guitar. Halloween night was dead, and Lindsey had talked him into coming down and playing some of the songs he'd learned for those who needed to hear something good. She tried to get Laurie to come too but couldn't get ahold of her.

"Come on, Frank! We love you. Now play us something already!" Lindsey playfully ordered as she sat on the counter and put her feet up on the bar.

Frank turned bashful like a kid and smiled as he finished tuning.

"All right, Lindsey, hold your horses." Then he proceeded to fumble through the opening notes of Jerry Jeff Walker's 'Night Rider's Lament' before catching his stride. Frank got a little more comfortable, and the song soon came to life. Frank sang easily. Like he'd been born a singer and just recently discovered his gift. It came to him naturally.

Frank's soulfulness moved Lindsey. She had spent the majority of the day trying to forget the day, and Frank's performance woke all the emotions that had been hiding in various parts of her heart over the years. Lindsey became mesmerized with his performance, living through every word Frank sang and every note he played. When Danny David came up to get another mojito, he had to ask four times before she even became aware of his presence. And then, while muddling the ingredients, Lindsey had to discreetly wipe away some tears so Danny David wouldn't ask any questions.

When Frank finished his three-song set (the only three songs he'd learned well enough to play in front of people), Lindsey had to take a pot break outside to keep from totally losing it.

"Goddamn. We've been through so much," Lindsey sighed as she took a hit.

She heard some laughter down the alley across the way and walked over in time to see some costumed college kids stumbling by.

"Be careful," she whispered, as she wondered what living so freely would be like without the memories of murder and mayhem implanted in your mind.

Lindsey put out her joint and added it to the collection of roaches in her coin purse. Before she reached the back entrance, she saw a shape move into the shadows by the cinder-block fence ten feet away.

Lindsey stopped.

"Who's there?" she called out. Her question only made her more fearful as it confirmed, at least to herself, the existence of a *someone*.

The hidden shape didn't answer. And Lindsey wondered, could it be *him*. And then she wondered, if it were *him*, could she make it to the door before he attacked. Or could she run to the end of the alley? Would he be able to reach her before she made it?

Lindsey's eyes remained on the dark space against the wall, but in her peripheral vision, she found a weapon by way of two boards nailed together leaning against the dumpster. Lindsey grabbed one board and used the dumpster as leverage to remove the other.

She gripped the board tightly. A nail stuck out the other side. She stepped toward the back door carefully.

As she got closer, she could see in the shadows, barely lit by the stray beams of moonlight, some strands of wiry hair rising into the air above the cinder-block wall. She did not need to see the pale gray mask beneath it to know *he* had come back.

Lindsey sprinted toward the door, holding the board with two hands like a baseball bat, ready to go. Her eyes stayed on the cinder-block fence as she ran.

She saw the shape in the shadows move. And then, a stream of liquid ran across the asphalt toward her. *Blood?*

The back door swung open just as Lindsey reached for the handle. Frank Hawkins waltzed out with his guitar, and Lindsey nearly took his head off with her board. As soon as she cocked her weapon, Frank ducked.

"Hey, it's me!" Frank called out.

"Jesus, Frank," Lindsey said as she turned back to the shadows.

"Sorry, Lindsey, I gotta split. One of the guys at the station's having cramps, and I—"

"Shhh…" Lindsey said as she pointed to the mysterious shape. "Someone is hiding there."

Frank focused on the direction of her finger. And then he saw the stream of liquid running across the ground. "Is that… piss?"

As soon as he said that, Danny David stepped out of the shadows, zipping up his fly. "What the hell are you two doing?" Danny David removed the cotton balls he'd stuffed into his ears to mute the loud music Lindsey had turned on as soon as Frank finished his set.

Lindsey breathed a sigh of relief. Which quickly turned to anger. "Danny David, there are plenty of stalls in the bathroom. What are you taking care of your business out here for? You almost gave me a heart attack."

"I get shy in there," Danny David said as he strolled back into the bar.

"You okay?" Frank asked with a comforting smile.

"Well, shit, I don't know, Frank. I guess not."

Frank laughed. "You and me both, right? But I had a good time all the same. Thanks for bringing me out. Let's do it again, all right?"

"Sure, Frank, let's do it again," Lindsey said, still attached to the anxiety that had come over her. "Do me a favor. Be safe tonight, all right?"

"Will do. You as well. I'll be at the station if you need anything."

Lindsey watched Frank disappear down the alleyway, then she turned to the shadowed wall. And then down to the river of urine inching closer to her feet.

"Jesus, Danny David," Lindsey sighed again. She chucked her board over to the dumpster and headed back inside.

*

Allyson spent her entire drive to Corey's trying not to give in to hypotheticals like the one that kept popping into her head, telling her that Laurie had lost her mind, taken matters into her own hands, and had somehow done something to him.

The rattle from Allyson's car rose in volume and sounded like a jackhammer beneath her. Her worries screamed to be heard over the noise.

Allyson pulled up to Corey's, startled to find the severity of the destruction the trick-or-treaters had created. She stepped out of her car and moved through the ribbons of toilet paper and burnt patches of grass across the lawn. The places where the firecrackers had been ignited.

A TV inside the home cast an eerie flicker across the curtains. Allyson knocked, but nobody came to the door. She looked through the curtains but couldn't see anything besides the glow from the TV. She checked her phone for the thousandth time. Still no word from him, only messages from Laurie.

Allyson felt certain that Laurie had done something to him. She grabbed the rings on her necklace and squeezed.

*

A glowing light radiated out of the dying community garden on the old Myers' property.

A small group of seventh graders, dressed in jumpsuits and masks to look like Michael Myers, gathered around a burning jack-o-lantern inside the garden to conjure the missing boogeyman. John had come up with the idea, and his best friend Debra put it into motion. She found the jumpsuits at Sears and convinced their friends Tommy, Nick, and Dean, to join the seance.

"Aren't you a little old for trick-or-treating?" Belinda asked her daughter Debra as she helped her make the masks.

"We're just gonna wear them at John's, Mom. To watch a movie. You're right. We're too old for that kids' stuff."

Belinda didn't buy it, but she didn't stop it.

"Just be careful, all right? Lots of weirdos like to come out on Halloween and look for trouble."

With their white papier mâché masks and bright blue jumpsuits (the kind typically worn by elderly men), the kids didn't quite look like Michael, but it was close enough to tell you who they were trying to look like.

John first conceived the idea while hiding in the storage closet to avoid the horrors of junior high lunchtime. John sat on the mop bucket eating a peanut butter and jelly sandwich when he overheard a teacher in the lounge say the name *Michael Myers*.

The geography teacher Mr. Zelikovic told Mr. Naylor and Mr. Murphy, "I wouldn't be surprised if Chandler's down at the old Myers house right now trying to find him," Mr. Zelikovic joked. The other guys laughed. "Think about what they could do if they had Michael Myers in their corner. Think we'd still be in a wage dispute? Hell no. Michael would be at each one of our doors, changing our minds. By killing us!" Mr. Zelikovic laughed.

"And you know they tried," Mr. Murphy added. "Greedy monsters. They would do anything not to give us more money."

"Michael Myers, please help us make these awful teachers go away!" Mr. Naylor jokingly imagined their pitch.

The bell rang, and John slipped out of the closet with a new idea about how to keep him and his misfit friends safe from the jerks at school who loved to terrorize them. Summon Michael Myers and bring him to their side. The teachers might have been joking, but it seemed like a real possibility to John.

Debra was in the moment John told her the idea because Debra loved scary stuff, and she jumped at any chance to get a little wicked. Their other friends took a little more convincing. Outwardly Tommy, Dean, and Nick dismissed the idea as pointless, but secretly they worried what might happen if, by some chance, it worked and Michael materialized. They worried about it in the same way they worried when Debra made them chant 'Bloody Mary' in front of the bathroom mirror. On one level they didn't believe it, on another they were terrified.

That's what brought them to the garden that Halloween night.

John lit the pumpkin, and they sat around it as Debra began the incantation.

"We all sit here, on Halloween night, before this burning pumpkin, asking the spirit of Halloween to grant us this wish. At this place where he once lived, we ask that Michael Myers appear before us and follow our orders."

Debra lifted her mask so she could see better as she removed a plastic vial from her bag.

338

"What the hell is that?" Tommy asked when he saw the red liquid inside.

"It's blood. From a sacrifice," Debra explained. Truth was, it was corn syrup and red dye, but Debra wasn't about to admit that. She knew mystery was a crucial ingredient for a scene like this.

Debra unscrewed the cap and poured her concoction into the pumpkin. The candle sizzled as the liquid splattered.

Dean got goosebumps. Not the kind you get when something frightens you, but the kind you get when something corny happens. The whole ritual just seemed so silly, and the dramatic way Debra acted made him roll his eyes inside his mask.

Dean might have not been affected, but Nick certainly was. The ritual tied his stomach into nervous knots, and his eyes would not stay still. They kept moving from the pumpkin to his friends to the surrounding darkness of the garden. That's when he spotted the shape of a person standing not too far away.

"Guys…" Nick whispered nervously.

"Shh, I'm almost done," Debra told him.

Tommy turned and saw the shape too. "Is that a person?"

Dean articulated the thing they did not want to consider. "No. It's him."

Debra and John removed their masks. They saw him too.

Michael Myers stood in the spot where his childhood bedroom once lived. Watching the children with their glowing pumpkin at the place where his sister's window would have been. Studying the masks that looked like the one that had been taken from him.

Debra started crying. She never expected her incantation to work, and now that it had and the boogeyman had arrived, she had no idea what to do.

Debra's fear elevated the rest of her friends' fear. If Debra was frightened, that meant they should all be frightened.

"Is he going to kill us?" John asked Debra. "Or is he gonna do what we say?"

"I don't know," Debra trembled.

The rest of the gang stayed silent. None of them for a minute believed the evil presence watching them would become their bodyguard.

They all stared at his dark, faceless silhouette.

And then, a light came over them.

"What's going on over there?" an adult shouted.

The kids turned to find two Haddonfield police officers approaching. And as soon they saw the officers, the kids sprinted toward them.

"He's here! He's here! Michael Myers is here!" Debra screamed.

"Over there!" Dean pointed.

The officers pointed their lights in that direction but saw no sign of anyone. Just overgrown weeds.

"You're not supposed to be in here after 8PM," one officer said as he aimed his light at their séance setup.

The other officer ran his light across their costumes.

"We saw him," Debra cried out.

"I'm sure you did," the officer responded. "And now that you all got your scare for the night, go on home. Catch you out here again, we're gonna give you a citation. Understood?"

The kids were halfway down the street before the officer even put the question mark at the end of his final word.

The officers lingered for a moment. One blew out the candle in the pumpkin. The other scanned the area once more.

Both felt the eeriness of the location and the night and hurried back to their car.

*

Laurie kept the stereo at full volume as she straightened things up in the living room. A small amount of Scotch sat at the bottom of her rocks glass. A more significant amount had been taken from the bottle. It had been a while since she'd had a drink and the sensation came over her warmly, but it failed to wash away her heartache.

Corey stood in the distance outside, watching Laurie through the window. Staring at her through Michael's mask.

And then he approached.

He ascended the steps to the porch with robotic precision. Graceful and angular at the same time. Transforming into the shape he'd studied. He moved to the side of the house and watched as Laurie turned off the music.

Laurie glanced to the window where a spider crawled up the glass. She could not see Corey's shape on the other side from her vantage point. Laurie finished her glass of Scotch and took her dishes into the kitchen.

When Laurie returned to the living room, she approached the window where Corey stood. He moved out of view just as she brought her cup to the glass, trapping the spider who had been searching for a way out. She cupped her hand over the rim and moved to the door.

Laurie stepped onto the porch and gently let the spider out of the glass.

"Hard world for little things," she said quietly. Her eyes remained on the spider as it cautiously exited her glass and crossed the porch.

Laurie came back inside and turned out the lights. She grabbed the bottle of Scotch, and walked upstairs.

Corey watched as her office light came on. Then he entered the house through the unlocked door. He stood in the entryway and then moved into the kitchen. He pulled open a drawer and removed a knife. He held it in his grip. Then he ascended the stairs.

Laurie studied the happy expression on one of the moldering pumpkins on her mantle and lit the candle inside. She took one last drink to steady her nerves. Then she pulled the key out from the doll and unlocked the safe in her cabinet. Her hand shook as she removed Frank's gun.

A heaviness fell over Laurie as she strategically

positioned the gun at several places around her head, considering the best angle.

Then Laurie set the gun down and made the call she had been dreading.

Nine-one-one.

"Yes, I'd like to report a suicide at 327 Mill's End Road."

Corey reached the landing and watched through the doorway.

Thunder rumbled outside as the storm moved closer.

Laurie hung up the phone and looked at her reflection in the window, wondering how Halloween night had once again become her nightmare.

Laurie removed her glasses, necklace, and sweater ritualistically.

And then Laurie placed the gun's nozzle beneath her chin.

Corey took a cautionary step back.

Laurie walked by the pumpkins on her mantle and moved past the doorway. Corey could no longer see her.

The gun *snapped* sharply, and bloody flesh splattered.

Corey looked at the chunky matter sliding down the wall, then stepped through the doorway and discovered pumpkin guts all over the floor. He turned and found Laurie Strode in the corner of the room, pointing the gun at him.

"God, I hate being right," she told him as she cocked the gun.

343

Corey stood still. For a moment. Watching her from within the mask. And then he raised his knife and charged—

CLACK! CLACK!

Laurie fired twice, hitting him in both shoulders. The force sent Corey crashing through the stair railing and falling to the ground below.

Laurie sighed heavily. *Why?* She tucked her gun into her belt and descended the stairs.

As Laurie reached him, Corey removed the mask and struggled for air. Blood filled his mouth and colored his teeth.

"Where'd you get the mask?" she asked.

Corey spat blood, and his head rolled in each direction, looking at the bullet holes on his body.

"You're not gonna die," Laurie assured him calmly as she stood before him.

Corey picked himself off the ground, wobbling on his knees.

Laurie put the gun in his face.

"I try so hard to have compassion and find mercy. I could've shot you in the head," Laurie lowered the gun to his chest, "or the heart, but what's the point?"

Corey slumped to his side and grabbed the knife.

Laurie's heaviness became heavier. "It can end here. It doesn't have to go any further."

Corey rose back to his knees with the knife in his hand. Blood spilled from his wounds and covered his Prevo jumpsuit.

Laurie turned her gun away from Corey and fired at the wall.

CLACK! CLACK! Click. Click. Click.

Laurie pulled the trigger until there were no bullets left.

"All right, now it's your move. Take the choice," Laurie said as she dropped the gun and kicked it away from her.

Corey looked over his shoulder as he heard the rattle of Allyson's car approaching. A bloody smile appeared on his face. Followed by a laugh that turned into a fit.

"Do you think Allyson is going to be with you?" Laurie asked him. "After all this?"

Corey shook his head as his laughter turned psychopathic. "No, I don't." Corey kept laughing, and then he sang the last bars of the vagabond's song:

> *When all is lost*
> *And the water won't stop*
> *We'll sing this song till it coughs us up.*

Laurie didn't know what to make of Corey's bizarre behavior.

"It doesn't have to be this way," she told him again.

But all Corey heard was Allyson's car door close, and as soon as he heard that, he ended his laughing fit and screamed, *"What have you done?"*

Corey jammed the knife into his neck.

"No!" Laurie screamed as Corey fell back. His blood spread across the floor.

Laurie frantically dropped to her knees and pulled

the knife from his throat as Allyson came through the door.

It took a moment to process what Allyson saw before her. Her grandmother holding a bloody knife, and Corey on the ground with his neck cut open, twitching horrifically. For a second, none of it made sense. Just puzzle pieces scattered randomly. And then, all at once, it came together and slammed into her.

"No, baby," Laurie quietly stuttered as she backed away.

"*Nooo!*" Allyson's voice shattered into a million pieces as she raced to Corey. She fell to the ground and looked into his eyes. The same way she had done at the end of their dance that night at Velkovsky's.

Corey did not smile. And he did not spring back. And Allyson watched his eyes dim. Until they were gone.

Allyson stumbled back to the door. Looking at the monster who had taken him away from her. The monster with his blood on her hands. Allyson could hardly breathe.

"Believe me," Laurie quietly begged. "I am so sorry, please, Allyson. I tried."

But Allyson heard nothing as she fell back into the hum.

Allyson reached for the door.

"Believe me. He did this," Laurie told her. But it failed to convince Allyson.

Allyson backed into the night and then ran to her car.

All she could see was the blood. And his face with no more life.

Laurie stood by the stairs, destroyed, as she listened to Allyson's rattling car fade into the night.

"Where did you get it?" Laurie's shaken voice asked Corey again about the mask. As if it mattered anymore.

A chill traveled through the home and gently blew the curtains. Laurie noticed the side door open.

"Allyson?" she asked quietly.

Laurie cautiously moved to the door as a light rain fell. Not the storm she'd expected.

Behind Laurie, a diseased hand reached out from the shadows and took the mask.

Michael Myers stood in the darkened living room, hidden from Laurie, pulling the mask over his face.

The faint sound of stretching latex caught Laurie's attention, but she saw nothing except for Corey's body when she turned.

Laurie stepped onto the porch and carefully scanned the area, aware of a presence.

As Michael retrieved Corey's knife, Corey shot back to life. Blood vomited out of his mouth as he cowered with terror at the shape above.

Michael wrapped his fingers around Corey's neck and gazed into Corey's bleeding eyes. Taking back the evil he had passed.

Flashes of his bloody violence appeared within the glassy reflection of Corey's horrified eyes. All of it coming back to him.

The fear.

The blood.

The death.

Michael's blank eyes darkened as he placed his hand on Corey's head. With a swift and muscular movement, he snapped Corey's slit neck in two. Then, he slipped back into the darkness.

Laurie closed the door and locked it. Corey's blood gradually consumed the floor, and Laurie's feet grew heavy as she moved in his direction. Like moving through quicksand. Sinking deeper into hell.

Laurie discovered both the mask and the knife were now gone. But she made no reaction to this discovery. Instead, she walked into the kitchen.

From the darkness, Michael watched Laurie move across the kitchen doorway. And then he approached. Gripping the knife.

Laurie removed some leftovers from the refrigerator and put them in the microwave, seemingly unaware that the boogeyman had arrived.

Michael entered the kitchen as the microwave hummed. But he did not find his prey. Silhouetted by the cold blue moonlight that penetrated the window, Michael hunted for Laurie.

Laurie watched through the screen door from inside the walk-in pantry as his head moved right to left, looking for her. She could feel her fear rising. Michael's true power.

Laurie considered the weapons at her disposal. A broom? Grill brush? Silver platter? Her eyes continued searching.

Michael turned to the pantry. And then he moved in that direction.

He reached for the door just as the microwave *dinged*.

Michael turned toward the sudden noise, and at that moment, Laurie kicked open the door and bashed his head with the fire extinguisher. Stunned, Michael dropped his knife, and Laurie hit him again. When Laurie reared for another blow, Michael grabbed her arm and drove her into the kitchen island, slamming her body into its edge. Knocking the wind out of her. Laurie collapsed to the ground, gasping for air.

Michael stepped forward and raised his boot to crush her head. Laurie caught it with both hands and fought his strength. The boot inched closer. The sole grazed her temple. He applied more pressure.

Laurie looked up at the soulless black eyes staring at her through the pale mask. The mask she'd known for most of her life. After all these years, the shape inside still watching her. And still trying to kill her.

Laurie roused her strength and put her boot into Michael's knee.

Michael stumbled back, and Laurie rushed to her feet.

Michael grabbed Laurie and flung her into the sink. Laurie smashed into the dishes drying on the rack. She clutched the drying rack and spun to strike, but Michael batted it away and threw her across the kitchen island.

Laurie crashed into the wall and dropped to the floor. Pain radiated through her body. Fear coursed through her veins.

Michael moved methodically toward her.

Laurie found her basket of knitting supplies and took the long needle.

When Michael appeared, she charged. Laurie lunged toward his neck, but he seized her wrist and redirected the needle back at her.

Michael pushed the needle toward her ear. Laurie could not stop his strength. A strength that seemed to have no end. As if he had acquired it from some supernatural realm. Michael just kept coming. No matter what she did, he just kept coming.

Laurie shuddered in agony as the needle entered her ear.

Michael placed his two-fingered hand on the thick wooden butcher block to give him more support as he shoved the needle deeper.

Don't fight it. Just let him win, Laurie's thoughts begged. *You'll never get rid of him. He's taken everything away from you. Let him win.*

His black eyes slowly consumed her. Telling her she could not escape. Telling her to give up.

"*Do it!*" Laurie screamed at her monster. "*Do it!*"

But something inside Laurie refused to let her surrender. If he had something mysteriously propelling him forward, so did she.

What happens when I'm no longer afraid… The words she had written in her memoir rushed back to her. Live or die, she was ready to take the choice.

Laurie's shape changed as fear gave way to resolve. As Michael became just a man in a mask, her posture hardened.

Laurie swept her hand across the floor and grazed the handle of the knife he'd dropped.

Once she got her fingers around the weapon, her strength returned.

Laurie pulled away from Michael's grip and jammed the blade through his hand. The knife sliced through his skin and buried itself into the butcher block, pinning him to the kitchen island. Laurie grabbed a stool and slammed it against his head. The force spun Michael around and landed him on his back against the island.

With one hand anchored, Laurie twisted his other arm back as she opened a drawer and grabbed another knife from within.

Laurie struggled to control his hand and screamed as she fought his power.

Sweat and blood poured from her face.

Laurie gripped the knife, and with explosive force, she drove the blade through his hand and into the countertop. She hammered it deeper into the wood with the palm of her hand.

Both Michael's hands were pinned.

*

Blocks away, Allyson idled at an intersection. Unable to find the motivation to move in any direction. Tears washed down her face.

A curious distant orange glow caught Allyson's

attention, and she stepped out of her car to find out what it was.

Above the homes across town, Allyson saw the radio tower engulfed in flames. Burning ferociously. Howling into the night. *Corey*.

*

Michael thrashed over the kitchen island as he tried to free himself. The blades ripped his hands as he pulled them.

Laurie grabbed the refrigerator and thrust it forward. The heavy appliance crashed onto Michael's legs, locking him in place.

Laurie moved back the drawer and pulled out *that* knife. The same knife Allyson had used in her fight with Michael. The same one Laurie used to chop up fruit for her smoothies.

She grabbed the handle with both hands and raised it over her head. Her face trembled with fury. Laurie's hands clenched the handle, securing it in her grip. And then she brought it down like a piledriver. Michael's ribs fractured as the blade speared his body.

He twisted unnaturally, and air hissed awfully from his punctured lungs as Laurie slowly drew the knife from his chest. Making him feel every single moment of the pain.

"I've run from you. I've chased you. I've tried to contain you, tried to forgive you," Laurie said as she tore the mask off his head.

Laurie observed his naked face and then brought

the knife to his neck. She pressed the blade against his carotid artery. "I thought maybe you were the boogeyman. But no. You're just a man who's about to stop breathing. Tonight, your darkness ends."

Laurie sliced Michael's neck and watched his blood drain. She studied his shape as the severed artery caused him to pull at the knives in his hands more desperately.

His blood poured out, coating the floor, but he refused to quit. His flesh tore as he ripped his hand free from its constraint.

Before Laurie could stop him, Michael had her by the throat. Crushing it in his grip. Choking the life out of her.

Laurie resisted his pull. And then she surrendered to his power. Her eyes lost their expression as they began to blacken like his. As she absorbed his darkness.

"It's over..." Laurie quietly submitted. "It's over..."

Laurie's posture went slack as Michael maintained his hold. Her eyes fluttered. Her breath slowed.

"*It's over!*"

Laurie opened her eyes to find her granddaughter running to her rescue.

Allyson wrenched Michael's hand from Laurie's throat and bent it back violently until she heard the bones in his shoulder break.

Laurie stumbled back, swallowing air.

Allyson held Michael's arm firm as Laurie grasped the knife.

Laurie limped slowly forward. She positioned the blade against his wrist. And then she sliced it open.

As the blood ran from his body, Michael stopped moving. Allyson and Laurie watched him die.

"Laurie?!" Frank Hawkins yelled as he burst through the door, responding to the suicide call the station had received.

Frank found Laurie in the kitchen. Bloody knife in hand. Standing over the body of Michael Myers with Allyson by her side.

"He's dead?" Frank asked.

Laurie nodded. Allyson shook her head.

"Not dead enough," Allyson told them.

*

Firefighters racing to the burning radio tower passed by Officers Richard Wright and Brody Docar, who were responding to the call that Michael Myers had been killed. The glow from the tower fire turned the night sky orange.

More reports came through the radio. Bodies had been found everywhere.

"We got another massacre on our hands," Richard said as his eyes looked at the porch lights coming on through the neighborhood. Word had gotten out. The boogeyman had struck again.

Richard wasn't one to believe in ghost stories or anything supernatural, but the idea of crossing paths with the boogeyman, even if that boogeyman had reportedly been killed, managed to get under his skin. Somewhere in the back of his irrational mind, he wondered if Michael's evil could still get out. And if so, could it infect him too?

Brody's phone buzzed. Again.

"We're fine. Everything is going to be okay. They got him," Brody told his wife when he answered. "We will. You just stay inside, keep the doors locked, and I'll be home soon." Brody turned his head away from Richard and whispered into the phone, "May God be with us."

Brody, who had quit smoking a year earlier, fidgeted with the pack of Marlboros he'd purchased after leaving the crime scene at Dr. Mathis's house. When Brody saw Deb's body stuck to the wall in Dr. Mathis's bedroom, he knew evil had returned to Haddonfield. And immediately upon leaving the residence, Brody made Richard stop at the Quickie-Go so he could restart his addiction. Before even walking out of the store, Brody tore the pack open and ripped the filter off a cigarette. After the horror he'd seen, he needed a direct line, no obstacles.

Brody was plagued with the same irrational thoughts as his partner. Only he worried less about becoming infected and more about the possibility of Michael suddenly coming back to life and killing him and everybody else. He knew what things Michael had survived in 2018, and even though he was a reasonably minded man, Brody could not stop thinking, *What if Michael had somehow survived this too? What if just when they believed he was dead, he came back to life and killed again?* The closer they got to Laurie Strode's home, the worse those thoughts became.

Brody's phone buzzed again. His wife sent him a *prayer hands* emoji. Brody sent her back a heart.

"Another Halloween in Haddonfield," Richard sneered as sirens throughout the town screamed.

"Hey, give me one of those," Richard gestured to Brody's cigarettes.

"What the hell is that?" Brody said as they turned onto Laurie's street, and he saw Officer Hawkins strapping Michael's lifeless body to the hood of a car.

"It's him," Richard replied as his mouth fell open. "It's Michael."

More police arrived behind them.

As Frank tied Michael's hands and ankles to the car, his eyes met Laurie's.

"Your prayers were answered, Laurie," Frank told her, remembering her confession four Halloweens ago when she told Frank how she wished he'd escape so she could kill him once and for all.

"This is the night we stop being afraid," Frank told her as he pulled the ropes tight.

"I'm sorry I didn't believe you." Allyson put her hand on Laurie's. She could feel Laurie's pulse beating steadily. Strangely calm.

"He killed them all," Laurie told Allyson blankly. "Michael killed them all. He infected everyone."

"Hey, Hawkins!" Officer Gray shouted angrily as he screeched to a stop behind Richard and Brody.

"Hawkins, this isn't how we do it! *This isn't how it works!*"

Before Frank could respond, another voice answered for him. "It is tonight."

Frank turned to find the former Haddonfield sheriff, Omar Barker, stepping out of his truck. He straightened his cowboy hat and approached the body on top of Allyson's car.

"Omar," Frank said with a grin.

"Tonight, it ends." Omar nodded as he looked around at the arriving officers. "Tonight, it ends."

Frank got in his car and looked in the rearview at Michael's unmasked face. Through the windshield he could see the shock on Allyson's face, but he couldn't see Laurie through the darkness within.

"All right," Frank sighed, "this one's for Haddonfield."

Frank announced into the radio, "Move it out."

The procession from Laurie's house began. Allyson followed Frank out of the neighborhood. A dozen police cars trailed behind them.

Laurie kept her eyes on the road. Staring vacantly at what lay ahead.

The news about Michael's demise spread quickly through Haddonfield, and more people joined the convoy. Every street they drove, more cars arrived.

Horns blared with excitement as the line of vehicles grew longer. Pedestrians ran alongside the caravan, hoping to catch a glimpse of the slain monster as the procession crossed the old bridge road.

Allyson tried to process the spectacle. Laurie made no acknowledgment of it. Her eyes remained on the dark road ahead.

Allyson followed Frank through the broken gate at the Prevo Auto Shop.

The caravan came to a stop behind them.

Police already at the location had removed the dead. Even though the scene had not been cleared, they made an exception when Frank called them.

Allyson looked at the swelling crowd. It seemed like everyone in Haddonfield had come to witness the disposal of Michael Myers.

"He tore us all apart," Frank told Allyson as he approached.

"Now he goes lights out, medieval motherfucker," Barker added as he climbed out of his truck.

The floodlights fired up, lighting the entire auto yard.

"Laurie?" Frank asked through the window. "Are you okay?"

Laurie said nothing. She just nodded. She noticed Veva, the woman who had verbally assaulted her at the grocery store a couple days earlier, watching from a distance. Veva's sister Sondra sat by her side, looking on.

Laurie recognized other victims in the massive group. People that had mostly remained out of focus as her world had closed in. Anyone who had been affected by Michael's evil came to the auto yard that night.

Lindsey stood in the pack anonymously. Watching quietly. Hoping this would finally be the end.

A group of firefighters emerged from the crowd and pulled Michael's body off Allyson's car. They dragged it through the auto yard, and the hundreds of people gathered at Prevo marched behind it.

Officer Wright, who had spent his late teens working at a junkyard, activated the impressive scrap metal shredder. The hulking machine pummeled the soundscape with roaring power as it woke. Richard pulled the lever and leftover pieces of yesterday's scraps traveled down the conveyor belt into the belly of the shredder, where they were digested and excreted as metal splinters onto a platform.

The crowd hoisted Michael onto the belt, and Richard relinquished control of the machine to Laurie. She placed her hand on the lever and looked at the faces in the crowd. Expressions that had been warped by years of living under Michael's reign.

"Tonight, we say goodbye to the boogeyman," Laurie said as she pulled the lever.

The crowd watched stoically as the body moved inside the machine. There were no gestures of triumph or celebration. There was only relief.

The shredder pulverized Michael's remains and sprayed his blood across the yard. Nobody said a word until he was no more.

Allyson took her grandmother's hand but felt no warmth. Only a frightening chill.

"I love you," she told Laurie.

Laurie gripped the lever tighter.

NOVEMBER 11TH, 2022

Allyson sat in the diner finishing a piece of pumpkin pie and trying to loosen the kink in her neck. She had been living on Lindsey's lumpy couch while figuring out what to do next with her life. The second their house was no longer deemed a crime scene, Laurie returned home. Allyson couldn't go back. And since she did not know where else to go, Allyson finally decided she would just start driving and see where she ended up.

Allyson folded her napkin into a plane and made a silent promise to live for those who couldn't.

"Your grandma's a real hero," the waiter said as she dropped off the check.

Allyson smiled and laid down a ten-dollar bill. "I know."

Allyson dropped the lucky penny she had found during her walk with Lindsey next to the tip.

"For good luck," Allyson told the waiter as she left.

*

A few days earlier, Allyson had returned to Prevo Auto Body Shop. Atilla and Simmons had taken over the business for now, and at the entrance to the office, they erected a memorial shrine to Ronald. They stuck Ronald's photo on the wall and surrounded it with Mountain Dew Code Reds and Ronald's favorite fedora. The one he wore to poker night. Nothing inside the shop told you that it was the place where Michael's body had been destroyed.

They put Allyson's car on a lift and tightened the exhaust system clamp to stop her rattle. While they worked, Allyson roamed around the yard.

The gate hadn't yet been fixed, and Allyson could see dots of red speckled around some of the cars where Corey had unleashed his terror.

Allyson found Corey's motorcycle leaning against an oil drum. She ran her hands over the chrome and then climbed on. Allyson gripped the bars as she looked over the horizon.

"You should take that," Simmons said as he came out of the garage, wiping his hands. "It probably means more to you than it does to us."

"I couldn't do that," Allyson told him. "What would I do with it?"

"You'd ride it, duh." Simmons smirked and laughed. "What else would you do with it? It's a motorcycle."

"I think it's a lovely idea," Atilla said as he approached. "And if Ronald were here, I know he would insist you take it."

"It's true," Simmons added. "You were pretty much the best thing to ever happen to that mixed-up, crazy kid."

Allyson smiled, not taking either of them seriously.

"No, we're serious. Ronald told us he'd never seen that boy happier—" Atilla got struck with some unexpected emotion, and the last word got caught in his throat. He smiled and tenderly placed his hand on her shoulder.

"I am sorry. Excuse me," Atilla told her softly and then walked away to release his emotions privately.

"Hey, your car's ready," Simmons said as he headed back to the garage. "But if I were you, I'd take that motorcycle."

*

Allyson stepped out of the diner and looked at Corey's motorcycle strapped to the trailer attached to her car.

She tugged at her leather jacket and then got inside.

Allyson started the car and let it idle for a few moments as she looked at the road ahead. She took a breath, and pulled forward.

Allyson drove by the WURG radio station and watched it disappear in her rearview. Then she passed by the clinic and crossed the bridge road. She turned onto Lampkin Lane and drove by the garden where the Myers' house once stood. Then she passed by her home. Once Allyson decided to leave, all the places that once felt so confining now seemed like distant memories.

Allyson flew right past the NOW LEAVING HADDONFIELD sign and disappeared into the other side.

The events of Haddonfield that created so much violence and bloodshed finally had been resolved. And each of us has a new beginning. The new horizons that lay ahead.

Laurie sat at her computer, bathed in the afternoon light. A light that did little to soften the dark look behind her eyes.

I've said goodbye to my boogeyman, but the truth is, evil doesn't die. It just changes shape.

Laurie stared at those words blankly. And then, she highlighted all the text and deleted the entire document.

Laurie opened her desk drawer and looked at the Myers mask stuffed inside. She removed it and studied the shapeless eyes looking back at her. She ran her finger across the latex. She felt its age in the rippled skin. She felt its pull.

The doorbell sounded and broke Laurie's gaze.

Laurie opened the door and discovered a tray of fresh vegetables sitting on her doormat. To her left, she found Frank Hawkins watching her.

"Just wanted you to know… I'm thinking about you," Frank said with a warm smile. Laurie made no reaction.

Frank continued, "Thank you for what you did. From now on, we can all breathe a little easier. And, hey, when you finish that book, maybe you'll let me take a look."

Laurie nodded. "Maybe someday."

Before Frank could reply, Laurie closed the door on him. Frank grabbed the vegetables and heard multiple locks relatching inside. Then he saw Laurie's shape move away from the window and disappear from his view. It caused a chill to run down his spine. A feeling he'd felt before in the presence of another shape.

Frank got inside his car and glanced back at Laurie's house, hoping he'd mistaken her look for something else. But something inside him wouldn't let him fully accept that. As the sunlight dimmed, Frank remained in his car watching the house. Promising himself he would never let it happen again.

A few shafts of stray afternoon light broke through the curtains and cut the darkness inside Laurie's home.

In every room, even when you could not see her, Laurie could be heard breathing. Watching from within the shadows. Unseen but felt.

Inside Laurie's office, his mask rested on her coffee table. Waiting for its new shape.

ABOUT THE AUTHOR

Paul Brad Logan is a writer and screenwriter known for *Manglehorn* (2014) and *Halloween Ends* (2022). His first novel *Hallelujah!* was published in 2021.

For more fantastic fiction, author events,
exclusive excerpts, competitions, limited editions and more

VISIT OUR WEBSITE
titanbooks.com

LIKE US ON FACEBOOK
facebook.com/titanbooks

FOLLOW US ON TWITTER AND INSTAGRAM
@TitanBooks

EMAIL US
readerfeedback@titanemail.com